CELIA'S JOURNEY

The Book in the Attic

CELIA'S JOURNEY

The Book in the Attic

by

Melissa Gunther

HA

Hayes-Allan, LLC
Colorado Springs, CO

Hayes-Allan LLC
www.hayes-allan.com
Hayes-Allan Internal ID: 70905-1207-351-3

ISBN: 978-0-9819470-4-4

First Paperback Edition, July 2012

To big dreams and daring to chase them

Table of Contents

Chapter One
The Discovery

"Don't slouch!" The hissed reprimand was followed by a sharp jab to the ribs. Celia Fincastle jolted upright, her back going straight, and pulled her elbows off the table, knowing that warning would be coming next.

"But Aunt Agatha, I'm tired of sitting here. We've been here for hours!"

"Really! What an exaggeration. I never! There are only a few more speakers and then we will depart. Now not another word from you!"

Celia tucked a strand of hair behind her ear and looked around. Seeing a mirrored pillar beside her, she studied her reflection. Although the light brown hair and dark brown eyes looked familiar to her, she hardly recognized anything else about her image. A purple chicken sat on her head, or at least it looked that way to her. Aunt Agatha called it a hat, but Celia called it atrocious. With a wide brim and feathers covering the crown, it closely resembled a bird nesting on her head. It matched her purple dress, which looked as if it had been in style some fifty or sixty years earlier. The dress was made of the itchiest fabric Celia had ever encountered, and she spent most of her time fidgeting because she was so uncomfortable, which only earned her more disapproving looks from Aunt Agatha.

Glancing over the shoulder of the girl in the mirror, Celia noticed her aunt looking with rapt attention toward the front of the room. Looking at her in the mirror gave Celia a chance to study her aunt unobserved for a moment.

Agatha Trowbridge was in her seventies, yet she didn't look a day over fifty. She had blond hair that, although it had faded some over the years, still had color left in it. She wore it in a high bun, always with some sort of fancy hair pin or decorated hat. Her wardrobe could only be described as elegant, and she fit into her high society social circle with ease. Although she had never married, she kept her calendar filled with dinners, luncheons, teas, fundraisers, and other pressing obligations.

Their tea that afternoon was a good example. Celia had been hoping to spend her Saturday morning sleeping in and the rest of the day just relaxing around the house. No chance of that when she lived with Aunt Agatha. Last night, just before bed, Aunt Agatha had blithely informed Celia that they were leaving at "eleven o'clock sharp" for another one of Aunt Agatha's dull-as-dirt meetings. They'd missed lunch, thanks to Aunt Agatha being on the preparation committee for this social gathering. Celia wasn't even sure what the tea was about. All she knew was that she would rather be in bed, and she certainly would rather have anything to eat but the food they had served, although she thought it was a stretch to call some of it "food."

The large room was filled with round tables draped with pink tablecloths. Each table had an elaborate flower arrangement at its center. One long table was set up at the front of the room, where all of the very important people were sitting. Tuxedoed waiters stood at attention along the outside walls, ready to jump into action at the slightest indication of a request. The lectern for the speakers stood off to one side, on the opposite end of the room from where Celia and her aunt were seated. Aunt Agatha had grumped about their seat assignments, mumbling something about deserving a better seat since she had done so much work, but Celia was quite happy to be across the room from the droning voices. This way she didn't have to worry about paying attention.

Celia sat glumly in her chair, her mind wandering as yet another person stood to make a long-winded speech about the value of something-or-other. Aunt Agatha had been irate when Celia had asked if she could stay home and not sit through the tedious afternoon. She didn't understand why her aunt had gotten so upset. After all, she was eleven now, since her birthday had been the week before. But Aunt Agatha would hear nothing of her staying home by herself. It wasn't the "done thing," and Aunt Agatha never did something that wasn't the "done thing."

Swinging her foot idly under her chair, Celia thought back to her birthday. It had been nine years since she had come to live with Aunt Agatha, her distant but only remaining relative. Though Aunt Agatha had raised her since she was nearly two, she had never been overly maternal. A series of nannies had cared for Celia until she started school, and birthdays were symbolic, rather than celebratory. For Aunt Agatha, each birthday brought them closer to the day she could send Celia off to boarding school. In her social circle, boarding schools were the "done thing," but not before sixth grade. Since Celia had just finished fifth grade, this birthday had been slightly more celebratory than previous ones. Celia was now getting tired of hearing about boarding schools.

There had been no pile of presents, no big party, just a quiet celebration with the two of them and a small cake in Aunt Agatha's favorite flavor (she didn't know Celia's favorite flavor). Only two presents waited on the hearth for Celia's birthday: one was the large, feathery hat currently residing on her head ("Oh, isn't it just lovely? My bridge club would be so jealous!"), and the other was a large stack of boarding school brochures ("It's so exciting that you'll be headed off to boarding school for next year!").

Her stomach growled, earning her a frown from her aunt. "Sorry," she whispered. The small finger sandwiches and light salad hadn't felt much like lunch to her, and her stomach obviously agreed.

Her mind wandered again, drifting through a random collection of things, but a tug on her arm eventually brought her out of her thoughts. "Get up! We must be on our way!"

She dutifully followed out to the car and politely agreed with all of Aunt Agatha's comments about the event during the ride back to the house. As the houses grew larger and the grounds more lavish, Celia knew they were close to home. Aunt Agatha's family came from old money, and since Agatha was the last living member of the family, she had inherited the family mansion. It was an old, large Gothic structure, very cold and austere-looking from the outside. The lawn would be perfect for games of tag or kickball, but Agatha forbade anything that might mar the immaculate landscaping.

The large windows in the front parlor were visible from the street, although the heavy draperies blocked much of the view through the panes. The design style inside was true to the period, with ornate antique pieces of furniture made of dark woods and fabrics. Aunt Agatha's décor was very proper, but left the large house lacking light and life. It seemed dull and dreary, much like the person who owned the property. Celia often felt as if she couldn't move in certain rooms for fear of disrupting the proper place of everything. Although nearly every room had floor-to-ceiling windows, very little light made it into the rooms due to the lace curtains and thick drapes artfully arranged on each window.

The car pulled through the wrought iron entry gates and into the curved driveway leading to the carriage house in back. Now used as a garage, the carriage house retained its old title, although no horses or carriages remained on the property. It was the proper title for the building, Aunt Agatha insisted.

Walking through the back door, Celia trudged up the back stairs to her room, pulling off her feathered hat as she went.

"Don't throw that on the floor somewhere! Put it on the hat rack in your room. I paid good money for that!"

"Yes, Aunt Agatha."

Once inside her bedroom, Celia shut the door and heaved a sigh of relief. Carefully hanging the hat on the rack on her wall, she quickly changed out of her itchy dress and into comfortable jeans and a T-shirt. Not totally heartless, Aunt Agatha gave her an allowance and let her buy whatever she wished with her money, and it usually went to her comfortable clothes. She had no choice of outfits for school, as she had up until now worn a uniform, but at home when company wasn't around, she could wear whatever she wanted.

Thanks to Aunt Agatha's disinterest in her tastes, Celia was allowed to choose the furnishings for her bedroom as well, or so Aunt Agatha maintained. She had handed Celia a book with a selection of furniture and color schemes and told her she could choose whichever option she wanted, as long as the decorator approved and Aunt Agatha wouldn't be embarrassed when her friends came over. Celia had chosen a white bedroom set from her limited options, including a wheeled desk chair that had always been a favorite of hers, and since she had only the choice of whatever pastel color she might like, she had selected purple and green, primarily because she had a vague memory of those colors in her room when her parents had been around and because it was a combination that Aunt Agatha would *never* choose.

Flopping on her back on her bed, she stared at the ceiling. She had placed stickers to represent the constellations there so she could feel like she was outside, instead of being stuck inside this fashionable but dreary old house.

"Celia!" Aunt Agatha screeched from downstairs.

Celia sighed as she walked out to the top of the stairs. "Yes, Aunt Agatha?"

"Dinner will be in two hours. The attic needs sorting this weekend. I need you to work up there this afternoon."

"But I–"

"No buts, young lady. Everything needs organizing. There are books stacked everywhere and boxes strewn all over the place. You need to stack the boxes and put the books on the bookshelves. And if you have the notion to pick a book to read, that would be most acceptable."

"Yes, Aunt Agatha."

Celia turned and dragged her feet to the door that led to the attic. It squeaked as she pulled it open and she coughed when dust swirled around her head. The rickety steps creaked as she slowly made her way to the top of the curving staircase where the attic light chain dangled in front of her. She carefully pulled the metal beaded chain and the few dim bare light bulbs flickered to life. Rubbing her arms, Celia stepped into the large open room in front of her.

The attic was Celia's least favorite place to be. Dark and dusty, it reeked of decades of neglect. Spider webs filled every nook and cranny, and odd trinkets in forgotten corners lurked like mysterious creatures. Old hat boxes, rocking chairs, dress forms, porch furniture, steamer trunks, leather suitcases, and wooden chests filled the space. Off to one side, a floor to ceiling bookcase held books piled high and crammed onto the sagging shelves. Late afternoon sunshine streamed through the small, high windows, creating sporadic beams of light through the dust-filled air.

Celia sighed and carefully picked her way around the piles towards the back corner. She started with a precariously stacked collection of hat boxes, restacking them so they looked less likely to tumble. Over the next two hours, she sneezed her way through the back half of the large attic, organizing the boxes and other assorted paraphernalia, until she reached the corner where the books were heaped.

Remembering her aunt's comment about reading, she figured she'd best choose her own book to read before Aunt Agatha chose one for her. She grimaced as she glanced over the titles. *Who reads these things?* she thought, seeing *Insect Taxidermy* and *Polishing Your Bowling Ball.* She swiftly pitched those onto a shelf, moving on to the next pile. Goose bumps shivered on her arms as she reached for the stack, but she quickly discarded the top few books after reading their titles. She felt a strange tingle in her fingertips when she touched the book at the bottom. Picking it up, it seemed like a peculiar energy was emanating from the book.

It was a large, heavy book, about an inch and a half thick. The cover was tattered, showing years, if not centuries, of use. The corners were worn and the spine was frayed in places. Carrying it over to one of the light bulbs for more light, she saw a thick coating of dust on the cover, obscuring what looked like a detailed design. She blew the layers of dust off the intricately carved leather cover and tried to decipher the title. The words were printed in unusual characters that she had never seen before. She was just about to open the cover and look inside when her aunt called from downstairs.

"Celia! Dinner is on the table!"

"Coming!"

She stood up and brushed as much dust off of her jeans as she could and carried the book with her. Pulling the chain that darkened the attic, she rushed down the curving staircase and closed the attic door behind her. She stopped off in her bedroom to set the book on her desk. She looked at it again and noticed carved motifs and flowers in the corners, colored with deep reds, greens, and purples, although some of the color had faded or worn off in places. Running a hand over the symbols on the cover, she felt a sense of excitement, although she wasn't sure why.

"Celia!"

Jumping, she hurried to wash up for dinner and slid into her chair in the dining room just as her aunt was checking her watch.

"You're late."

"I'm sorry, Aunt Agatha. I was cleaning off all the dust from the attic."

"Hm." Dishing up food onto Celia's plate, Agatha glanced at her grand-niece out of the corner of her eye. "Did you finish straightening up there?"

"Not quite. I was just working on the books when you called me for dinner."

"And did you find something to read?"

"Yes, I did, actually. I found a really old, big book that looks like—"

"I don't care what you read, as long as it's something respectable. You know it's not the done thing to read things like those horrible tabloid magazines."

"No, it's nothing like that, Aunt Agatha. It looks like it might be about history." It was only a guess, but surely something that old had to have something to do with history.

"Very good. Young ladies must be well-read lest they sound uneducated in conversation. You don't want someone to think you stupid."

Celia merely nodded. School had just gotten out for the summer, and while she was looking forward to a few months without classes and homework, it was almost as bad spending the summer at home with Aunt Agatha. During the school year Celia could use homework as an excuse to escape to her bedroom. But during the summer, there was no avoiding the endless litany of corrections and advice that Aunt Agatha doled out on an hourly basis. Dinner tonight appeared to be no exception.

"Have you looked through the school brochures, Celia?"

"I started. I'm only partway through the stack."

"Well, we must hurry and decide before all the good schools are filled. It wouldn't do to miss out on a good school simply because you wanted to take your time."

Celia twiddled her fork. "Aunt Agatha, I'm not sure about boarding school. Couldn't I just stay at the school I'm in now?"

"Oh, fiddlesticks. I went to boarding school myself. You'll love it there."

"But I'm not sure I want to go away to school."

"You'll do just fine. It won't be a problem at all. You'll see."

Knowing that any further discussion would meet with the same answers, Celia sighed and focused on her plate. Agatha had her heart set on sending Celia to boarding school, and nothing was going to stop her from getting her way.

A few moments later, Celia spoke up again. "Aunt Agatha? What do you know about my parents? Did they go to boarding school?"

"My heavens, what brought that up?"

Celia shrugged. "Just curious."

Agatha looked up as she thought. "Well, I wasn't all that familiar with your parents. We were only related by marriage, after all. But I seem to recall that at least your father went to boarding school. I'm not certain about your mother."

"Were they nice people?"

"Oh, I suppose. As I said, I didn't know them very well. I do remember that they were a trifle peculiar, involved in something or other that your mother's family had been involved in. It seemed that your father's family wasn't too happy about all of it, but they never really spoke to me about anything."

"Do you remember anything about what happened to them?"

Aunt Agatha sighed. "Celia, you have asked that question hundreds of times, and I'm sorry, but the answer remains the same. I was out of the country, as you know, and by the time I returned, they were already gone. The officials who talked to me couldn't tell me anything. I don't know anything more than you do."

"But they couldn't have just disappeared! *Something* had to happen to them. People don't just vanish."

Agatha frowned at her. "Don't forget that curiosity killed the cat, Celia. If you go poking your nose into things, you'll find yourself in deeper trouble than you could ever dream of. It's not a wise thing to do."

Celia looked at her. "What do you mean? Do you know something?"

"Of course not. Don't be ridiculous!" Aunt Agatha patted her hair and smoothed her skirt in her lap. "Now finish your dinner. It's getting late and you have a busy day tomorrow."

"Doing what?"

"First you must finish the attic and then you must study all of those school brochures. There's no time to waste. You need to decide quickly."

"Are you sure you don't know anything about my parents?"

Aunt Agatha gave her a sharp look. "I will have no more of your nosing around, do you hear? I have told you everything I know, and the subject is closed. Is that clear?"

"Yes, Aunt Agatha."

Celia remembered very little about her parents. She knew her father had been tall and had dark hair, and her mother had blond hair and laughed a lot. She had no memories about their disappearance, though she had tried long and hard to come up with something that might tell her what had happened to them. She had searched the house long ago for clues about them, but had found nothing, unless Aunt Agatha was hiding things somewhere Celia didn't know about. Each and every time Celia had questioned Aunt Agatha about her parents, she had gotten the same response, and it always seemed as though Aunt Agatha was hiding something.

Later that evening, Celia finally managed to get away to her bedroom. She fell onto her bed again and looked up at her constellation stickers. Normally the stickers helped her relax, but tonight something seemed different. The back of her neck started to tingle and a shiver went down her spine. While she looked at the stickers, she thought it was almost as if they were glowing. Studying them, it seemed like the ones over her desk were glowing brighter than the rest. Sitting up, she looked over and spied the large book she had discovered in the attic resting on her desk where she had left it before dinner. As if drawn by an invisible force, she stood and walked over to the desk.

Standing in front of it, she saw that a blue glow was coming from the book. She eagerly picked up the book to study it. Although the symbols on the front still made no sense to her, she couldn't help but examine the design on the richly-colored cover and wonder what the musty-smelling pages might contain. Excited, she sat down at the desk, set the book in front of her, and flipped open the cover.

A wind rushed through the room and she jumped back, the chair rolling away from the desk. The wind blew the pages of the book and left them open to a point near the middle. It seemed like the pages were quivering, as if vibrating with excitement.

Celia leaned forward to see what was on the page, only to be jolted back again when a shaft of bluish light beamed from the book toward the ceiling. She watched with wide eyes as the light spun and flashed, growing wider and brighter. Small dots of light flung out from the center beam, flecks of blue that spiraled out from the center and into her bedroom. It was like watching the night sky move at lightning speed, with sparkling pinpoints of light spinning around the room.

Her heart pounding in her ears, she stared at the book as something started to take shape in the center of the beam of blue light. Rotating in the light, a figure started to appear, as if each particle of light combined with the others to build a person. It seemed fuzzy at first, but grew sharper with each passing moment until finally the figure was clear, hovering over the center of the book.

Standing in miniature above the still-quivering book was the image of a man, seemingly created out of the blue light that illuminated him. He looked dignified, clothed in a three-piece suit and wearing round spectacles and a derby on his head.

"Good evening, miss," he said, nodding his head to her.

Chapter Two

A Visit From Mr. Morven

Celia gulped. "Who-who are you?"

"Higby H. Snodridge, at your service."

"How did...what are...did you...?"

He chuckled. "Never fear, Miss Fincastle. I know I must come as a bit of a surprise to you."

Her eyebrows flew upward. "A bit? Not one for understatement, are you? And how do you know my name?"

He smiled wryly. "You sound just like your father."

"You knew my father?"

"Absolutely. He was one of the brightest students to ever walk through our doors. Your mother was another."

"Wait. You knew *both* of my parents? You said students. Are you from a school? What school was that? How come nobody's told me about my parents? What happened to them?"

Laughing, he held up his hands as if to stop her. "Slow down, slow down! Unfortunately, this is not the time or place to discuss all of that. Your aunt will likely be coming up here soon, and we mustn't let her see this."

Celia snorted and rolled her eyes. "She'd flip out."

"Yes, well, while I'm sure that translates to her being quite alarmed, that is exactly what we must avoid if things are to work the way they should."

"What do you mean?"

"I have been sent as an official messenger for the Renasci Academy for Gifted Students. It has come to our attention that you are now of age to attend our school, and the headmaster would like to extend an invitation to you. All of us would be delighted to have you there."

"Renasci Academy for Gifted Students? I've never heard of it."

He nodded his head knowingly. "Yes, we figured as much. Agatha Trowbridge is not exactly on our list of benefactors."

Celia frowned with confusion. "Aunt Agatha knows about your school?"

Mr. Snodridge wagged his head from side to side as if trying to think of the proper words to say. "Not exactly. Well, no, let me rephrase. She has likely never heard of our school, but even if she had, she isn't the type to approve of us."

"I don't understand."

"Not to worry. There will be plenty of time to explain everything to you. For now, though, we must convince your aunt to let you come to our school."

"Is it a boarding school?"

"My dear, it would be impossible for it to be anything else."

"Then it won't be nearly as difficult as you're thinking to get Aunt Agatha to agree. As soon as she hears that I've picked a boarding school, she'll be so happy she won't care about anything else."

"Surely she'll want to know something about the school?"

"Only whether it gets me out of her hair. The rest won't matter."

"If things work that smoothly, Miss Fincastle, then you'll know that you were meant to come to our school, which I sincerely hope to be the case. I shall leave you our brochure," he said, and with a wave of his hand, blue light sparkled on the top of the pile of school brochures as a shiny leaflet materialized. "I encourage you to peruse it at your leisure—"

"Huh?"

"Ah, look it over."

"Oh."

"See what you think and decide if it is somewhere you'd like to attend. I have every confidence that you will decide in favor of coming to our school. Be careful what you mention to your aunt. There isn't much in the brochure that will seem out of place to her, and that is precisely what you want." He scratched his forehead. "Be aware, however, that things are not always what they seem, Miss Fincastle."

"Like this book, you mean?"

"Exactly. I shall not say any more for now. If you decide you'd like to attend the school, simply fill out the card in the brochure and drop it in the mail. It will get to us." He nodded to her in a gracious manner. "I must be leaving for now. I sincerely hope to see you this fall." With a twirl of his hand in the air by his head, the blue lights above the book swirled up like a flame and disappeared.

Celia blinked and glanced around. The brochure sat on the pile right where it had appeared, but there was no sign of the figure or the blue light. A bit unnerved, she rolled her desk chair back to the desk and leaned forward to look at the book. Getting her first glimpse of the pages inside the book, she was disappointed to see that they were filled with the same kind of symbols that made up the title on the cover. Try as she might, she couldn't decipher any sort of pattern to the symbols that might help her discover what they said.

A sharp knock on her door made her jump in her chair. "Celia? It's nearly ten, and we must be up early tomorrow, don't forget."

Chapter Two

Celia headed over and opened her door, finding her aunt standing in the hallway. "I was just about to get ready for bed, Aunt Agatha."

"Very well." Peering over Celia's shoulder, Agatha spied the pile of brochures on the bed. "Have you made any decisions about schools?"

Celia shrugged. "I'm starting to narrow down the choices."

"Excellent. Well, remember that you must decide quickly before all the good schools are filled."

"I know."

"Hmm. Well, I'll leave you to your nighttime routine. Good night, Celia."

"Good night, Aunt Agatha."

Agatha spun on her heel and marched to her room, her shoes tapping out her footsteps on the floor. Celia hurried to get her teeth brushed and wash her face, easing the door shut behind her as she slipped back into her room.

Spying the brochure that Mr. Snodridge had left for her, she flopped on her stomach and picked up the flyer. The glossy paper had small pictures of the campus, classrooms, and dormitories, all of which looked like they might be located anywhere, but were too small to see many details. Large trees provided shade for the commons, where students were pictured eating lunch or studying on the large open grassy area. The classrooms appeared to be small lecture halls with curved rows of desks or tables set up on tiers. Each of the pictures of the dorm rooms showed comfortable areas for students to study and relax.

The description of the school was rather bland, stating things that could apply to almost any school. Nothing seemed to jump out as a feature that would make someone choose that school over any other, but for some inexplicable reason, Celia was drawn to the campus. She somehow felt like that particular school was where she belonged, as if there were an adventure waiting there for her to experience. Her mind made up in almost an instant, she grabbed a pen and filled out the form requesting more information. Carefully tearing it out of the back of the brochure, she flipped it over to check the address. Oddly, there was only one line on the card. "Renasci via BUS, 4th Station," it read, and Celia's brow furrowed as she read it. Would the post office know where to send that?

Deciding to talk her decision over with her aunt in the morning, she piled everything on her desk, flipped the light off, and went to bed.

As she shuffled into the kitchen the next morning for breakfast, she clutched the brochure and card in her hand.

"Good morning," Aunt Agatha said to her.

"Morning."

"Eat quickly, because we leave in fifteen minutes."

"Okay."

Agatha sipped her tea. "What's that in your hand?"

"I think I've picked a school. This is the brochure," she said, handing it to her aunt.

Aunt Agatha perched her reading glasses on her nose and peered down at the paper. "Hmm," was all she said. Celia poured a bowl of cereal and began eating while glancing out of the corner of one eye as her aunt flipped quickly through the pamphlet. When she finished, she set the paper down and pulled off her glasses. "Well," she said, "I see you have filled out the card already. It seems to be an acceptable school, so I suggest you put that card in the mail first thing today."

"Do you think it's a good choice?"

"I have never heard of this school specifically, but some of the references are certainly familiar to me, and I approve of their recommendations. I expect to hear more about this school when someone contacts you, but as long as they can assure me that the school will provide a decent education in the things that one must know for a productive life, then I know of no reason why this school shouldn't be a perfectly acceptable choice."

Knowing that her comment was as close to approval as Aunt Agatha was likely to get, Celia nodded. "Okay. I'll drop the card off at the mailbox when we leave."

"Very well." She rose, carefully collecting her teacup and saucer. "Don't be late." With that, she left the room.

Celia looked again at the address on the card. Recalling Mr. Snodridge's words about dropping the card in the mail, she shrugged and figured that given everything else surrounding this school, anything was possible. After all, how many other schools would send a messenger out of a book to drop off a brochure out of thin air? Grinning to herself, she cleared her dishes and went to get ready.

Two weeks after Celia sent her card to the Renasci Academy, a large envelope addressed to her came in the mail. Seeing the formal-looking seal on the back and the unusual return address, Celia grew excited as she brought the mail in from the mailbox by the front door. Setting the rest of the mail down on the sofa table, she carried her envelope over to the mauve wing back chair by the grand piano.

"What's that you have?" Aunt Agatha asked, eyeing the envelope over the edge of her reading glasses. She had been working on a floral needlepoint while overseeing Celia's dusting job in the front parlor.

"It's from the Renasci Academy."

"Oh? How lovely!" Aunt Agatha had been in a particularly cheery mood lately every time the subject of school came up. "Well, are you going to open it?"

"Of course."

Celia turned the envelope over on her lap with some trepidation. Although she still felt that this school was where she belonged, she was a little anxious about what Mr. Snodridge had said about Aunt Agatha's approval. And there was a small part of her that wondered if she had imagined the whole encounter with Mr. Snodridge. During the past two weeks, she had often thought that the blue light and the figure had just been a dream, and any day now she would have to choose some other school to attend that fall. She had looked at the book many times, but nothing seemed to change and the symbols just started to look like some foreign language instead of something mysterious. Even looking at the brochure hadn't convinced her that it had all been real. But now, holding the solid evidence that the school must exist somewhere, she felt a rush of excitement again.

Carefully tearing open the envelope, her fingers tingled the same way they had when she'd first held the book that was now sitting on her bookcase. She slid a thick stack of papers out of the envelope and settled them on her lap. Looking at the first page, she read the following letter:

Miss Celia Fincastle:

Thank you for your interest in the Renasci Academy for Gifted Students. We would be delighted to have you as a student in our hallowed halls. Enclosed you will find more information about registration and enrollment, as well as a list of materials and provisions required for the first year of schooling, should you choose to attend.

Mr. Morven, our new student advisor, is available to assist you in any way, and will be contacting you in a few days as a follow-up to this information packet. Please ask him any questions that will aid you in the decision-making process.

We sincerely hope that you will select our school for your continuing education, as we offer programs that are found at no other school. Thank you for your interest.

Warmest regards,

Headmaster Doyen

Tucked just behind that letter was one addressed to her aunt. "There's a letter here for you, Aunt Agatha."

"For me? Well then, hand it over here," she said, setting her needlepoint aside.

Celia flipped through the other pages while her aunt read the letter. There were lists of required books for every possible class offered and page after page of information about the school and its programs.

"Oh, isn't that nice of them to send me a letter! This says that someone will be stopping by in a few days to answer any of our questions. I expect that I shall be able to finish all of the paperwork for your enrollment at that time, so you'll need to fill out all of the forms by then, Celia."

"Don't you want to read the rest of this?"

She waved her hand as she shook her head. "Oh, that isn't necessary. I'll just talk to the representative when he comes."

"Aunt Agatha, I really think—"

"And I really think that I have made up my mind. Please do not pester me about this."

"Are you sure?"

"Of course I'm sure! I am not a wishy-washy, indecisive nitwit! Now, enough about this!"

Celia bit her lip as she looked back at the paper in front of her. Her eyes widened as she read the last paragraph on the page, and she bit her lip to keep from laughing out loud. Surely Aunt Agatha wouldn't agree to this school! At least not if she actually read all the paperwork. However... if she refused to read anything and agreed to let Celia go without understanding what the school really was... Mr. Snodridge's words replayed in her head as a shiver traveled up her spine.

The phone trilled and Aunt Agatha said, "Answer that, please, Celia," so Celia piled her papers and stood to get the phone. Aunt Agatha didn't own a cordless phone (she thought they were "too newfangled and unnecessarily complicated"), so Celia had to walk across the room to the phone table.

"Hello?"

"Good evening. Is Miss Agatha Trowbridge there?"

"May I inquire who is calling?"

"Of course. This is Mr. Morven from the Renasci Academy. Is this Celia Fincastle?"

"Yes."

"Nice to meet you, Celia. I trust you have received the paperwork stating that your advisor would be calling?"

"It just came in today's mail."

"Ah, splendid. Have you decided to attend our school, or am I being presumptuous?"

"Well, I'd like to go, but..."

There was a moment of silence. "Your aunt." The words were heavy with unspoken meaning. "Has she expressed disapproval of our school?"

"Not yet, but the paperwork just came today, and..."

"Very well. May I speak with your aunt to set up a time to visit you?"

"Of course." She placed her hand over the mouthpiece as she turned to her aunt. "Aunt Agatha? It's someone from the

Renasci Academy who would like to ask you about setting up a visit at our house."

"Someone from the school? How prompt!" She walked over and took the phone, then shooed Celia away before she turned her back to the room and spoke quietly into the phone.

Celia gathered up the papers and took them up to her bedroom, returning downstairs in time to hear her aunt say good-bye and hang up the phone.

"My, they certainly are on top of things, aren't they?" she said as she settled in the chair again. Aunt Agatha picked up her needlepoint, replaced her reading glasses, and scrutinized Celia. "That nice young man will be stopping by tomorrow afternoon, so please try to look decent for his visit."

"He works at a school, Aunt Agatha. I'm sure he's seen kids wearing jeans before."

"I'll have none of that, young lady. You will wear a skirt or a dress, and you will look presentable, or you won't be allowed downstairs to meet him. Is that clear?"

"Crystal." She received a disapproving look for her reply, but no more was said.

The following afternoon, Celia was ordered to wait in the front parlor until Mr. Morven arrived. She was lying on the sofa, staring at the ceiling, when she thought she saw a flash of blue light. Sitting up, she looked around to see where it came from, but saw nothing out of the ordinary. She was startled by a knock at the door, and her heart began to pound as she stood to answer. She wiped her hands nervously on her skirt before she opened the door.

A dapper man stood on the front steps, his wire-frame glasses gleaming in the late afternoon light. He carried a slim briefcase, and somehow Celia felt oddly reassured by the expression on his face, as if he knew exactly what was going on and he was on her side.

"I am Mr. Morven. Miss Fincastle, I presume?"

"Yes. Hello, Mr. Morven," she said politely. "Please come in."

"Thank you. It is a pleasure to meet you in person. I've heard so much about you."

"You have? How?"

"Ah, well, let's just say that there is much that you don't know about yet. Nothing to worry about, however, so please settle your mind."

"Uh...okay. Um...you can have a seat while I get my aunt."

"No need, Celia!" Aunt Agatha said as she breezed around the corner and came down the stairs. "I'm right here. Ah! And you must be Mr. Morven!"

"Indeed, Miss Trowbridge. Pleased to meet you." He kissed the back of the hand she extended. "I do hope this visit wasn't too short a notice. Normally there is not such a rush to admit a student, but seeing as the semester begins in a matter of weeks, we felt it would be better to talk with you without delay."

"Oh, it isn't a problem at all. I have been after Celia to select a school for months now, but she simply wouldn't make up her mind, and I wasn't about to force *my* decision on her." Aunt Agatha made it sound as if Celia had dragged her feet, when she had only received the brochures a few weeks ago.

Mr. Morven winked discreetly at Celia. "Yes, the choice of a school is rather important. I'm glad Celia didn't rush the process and make a hasty decision."

Flustered, Agatha fingered her necklace. "Well, of course. Ah, shall we sit down? Celia, please fetch the tea cart."

"Yes, Aunt Agatha." She hurried into the kitchen and carefully pushed the cart into the parlor. The teacups rattled as she drove over the edge of the rug, but the cookies remained piled on the plates. She quietly poured three cups of tea and served them, then perched on the edge of the wing back chair as she tried to pick up the ongoing conversation.

"Thank you, Celia," Mr. Morven said as he sipped his tea, then turned back to Agatha. "Ma'am, have you read the paperwork?"

"Oh, posh! I don't need to wade through all that. Can you tell me that this school is reputable?"

"Of course it is, ma'am."

"And my grand-niece will receive the best education possible?"

"Absolutely. In fact, we are the leading school for gifted students in the country, if not the continent."

"Then I don't need to hear anything more. As long as I'll not be embarrassed in front of my friends, and Celia will be able to achieve a high level of success at this school, then I give my complete approval. Just hand me the paperwork and I will sign whatever I need to sign."

He shuffled through his portfolio and pulled out a stack of paper. "Ma'am, I must mention one more time that you should read this completely before you agree. Once you sign this paperwork, it is a legal, binding contract."

"Mr. Morven, I assure you that I am not concerned about the specifics about your school. You seem like a trustworthy young man, and I believe you will not do anything that is not in the best interest of my grand-niece."

"If you are certain that you will abide by the terms of this agreement, Miss Trowbridge, then I cannot force you to read the rest of this information. I caution you that our school is not the average school, but as long as you are aware of that, I can only stress that you should read through the information. If you choose not to, then we cannot be responsible for that decision."

Agatha waved her hand as if swatting a fly in front of her face. "I am not concerned. I think it will be very good for Celia to go to a school that's not average. Her previous schools have all been too lenient. Please hand me the things that I need to sign and I will be on my way."

He nodded his head to her. "Very well, then, ma'am." He pulled a couple of sheets out of the stack of papers. "If you will sign these forms then I can be out of your way."

As Agatha bent over the table to sign the papers, Celia sat in slight disbelief at the fact that she was actually going to be able to go to the school. Surely this would all turn out to be a big mistake, and Aunt Agatha would slap the pen down and refuse to sign the paperwork. She'd see something that would make her ask questions and Celia would never be allowed to go to Renasci Academy. But then again, Aunt Agatha would never admit she had made a mistake by agreeing to let Celia go before reading through the paperwork. People like her just didn't make mistakes like that.

Celia jolted out of her thoughts when Mr. Morven snapped the portfolio shut. "Very well, Miss Trowbridge. Your grand-niece shall attend our school this year. Our school year begins on August second. We shall send someone to pick Miss Fincastle up the day before, on August first. Please see that her things are packed and ready to go. As we have a rather long journey to the school, we won't have time to wait for last-minute preparations."

"Not to worry, young man. She'll be ready with plenty of time. I will see to it myself."

He nodded, then turned to Celia. "May I speak with you briefly, Miss Fincastle?"

"Me? Uh…"

"Don't stammer, Celia. It's not polite," Agatha said. She shook her head. "I have to prepare for this evening anyway, so please stay in here and talk. And Celia, stop being so rude!" With that, she breezed from the room, her shoes clicking on the wood floors.

"What did you want to talk to me about, Mr. Morven?"

"I merely wanted to caution you."

"About what?"

"Things are not always what they seem. You know very little about the things going on. I know you are curious about the school, but I must stress that you not explore things too much before you reach the school. As you know, your aunt is suspicious about anything out of the ordinary, and she will not hesitate to forbid your attendance."

"I thought you said it was a binding contract, or something like that."

"Oh, it is, but your aunt is your legal guardian, and as such, she retains final say on decisions." He stood and collected his hat. Spinning it in his hands, he looked at her carefully. "You'll need to go into this with an open mind. As I said, there is much you do not understand yet. It is not my place to tell you any of what is going on."

"I read in the paperwork..."

"Yes, I'm sure you did. However..."

"Are you sure I should be going to this school, Mr. Morven?"

"Absolutely. The fact that you have the book in your possession guarantees that." He studied her again. "It is important that you keep that book with you."

"All the time?"

"No, no, of course not. But carry it with you when we come to pick you up in August. It is useless in the wrong hands, but a necessity for your success. Without it, you face almost certain disaster."

"Disaster? What do you mean?"

"I have said too much already. I must be on my way." He picked up his briefcase and placed his hat on his head. "Good evening, Miss Fincastle. I look forward to seeing you this fall."

"But..."

"I'm sorry, Celia. I know you will grow tired of hearing this, but you need to be careful. You're very important to everyone in our demesne."

"Huh? What's a da-main, or whatever you said?"

"Demesne. It's our world, or our realm, you could say."

"Wait a minute. I'm getting more confused. And did you say I'm 'very important' to all of you?"

He sighed. "This isn't the time to go into all of this, Celia. I'm terribly sorry, but you'll just have to wait until you come to the school. Please be patient, and don't talk to your aunt about all of this, or all hope is lost." He opened the door and stepped outside. "Don't forget to pack up those cookies," he said, gesturing to the tea cart.

Celia turned to look at the cart, and saw a quick blue light flash on the wall of the parlor. She spun around and thought she glimpsed a couple of twinkles of light like the ones that had appeared with Mr. Snodridge, but Mr. Morven had completely vanished.

As the weeks crept by, Celia could hardly wait until the day of her departure. Neither, apparently, could Aunt Agatha. Each morning, she would sit with her nose in the paper and ask, "How many days until you head off to school?" And Celia would always reply with one fewer day than the number from the day before, which she knew because she was counting the days off on her calendar.

The summer passed slowly, with many of Aunt Agatha's torturous meetings and get-togethers, including one particularly notable afternoon when the fourth player couldn't make it for their bridge club game. Aunt Agatha had insisted that Celia play in the empty chair. Since Celia had never played bridge before in her life, and she certainly wasn't as cutthroat as the ladies in Aunt Agatha's bridge club, the game had been a disaster. Celia might have had some difficulty concentrating on the game, however, due to Aunt Agatha's request that Celia wear her awful purple chicken hat and dress ensemble again. The other women had predictably fawned over the hideous creations, and Celia had been forced to endure the entire afternoon in the itchy dress with feathers poking her in the face.

By the end of the summer, Celia had cleaned the attic twice, sorted the clothes in her closet, alphabetized the spices on the shelves in the kitchen, and arranged the books on the shelves in the library by size and color. She had found any activity that would keep Aunt Agatha from finding something for her to do, for fear that Aunt Agatha might make her play bridge again or find some other horrible task for Celia to complete.

After nearly six weeks without word from the Renasci Academy, Celia was now starting to wonder if she was really going to the school or if they had somehow overlooked her on their lists. She started checking the mail carefully every evening, hoping to hear something that would give her some hope that she was going to get away from Aunt Agatha.

When she checked the mail carefully for six days straight and sill found nothing from the school, Celia entered her room and closed the door behind her, feeling dejected. Slipping her sneakers off by the closet door, she glanced over at her desk, and noticed something sitting on the top that she had cleared off that morning. Walking over, she found an envelope that said "Miss Celia Fincastle" on the front. She picked it up, noting the heavy parchment and the detailed design printed in red ink on the back flap. She slipped a finger under the red wax seal holding the envelope closed.

Sliding out a thick sheet of paper, she felt a rush of excitement as she recognized Mr. Morven's handwriting. Eagerly opening the single sheet, she read:

Dear Celia,

I trust this letter finds you well and ready to leave for school in a week's time. Your information packet contains a list of required items for your first year at the school so you can pack appropriately. I wanted to write and inform you that the headmaster has asked me to personally escort you for your first trip to the school. Be prepared for a long trip, as the distance we must travel is considerable. I hope you are excited about your first year of school and all of us here wish you the best of luck and great success. I shall see you next Wednesday at eight-thirty A.M. sharp. I am quite certain that your aunt will not allow you to be late!

Sincerely,

Mr. Morven

Celia nearly squealed with delight when she read the letter. They hadn't forgotten about her! She was really going to the Renasci Academy! Running out the door and down the hallway, she called, "Aunt Agatha! Aunt Agatha!" She thundered down the stairs and came to a screeching halt when she rounded the corner and came face to face with a stern-looking Agatha.

"It is not proper for young ladies to run and scream, and *especially* not inside the house!"

"I'm sorry, Aunt Agatha, but I got a letter from Mr. Morven. He says he's coming to pick me up next Wednesday at eight-thirty to take me to school!"

Her aunt looked as if she was warring between disapproval over Celia's actions and delight over the news about school. "Well, we shall see to it that you are ready on time. But no more running and yelling in the house!"

"Sorry."

"Hmph." She turned and left the room.

Celia spun in a circle with her arms wide, giggling with delight. Finally, she was going to be off on her own, well, sort of, and free from Aunt Agatha's stuffy rules! And it was all happening in seven days!

Chapter Three
Off to the Station

Wednesday morning found Celia sitting on the front porch steps with her packed belongings when Mr. Morven pulled up in a white van. Celia pushed to her feet, shading her eyes from the morning sun as she watched him exit the vehicle and walk around the front.

"Good morning, Celia!"

"Good morning, Mr. Morven."

"I see you are all packed and ready to go," he said, looking over her steamer trunk and duffle bag.

"Yup."

"Celia," Aunt Agatha reprimanded sharply, coming out the front door.

"I mean, yes, I am."

"Ah, Miss Trowbridge. So nice to see you again."

"You, as well, Mr. Morven."

He glanced at his watch. "I would love to stay and chat, but we do have a schedule to keep, so we must be on our way." He turned to Agatha. "Thank you so much for making sure your niece was ready to leave on time. I'm sure we'll be in touch again, as we will send progress reports about Celia's schooling."

"Yes, of course."

Celia looked over at her aunt. She'd never seen Aunt Agatha so excited. While she knew that Aunt Agatha had never really been thrilled to have her in her house, Celia had never before sensed that she had been such an imposition on her.

"I'll go load your things in the van, Celia, if you'd like to say good-bye to your aunt."

Celia nodded and watched as he effortlessly lifted her trunk and carried it on one shoulder to the back of the van. Turning to Aunt Agatha, she stood awkwardly, unsure of what she should do.

"Well, Celia, I hope you enjoy your new school," Aunt Agatha said. She fussed with her hair, then held out her hand. "I trust you will work hard and not cause any trouble."

Uncertain, Celia slowly slid her hand out and shook Aunt Agatha's. She felt more like she was at one of Aunt Agatha's tea parties than saying good-bye to the person who'd been raising her for years. "Good-bye, Aunt Agatha."

"Good-bye, Celia."

Celia picked up her duffle bag and turned to walk down the pathway. As she reached the bottom of the stairs, she could have sworn she heard Aunt Agatha say, "And good riddance," but when she whirled around to look at her, Aunt Agatha was standing with a polite smile plastered on her face, her hands clasped properly in front of her. When she saw Celia looking back at her, she gave a small wave. Celia waved back, a little confused, and then turned and headed to the van.

"Would you like that bag in the back, Celia?" Mr. Morven asked.

"That's fine."

Soon they were seated in the van and pulling away from the curb. Celia waved to her aunt one last time, but she had already turned around and was walking through the front door. Celia faced front again and let out a big sigh.

"Are you nervous about going to your new school?" Mr. Morven asked.

"A little."

"Ah, well, don't be. I'm sure you'll fit in just fine, and I don't think you'll have any trouble with the curriculum."

Celia thought for a minute. "Can I ask you a question, Mr. Morven?"

"Just one?" He laughed. "I was pretty sure you'd have more than one question for me, but go ahead."

"I don't feel very gifted. How did I get into this school?"

"I assure you, Celia, that you have been on the list for Renasci since the day you were born. Your parents were two of the most accomplished students that Renasci ever saw, and the events that happened long ago made it an almost certainty that you would be attending."

"What 'events'? What happened?"

He was silent as he changed lanes and merged onto the highway. "I don't know all of the details, so I'm not going to be much help to you. I just know what was told to me when it all happened. I was out of the country at the time, finishing my schooling, but it was all anybody could talk about for months, maybe even years."

"What do you mean?" Celia started feeling uneasy.

"Well, I guess now might be a good time to tell you that the Renasci Academy exists in a different demesne from the world that your aunt and nearly everyone else lives in."

"Wait. You used that word before: demesne. You said it was like a different realm or something."

"That's correct."

Celia scrambled to try to fit all the pieces together. "So...Renasci is in a different *world*? Like an alternate universe or something?"

"Not quite. We exist in the same world as everyone else, but while we are very aware of the rest of the world, they don't seem to realize we exist."

"Hold on a minute. I thought those kinds of things only happened in books and movies."

"No, no. It's all very real. I know this must sound strange to you, but I would guess that if you stop and think about it a little, you'll find that maybe it doesn't seem so weird after all. Haven't you ever felt like you didn't belong where you were? Like you just didn't fit in anywhere?"

"Sort of, I guess."

"It's because you belong somewhere else. It's not that you can't live in the rest of the world, it's just that your place is in our demesne."

"Maybe. But what happened to my parents? If they lived there and I belong there, why did I spend all this time with Aunt Agatha?"

"I'm sorry, Celia. I really don't have all the answers for you. I'm not sure anyone does, at least not anyone you'd want to talk to. All I can tell you is that you went to live with Agatha because she was your last remaining relative. Everyone else just... disappeared."

"But that doesn't make sense!"

"I know. Again, I'm sorry. Maybe you can find some answers on your own once you get to school."

They rode in silence for a while until they pulled up to a large building in the center of the city. It looked rather nondescript, with beige bricks on the outside, small rectangular windows placed high on the walls, and a flat rooftop. It was a single story high, and had very little ornamentation on the outside of the building. A single concrete pathway led to a door in the front, and immaculately mowed grass covered the rest of the property.

"What is this place?" Celia asked, straining her neck to see the roofline.

"The bus station."

"Right. I've been to the bus station. You don't expect me to believe you, do you?"

Mr. Morven chuckled. "Higby warned me that you wouldn't just come along quietly." He waved his hand to indicate the building. "This is the bus station for the demesne. Most people walk past this building every day and think it must be an office building, or a historical center, or something similar. They never stop to notice that there are no signs on the building and only one door." While he spoke, they both exited the van and walked around to the back door.

"Oh, yeah."

"And since they never really stop to wonder about the building, they never set foot inside it." He winked at her. "So they miss all the fun!" He opened the back doors of the van and pulled out her trunk and duffle bag. "We're a little early, so we've got plenty of time to get in and find you a good seat."

He carried her trunk up the walkway and front stairs and set it down. Celia noticed that there was no handle or knob on the only door, and she wondered how they were going to get inside. She watched as he reached over to one side, carefully pivoted a brick out, pressed the button concealed behind it, and replaced the brick. If Celia hadn't been paying attention, she never would have known which brick he moved.

Moments later the door swung inward and they stepped inside. Celia looked around, but after the brightness of the sun outside, it was hard to see anything in the dim light inside until her eyes adjusted. She had a glimpse of a hallway off to the right before Mr. Morven ushered her forward. At the end of a short hallway, she came upon a wide staircase off to the left. With gold handrails, plush red carpeting, and footlights on every other step, it looked more like it belonged in a fancy theater than the plain-looking building they were in. Celia looked down the stairs and tried to see where it went, but she couldn't see the bottom.

"Where does this go?" she asked.

"To the bus platform, of course," Mr. Morven replied.

Celia turned toward him and nearly jumped out of her skin when she saw another man standing beside him. "Oh! You scared me!"

"So sorry, miss," he said, dipping his head to her. "I thought you had seen me when I opened the door." He wore a navy uniform with gold buttons and gold bars on his sleeves. On his head was a conductor's hat, with its stiff, square shape and hard brim.

"Celia, this is Zosimo Bearden. He's the conductor of the bus."

"What kind of buses run underground?" Celia asked.

"Ah, it's your first time on the bus, I see," Zosimo said, his hands clasped behind his back as he rocked onto his heels.

"I'm sorry, Celia," Mr. Morven said. "I didn't explain. They're not really buses like school buses. BUS stands for Below-ground Ushering System."

"Oh." Celia was a little overwhelmed with all of the new things going on around her. She'd expected to feel a little out of place at a new school, but she'd never thought that everything would be so different.

"Are the cars open yet, Zosimo?" Mr. Morven asked.

"Sure are. In fact, a few others are already down there. Help yourself," he said, gesturing down the stairs.

They started down the long, wide staircase. Celia had been certain that the bottom was just out of view, but they kept going down and down until she started to wonder if the stairs would ever end. Finally, what seemed like fifty stories below ground, Celia spotted something besides stairs. As they continued down the remaining steps, her eyes widened as she took in the scene in front of her.

They were approaching a platform that looked similar to a subway station, with a tunnel on the right side. Sitting on what she assumed was a set of tracks was a long caterpillar-looking vehicle made of connected bubble-like cars. Each one had a large window, and every ten cars or so there was one with a door. The cars were bright blue and shiny, and Celia could see people sitting in a few of them. On the opposite side of the platform was a row of booths selling everything from magazines to meatball subs.

"Welcome to the BUS station, Celia." Mr. Morven set her trunk down. "I think it might be best if we choose a compartment and get your gear stashed; then you can feel free to check out the rathskellers."

"The what?"

"Rathskellers. That's what all the stalls on the other side are called."

"Why don't you just call them 'stalls' or 'shops' or something?" Celia grumbled. She felt like she was in a foreign country and didn't know what anyone was saying with all of these new words she kept hearing.

"I know it's a lot to take in, Celia, but don't worry. You'll figure everything out in no time." He gestured to the blue train. "Would you like to pick a compartment?"

She shook her head. "If you don't mind, I think I'll let you pick."

He lifted her trunk again. "Not a problem." He strode over to the closest door and stepped onto the train, and Celia hurried to follow him.

When she stepped on the vehicle behind him, she noticed that the inside was a paler shade of the blue on the outside.

Chapter Three

A long aisle ran down the middle of the cars, with sliding doors heading to individual compartments on each side. Mr. Morven walked down to an open door about halfway down the car and stepped inside the compartment. Celia followed, and found herself facing the platform from the other side of the window. The compartment had a bench on either side, each covered in pale blue fabric. Mr. Morven stashed Celia's trunk under the left bench and fastened it in place. Her duffle bag went on the rack above the bench.

"Would you like to get anything to eat or something to read for the trip, Celia?" Mr. Morven asked. "It's a rather long trip."

"Sure, but..."

"Is there a problem?"

"I didn't bring any money."

Mr. Morven put a hand on her shoulder and steered her toward the exit. "Don't worry about that, Celia. It's all taken care of."

"What?"

He put a finger to his lips. "Shhh. Can't talk about it here."

Stepping off the train, Celia looked up and down the platform at the booths to see what they were selling. One place had books, another sopapillas. At one end was a booth advertising music, while another was promoting their new fruit drinks.

"What did you say these were called, Mr. Morven?" Celia asked.

"They're rathskellers." He rummaged in his pocket and pulled out a plastic card the same size and shape as a credit card. "I have to go check on something for just a minute, Celia. If you see anything you want to get, within reason, of course, hand this over and they'll take care of it."

"Okay." She watched him hurry off across the platform, then turned her attention back to the rathskellers. Wandering over to the one selling sopapillas, she asked for a small order from the friendly man behind the counter.

"Would you like honey with those, miss?"

"Yes, please."

She waited a few moments while he prepared the fried dough pillows and drizzled honey on the top. He set the container on the counter with a flourish. "There you go, miss. That'll be fifteen thirty." She cautiously handed over the card. "Well, you're all set, then," the man said, glancing at it and then handing it back to her. "Have a great year at school."

"Thank you," she said, taking the card and tucking it into her pocket. She nibbled on her sopapilla as she ambled down the row of booths. Spying a stall selling books and magazines, she headed inside and looked around. Instead of the regular best-sellers as she expected, the displays were filled with books from authors she had never heard of and magazines she had never seen before. Although there were a few shelves with things for the parents of students to read, the majority of the items were obviously aimed at the crowd headed off to the school. There were teen magazines and comic books, books of puzzles and magazines about music and movies. Books about study habits sat next to books touting courageous stories of adventurers and books giving beauty advice.

"Hello, there!" Celia turned to find a woman standing behind her with a smile on her face. "Are you looking for something in particular?" she asked.

Celia shook her head. "Not really."

"First year at Renasci?" When Celia nodded, she pointed to the display of magazines. "There are some popular magazines over there, if you'd like to check them out." She walked over and picked up one showing a smiling teenager on the cover. "This one's always a big seller with the tween crowd."

Celia glanced at the cover but didn't recognize any of the names listed. "Are these people stars or something?"

"Or something. They're just the biggest celebrities in the demesne!" She smiled at Celia. "You must be new to our world. Most of the other girls your age that have come through here have grabbed this up like it was the last copy in the world."

"Yeah, well, I guess it's obvious that I'm not used to all of this. But I'll go ahead and get this and see what I think."

"Sure thing. Or are you more of the bookworm type?"

Celia shrugged. "A little of both, I suppose."

"I might suggest this book for you, too, then," the woman said, picking up a thick book titled *The Roots of Renasci*. "It's all about the history of your new school."

"Sure. That sounds good."

"I'll ring you up right over here." Celia followed the woman over to a register. After a few moments, the woman said, "It'll only set you back ninety-three forty-four."

Celia had wondered about the price of the sopapillas, since they seemed a lot more expensive than the price of snack food she was used to, but the total for her reading material seemed a bit excessive. "Ninety-three forty-four? Dollars?"

The woman laughed. "No wonder you looked so shocked. I forgot you're not from around here. No, it's not dollars. We use a different kind of currency here, called the konig. One dollar is approximately equal to three konigs. So if you were going to convert this to dollars, it would be, let's see..." There was a pause as she did a quick calculation in her head. "About twenty-eight dollars and change."

"Oh. I didn't know."

"No problem. Most of us here at the BUS station take both kinds of money, so don't worry if you don't have konigs."

"No, I've got this card..." Celia fished it out of her pocket and handed it over.

"Ah, now that's something special. I guess it's all paid for then. You have a great year at school, and hopefully I'll see you again soon!"

"Um, thanks." Celia picked up her bag of books and turned to leave.

"Oh! Don't forget your card!" the woman said.

Celia turned back to her. "Oh, thanks. I wouldn't want to lose that."

"No," the woman said, eyeing her speculatively, "you wouldn't."

Celia took the card from her and put it back in her pocket, feeling a bit like there was something going on that she didn't know about. "Thanks."

"No, thank *you*."

After buying a raspberry drincan, which reminded Celia of a smoothie, she headed back to the train. It took her a few moments to figure out which door she needed to go through to get to her compartment, especially since the platform was now getting busier. She jostled her way through the people milling about on the platform and made her way onto the train. She squeezed past the crowds of people blocking the aisle, but she finally found the correct compartment, closed the door to block the noise of the hustle and bustle, and sank down on the bench below her duffle bag.

She watched people on the platform, some waving to friends, others saying good-bye to parents and siblings. Many were lugging suitcases, trunks, and large bags onto the train, while others seemed to bring very little with them. The parents looked just as frantic as the students, some of them running around to make sure all of their children were safely on the train with all of their possessions. Some, however, were sitting on benches and looking rather relieved to be sending their children off to school for another year. Celia noticed a few kids who were looking bewildered and figured it must be their first time heading to the school, too. Most of them had a dazed look as they tried to find their way around the platform and onto the cars. She was thankful she had Mr. Morven there to help her find her way through the chaotic situation.

Remembering the reactions she'd gotten to the card Mr. Morven had given her, she pulled it out of her pocket to study it. There was a stylized ram drawn in red, with an unusual-looking crest in the top right corner. On the back was the standard magnetic strip that was on most credit cards, and a one-line address similar to the one that had been on the card in the school brochure. It didn't seem so peculiar to her.

The door to the compartment opened and Mr. Morven walked in. "Hey, Celia. I see you found some rathskellers to visit."

She nodded. "Here's your card back," she said, holding it out to him.

"Actually," he said as he sat down opposite her, "it's yours."

"Mine?"

"Yup. It's linked to an account that's set up for you to use while you're at Renasci."

"Really?"

"Really. But don't expect to go on a wild shopping spree. It's limited to certain amounts of money each week, and only at certain locations." He leaned forward and rested his elbows on his knees. "It's probably best if you don't mention it to the other kids for now. It might make them suspicious."

"Okay."

Mr. Morven glanced at his watch. "We've only got about fifteen minutes until we leave. Are you all set for the trip?"

Celia nodded.

"Great. Zosimo always leaves right on schedule, so in the future, make sure you get here with plenty of time. When your ticket says 10:37, it means 10:37."

"Ticket?"

"Oh, almost forgot," he said, rummaging in his jacket pockets. He pulled out two long strips of paper and handed one to her. "Zosimo will come around and punch these once we get on our way."

"If he doesn't check the tickets until after we leave, doesn't anyone ever sneak on the train?"

"It's never happened that I know of." He shrugged. "I guess it could happen. But Zosimo is on top of things here. Nothing's usually a problem."

An announcement came out of the speakers on the ceiling. "Ten minutes until departure, everyone. Ten minutes until departure."

Celia watched out the window as the pace of the crowd picked up to a frenzy. From her seat, she could see the bottom of the staircase, and a few stragglers were now running down the stairs to get to the train on time. The aisle outside their door was packed with people rushing both directions, and every once in a while the train shifted as the cars rocked with people jumping on or off. Still looking out the window, Celia noticed the book and magazine rathskeller she had shopped in earlier. Remembering the woman's reaction to her card, she turned to Mr. Morven.

"Is there something unusual about this card, Mr. Morven?" she asked, holding up the card she still held in her hand.

"Somewhat," he replied cautiously. "Why do you ask?"

Celia looked at it. "I guess I figured that to pay for anything, someone would have to run this through a machine or something."

"They didn't swipe the card? Like a credit card or a gift card?"

Celia shook her head. "No, and some of them acted kind of weird when I gave it to them. Like it was something really strange."

Mr. Morven sighed. "I'm sure they haven't seen one in a while. But they should have swiped it. Otherwise you technically didn't pay for anything."

"But I gave them the card and..."

He held up a hand to stop her. "No, no. You didn't do anything wrong, Celia. We'll just have to make sure they get reimbursed for the things you bought, that's all. It's...well, not many people have a card with that particular design on it, and sometimes people get carried away when they see it."

"Why?"

He drummed his fingers on his knee. "It's special, I'll say that much. For now, it would be best if you put it back in your pocket and we'll figure it all out later."

"But—"

"I'm sorry, Celia, and I know you'll get tired of hearing this, but I really can't say anything more."

"Five minutes until departure, everyone. Five minutes until departure," came the announcement over the loudspeaker.

"Do I need to bring my lunch with me?" Celia asked, the thought suddenly popping into her head.

"Nope. There's a dining car about three back from ours. You can get whatever you'd like to eat there once we're underway."

"How does this thing travel, anyway?"

"It's a lot like a train, really. It's got tracks, but the design of the vehicles lets us take very sharp turns."

"Because of the little, um, bubble cars?"

"Exactly. I don't know what the proper term for them is, but that's probably as good a description as any."

"Do we travel underground the whole way?"

"No, only when we're near cities and towns. Most people aren't accustomed to seeing a bright blue train heading down the tracks. All our stations in towns are underground, most of them underneath very boring-looking buildings like the one above us now."

"It sounds neat."

"There's no better way to travel! Well, maybe one better way, but this is the best way to get to school with all your stuff."

"Does everyone get to the school on the train?"

"Not everyone takes the BUS. Some kids live close enough to the school that their parents can drop them off, but for most, the BUS is the only way to get there."

"Is this the only BUS, or are there different ones from different places?"

"There are five main BUS routes that run throughout the country, with stops of varying sizes all over the place. Some areas have developed smaller routes to get to the stations, but most people just find their way to a major station. There are also different kinds of services on the tracks, depending on the destination and purpose of the trip, like an express passage, or EP as we call it, which is what we're going on today to Renasci."

"How does everyone get to the stations if they live far away?"

"Lots of different ways. Some—"

"ALL ABOARD!" The loud voice over the loudspeaker made Celia jump. "ALL ABOARD!"

"You'll want to hold on the first time we start up, Celia," Mr. Morven said. "It takes a little getting used to."

There was a mad dash to the platform by those who were not going on the train, and parents lined the edge of the platform to wave one last time. A whistle blew and there was a loud hiss, followed by a clunk. The cars jerked forward and Celia grabbed for the armrest at the end of her bench. There was no turning back now. They were headed for Renasci.

Chapter Four
Secrets Revealed

Celia watched the platform start moving slowly off to her left, and soon the people became a blur. After a moment, the platform disappeared and the view out the window changed to a concrete wall. The train sped up, and Celia held on tighter. Faster and faster they went, until finally it seemed that their speed leveled off.

"How fast are we going?"

Mr. Morven shrugged. "Pretty fast. I don't know for sure. We go at a decent clip for a while, but then we have to slow down when we hit the mountains because of the tight turns."

"Mountains? Where are we going?"

"Tickets!" someone called, followed by a knock on the door. The door slid open and Zosimo stuck his head in. "Got your tickets?" he asked.

They both held out their tickets, Celia still holding tightly to the armrest with her other hand. How Zosimo was standing up, she wasn't sure, as the train was moving quite fast. He punched their tickets and handed them back, tipped his hat, closed the door, and headed on down the aisle calling, "Tickets!"

Celia sat on her bench and studied the ticket in her hand. It was long and thin, and now had a punch in the upper left-hand corner. It read:

ONE-WAY TICKET
C-BUS 1ST STATION TO RENASCI 4TH STATION
10:37 A.M. AUGUST 1ST EP

There was a coat of arms on the left side of the ticket and a symbol that Celia didn't recognize on the right, and all the printing was done in green iridescent ink.

"Where is the 4th Station, Mr. Morven?" she asked, looking at the text on the ticket.

"At Renasci," he replied absently as he pulled out a thick pile of papers from his briefcase and set them on his lap.

"Yeah, but where is Renasci?"

"Um, I guess it's in the middle of the Rocky Mountains somewhere."

"You don't know for sure?"

"Well, it's never been plotted on a map."

"Why not?"

"No one outside of the demesne knows it's there. The only way to get there is by this BUS. None of the roads in the area connect to anything outside the demesne, so it's kind of hard for anyone to just stumble across it."

Celia thought for a moment. "So we're going from the east coast all the way to the Rocky Mountains?"

"Pretty much."

"Wow. We must be going really fast."

"Yup, pretty much." Mr. Morven was reading his papers as he answered her questions.

Celia watched out the window as the concrete wall moved away from the side of the train and slowly tapered off to ground level. Sunlight came through the windows and lit the compartment as they moved from underground to above ground. She tried watching the scenery, but they were traveling so fast that it all seemed to blur together. Feeling her stomach roll, Celia moaned and turned away from the window.

"Doing okay?" Mr. Morven asked, looking at her. "You don't look so great."

"I'm feeling a little sick."

"A lot of people have that problem their first time on the BUS. The super-fast speed gets to them. You might try lying down. Sometimes it helps if you can't see out the window."

Celia stretched out on the bench and closed her eyes, and before she knew it she had dozed off. When she woke up, the pile of papers on Mr. Morven's lap had dwindled to a small stack. She sat up and stretched.

"Hey," he said, noticing that she was awake. "Feeling better?"

"Yeah." She looked out the window at the flat plains they were speeding across, her eyes trying in vain to focus on the scenery. Glancing out at the horizon, she took in the wide open sky and a view that seemed to stretch forever.

Celia's stomach growled and Mr. Morven laughed. "Guess you're getting hungry, huh?" he asked.

"A little," Celia admitted.

"Feel free to run back to the dining car and grab a bite to eat."

"I think I will," she said, carefully standing up. She still wasn't quite used to traveling at such a fast speed. "I just head to the right and I'll find it?" she asked.

"Yup. It's about the third car back. You can't miss it. And just hand them your card to pay. You shouldn't have any trouble."

"Okay."

Celia slid the door open, stepped out into the hallway, and closed the door to the compartment. Turning toward the back of the train, she walked carefully along, keeping her hands out to the sides to catch her balance when the train shifted. She tiptoed across the connector disks between cars and made her way down to the dining car. When she finally looked up after making sure her feet were firmly planted on the floor of the car and not on the shifting expansion disk, she could hardly believe what she saw.

It was unlike any dining car she'd ever heard of. On the right side next to her was a curving wooden counter, with a friendly-looking man dishing up food and drinks. The counter made an L-shaped area where the man was moving around, then curved and ran along the rest of the right wall on the outside edge of the car. Round stools covered in blue fabric sat in front of the counter. The entire left side of the car was a row of circular booths, complete with round tables and curved benches, all in shades of blue.

"Howdy, miss," the man behind the counter said as he flipped a glass in the air and caught it with one hand. "Can I getcha something?"

Celia stepped over to the edge of the counter and leaned on her elbows. "What do you have?"

"Anything you'd like," he replied. "You name it, we can get it."

"But how... ?" Celia began, then thinking about everything else she'd seen today, shook her head. "Never mind. Can I have a turkey sandwich?"

"Sure can. Cheese?"

"Swiss, if you have it."

"Absolutely. Anything to drink?"

"Um... I had a raspberry..." She couldn't remember the name. "...something that I got at the station before we left. Can you make one of those?"

"A drincan?"

"That's it."

"No problem. Anything else?"

"No, thanks."

"All-righty. That's a turkey sandwich with Swiss and a razz drincan. Comes to twenty-two twenty-five," he said, ringing her order up on an old-fashioned cash register. Celia handed him her card, trying to cover it with her hand so no one else would see it. He took it, glanced at the front, and gave her a wink. He turned to the back and Celia saw him swipe the card through a machine, then he spun back around and handed the card back to her. "All set. Order's number fifty-three. I'll call you in a minute."

"Thanks."

She turned and glanced around the room. She didn't really feel like sitting at one of the big booths by herself, so she made her way down the car and found an empty stool at the counter. Slipping onto it, she had to turn away from the window in front of her, since the rapidly moving scenery was making her feel nauseous.

As Celia was looking around the dining car, she noticed a blond-haired girl sitting two stools away, watching her. When she saw Celia looking at her, she smiled. Celia noticed she was eating by herself, as well.

"Hi," the girl said. "First time on the BUS?"

Celia nodded. "Yours, too?"

"First time for a trip this long. I get to be the guinea pig for our family. I've got three younger brothers and sisters, so I'm the first to head off to school."

"It's a little faster than I'm used to traveling," Celia said, trying to avoid seeing anything out the window.

"I know what you mean. The local trains don't usually get up to speed before they have to slow down." The girl turned to face Celia. "I'm Maddie," she said.

"Celia."

"Number fifty-three!" the man behind the counter called out.

"That's me," Celia said, hopping off the stool. She headed up and grabbed her order, then returned to her seat.

"I'm starved," she said, climbing back on the stool. She took a big bite of her sandwich, and saw out of the corner of her eye that Maddie was staring at her. "What?" she asked, her voice muffled by the mouthful of food. It was only then that she noticed Maddie holding her card.

"You said 'Celia.' Are you Celia Fincastle?"

"Yeah. Why?" Celia carefully set her sandwich back down.

"Do you know who you are?" Maddie squeaked. "I mean, I've heard about this symbol, but I've never seen it in person before, only in pictures," she said, staring at the card she still held.

Celia chewed slowly and swallowed, then wiped her fingers on her napkin. "What do you mean? There's nothing special about me."

Maddie's eyes widened. "You mean you don't know?!"

"Know what? Mr. Morven gave me that card. I don't know anything about it."

"Oh, here," Maddie said quickly, holding the card out to her. "You'd better take this back."

"Thanks," Celia said, taking the card and putting it back in her pocket.

"Oh, wow, I can't believe I'm actually talking to you. I've heard so much about you, but nobody's known where you've been for the last nine years. I mean, it was a big deal for me, because you're my age and everything, but everyone knows about you. Or, at least, what there is to know about you."

"Maddie!" Celia said, stopping the torrent of words. Maddie stared at her with wide eyes. "I have no idea what you're talking about, but I don't think there's anything that great about me. There must be someone else with the same name or something." She picked up her sandwich and took another bite, thinking the conversation would move on to some other topic.

Maddie shook her head wildly. "No, no. I'm certain it's you. There is no other Celia Fincastle in the demesne. You're the one who was chosen. I know it!"

"Chosen?" Celia started to get nervous. "What are you talking about?"

"The Overseer. He picked your family! And you're the one he said was coming."

Celia took a sip of her drink and forced it down her dry throat. Could what Maddie was saying be true? Surely not. Wouldn't Aunt Agatha have known something about it?

"I'm sorry. I shouldn't be going on about this. Hasn't anyone told you this before?"

Celia shook her head. "I... I have to go," she said, picking up her sandwich and drink. "Nice meeting you, Maddie."

"Oh, you, too, Celia. Maybe we'll see each other at school!"

Celia just nodded as she headed for the door. She noticed that a few of the people who had been sitting across the car in a booth were giving her odd looks and whispering to each other. Hurrying out of the car, she kept her head down and made her way back to the compartment where Mr. Morven was still working on his paperwork. She walked in and dropped onto the bench.

"Uh-oh," Mr. Morven said, looking up from his paperwork. "You don't look so good. Still feeling ill?"

Celia shook her head. "Someone... this girl..."

"Did someone say something to you?"

She nodded. She noticed he had a worried look on his face. He moved his papers off to one side and focused only on her.

"What did she say?"

"Something about...she thought I was someone famous or something. My card fell out of my pocket when I went to get my food. Something about an Overseer and my family and I was the chosen one."

Mr. Morven sighed. "I told them we should tell you right away..." he said quietly, glancing off to the side.

"You mean it's true?!"

"To a certain extent, yes," he said, looking back at her. "I assume this girl found your card and recognized the symbol on it." When Celia nodded, he continued. "The stylized ram and the crest that are on that card are very important symbols, Celia. It's probably hard for you to understand all of this, since you grew up outside the demesne, but your parents...your whole family, really, hold a very important position in our world."

"Are my parents still in this other world?"

"I don't know."

"Why not?"

"I think perhaps I should start at the beginning. In the demesne, there is a leader called the Overseer. He is very powerful, more powerful than you can imagine. He chooses people to represent him and lead the rest of us, and your family was the one he chose for our country."

"So my family is like royalty or something?"

"Not exactly, but similar, I guess. It is a huge honor to be chosen as the Overseer's princeps. The Overseer chooses a new family every fifty years, but often the same family is chosen again and again. When the new family was to be chosen the last time, another family, the Coridans, was trying to take your family's place. When the Overseer chose your family again, the Coridans became very upset, and tried to take over your family's position by force."

"What happened?"

"Unfortunately, no one knows for sure. Security was obviously tight around your family, but somehow someone from the Coridans got past the guards and into your family's quarters. When everyone realized what was going on, the guards went to check on all of you, but you were the only one left. There were no clues about what happened, no evidence of any sort to work from. They sent you to your aunt, as she was the only person left even distantly connected to your family.

"It was, understandably, the biggest news at the time. No one could figure out why the rest of your family disappeared but nothing happened to you."

"So Maddie was right. Everyone knows about me?" Celia glanced at the door and was startled to see that people were looking through the door curiously as they walked past. "Why didn't anyone tell me?"

"Your aunt wouldn't let us."

"Aunt Agatha knew about this?"

"Not entirely. She was given a brief outline of events, but no details. When we asked that we be able to contact you as you grew older, she refused."

"Is everyone going to start staring at me?" she asked, looking at the door again.

He shook his head. "It's been a long time since anyone in the demesne has seen you. Almost everyone knows you by name only, but I'm sure that once word gets out you'll probably get your fair share of attention. People are going to be curious."

Celia groaned as Mr. Morven stood up. "I'm sorry, Celia. I hadn't planned on you finding out like this. I'm going to grab something to eat and let you have a few minutes to yourself." A moment later, he was gone.

Celia sat on the bench and stared at the wall in front of her, her mind reeling with what she'd been told. Surely there was some mistake. She'd thought it was rather strange that she'd been asked to attend this school in the first place, but now, to find out all this... it just seemed like too much to believe.

The original paperwork she'd received from Renasci had mentioned that it was a school for the gifted student, but not in the traditional sense of the word. In this case, "gifted" meant someone who had extraordinary abilities, things that most people could only dream of doing. While Celia had been uncertain that she fit that description, Mr. Morven had assured her that she was indeed qualified to attend.

Knowing now that Aunt Agatha had some idea about where her parents were from and who they were, she understood the concern about her approval of Celia's attendance at Renasci. If Aunt Agatha knew what Renasci really was and where it was, she would never have let Celia go.

Celia's stomach started to feel queasy again, but this time not from the movement of the vehicle. If everything Mr. Morven had said was true, then going to school just got a lot more complicated. What if people were expecting her to be really good at something, and she ended up being horrible? What if she messed up?

There was a knock on the door and Celia looked over to see Maddie on the other side. Sliding the door open, she said, "Hi, Maddie."

"Hi, Celia. Can I come in?"

"Sure."

Maddie took the bench across from her. "I hope I didn't upset you before," she said, a worried look on her face. "My mom says I talk before I think sometimes."

"It's okay."

"Have you been to Renasci before?"

Celia shook her head. "I've been living with... well, I call her my aunt but she's not really my aunt, exactly. Anyway, she's not part of the demesne."

"Oh, too bad. It must have been horrible being stuck there."

Celia just shrugged. It was all she really remembered, so she had no way of knowing about anything else.

"Anyway," Maddie continued, "everyone's talking about what coterie they're going to be part of. My mom says there's no way I'm going to make it into Mensaleon, but that's the one I think is the coolest. Not that there's much difference, of course, but their gifts are the ones that sound the most fun."

"Um, Maddie?" Celia interrupted her.

"What?"

"What are you talking about?"

Maddie looked at her strangely. "You really don't know much about the demesne, do you?"

Celia shook her head, growing frustrated. "I told you, I've been living with my aunt."

Before either one could say anything more, the voice came over the speakers again. "We are approaching the mountains. Please find your seat and remain there until we arrive at the station. It is unsafe for passengers to be moving about the train while we travel through the mountains. Thank you."

Maddie jumped to her feet. "I'd better go. See you when we get there!" She headed out the door.

Celia noticed that the aisle outside the door had gotten busy and was glad she wasn't trying to get through the crowd of people out there. In a few moments, Mr. Morven returned carrying a wrapped sandwich and a drink. Seeing his meal, Celia remembered the remainder of her sandwich she had brought back from the dining car, so she pulled it out and took a bite while Mr. Morven settled in his seat again.

"Did you hear the announcement?" Mr. Morven asked.

Celia nodded. "You said the school was in the Rocky Mountains. Are those the mountains we're getting near?"

He nodded. "Yes. We have to zigzag our way through the mountains while we climb, which is why the trains are designed the way they are. The rounded cars make it easier to go around the switchbacks."

"Oh." Celia chewed for a minute. "Mr. Morven?"

"Hmm?"

"Maddie said something about a . . . coterie, or something?"

He nodded. "Students are divided into coteries for dorms and classes. It will all be explained when you get to the school."

The train gave a lurch and Celia looked out the window. The scenery, which had been whizzing by at an alarming rate, was becoming clearer. "Are we slowing down?" Celia asked.

"We have to. The sharp turns make it impossible for us to keep going at our normal speed. We'd fly off the tracks."

"Oh."

Soon after, the train reached the start of the first incline, and then the first of many switchbacks. After a couple, Celia laid back down on the bench and closed her eyes, certain that the turkey sandwich she had eaten was going to reappear in a less appealing form. She quickly dozed off again, and when she awoke, the lights were on inside the train again and the windows showed nothing but darkness.

"How long was I asleep?" she asked.

Mr. Morven jumped a little at her voice. "Oh! You're awake again. I was just thinking I'd have to get you up soon. The ten minute announcement just came over the speakers. We should be pulling into the station soon."

"Is it nighttime already?"

"No, no. We went back underground, that's all."

"Oh."

A few minutes later Celia had to squint her eyes when the train popped above ground again and bright sunlight filled the car. Looking out the window, she saw tall, rocky peaks and towering pine trees. It was unlike any place she'd ever been. As the train continued to climb, her ears popped, and she felt her stomach tightening into a knot, although she was pretty sure it wasn't from motion sickness this time.

"We are approaching the Renasci Station," the speaker squawked again. "Please remain in your seat until the vehicle comes to a complete stop, then proceed in an orderly fashion to the nearest exit. Your belongings will be delivered to your dorms. Seventh-years should gather on the right side of the platform, as indicated. Thank you."

"That's you," Mr. Morven said.

"What's me?"

"Seventh-years. Students are referred to by the number of years they have remaining until their schooling is finished. Since this is your first year, you have seven years left, so you're a seventh-year."

"Oh."

The train slowed further and Celia noticed that there was nothing but a steep drop-off on her side of the train. Glancing across the aisle, she could see the platform coming into view. The vehicle slowed to a crawl and people started to fill the aisle outside their door, despite the instructions to remain seated. When the train jerked to a stop, the people in the aisle fell toward the front of the car, and there was a scramble as they tried to regain their footing.

Mr. Morven shook his head. "I don't know why they bother to make that announcement. No one ever stays in their seat, and they always have the same problem in the aisle when we finally do stop." He collected all of his papers and put them back in his briefcase. "Well, it looks like the main rush of people has passed. Are you ready?" he asked Celia.

She nodded her head, too nervous to speak. Rising slowly to her feet, she stepped toward the door, but Mr. Morven stopped her.

"Is the book in your duffle bag?"

"Y-y-yes."

"You're not supposed to take any of your things with you, but I really don't think you should leave that book here. Would you like me to take it into the school for you? That might be the best solution." At her nod, he reached over her head and grabbed the bag off the shelf. "After you," he said, gesturing to the door.

Celia walked over and opened the door. There were a few stragglers in the car, but most of the people had already left. Turning to her right, Celia walked toward the door of the car, then turned left toward the exit. Taking a deep breath, she stepped through the door and onto the platform of the station.

Chapter Five
Welcome to Renasci

The busy platform was brightly lit with sunshine, and Celia had to shade her eyes to see anything. There was a small building at the back edge of the platform, with wide double doors on either side of a ticket window. The crush of people flowed through the doors, but Mr. Morven directed Celia toward the right side of the platform where a group of students were waiting. Celia noticed some of the same kids who had looked so nervous on the last platform, and felt somewhat reassured that she wasn't the only one who felt that way.

"Seventh-years, please gather around!" someone called from the back of the group. A head popped over the crowd, as the person jumped onto something so they could see over the heads. Celia felt as though she recognized the man, but she couldn't quite place him. It wasn't until he turned and spotted her walking toward the group that she figured out who it was.

"Ah, Celia! I see Mr. Morven escorted you safely from your aunt's house. Quite the trip, is it not?"

Celia smiled at the familiar face, even though the last time she had seen that particular face it had been in miniature and made of blue light. "Yes, it was, Mr. Snodridge."

"Oh, none of that, Celia. Everyone here calls me Higby."

"But Aunt Agatha says..."

He smiled at her. "Yes, I'm sure she does, but it's quite a mouthful to say Mr. Snodridge every time you see me, so it's much easier to just call me Higby. I assure you, nearly everyone here addresses me that way."

"If you're sure..."

He nodded decisively. "I am. Now, if you will be so kind as to join this group over here, I am in charge of getting all of you neophytes through orientation this year."

"Uh...'neophytes'?"

"Sorry. New students."

"Oh."

"Celia," Mr. Morven said next to her. "I'm going to head up to the school. I'll bring your bag up to your dorm later this afternoon. Higby will get you from here."

Celia nodded. As she watched Mr. Morven stride away toward the station, she felt very apprehensive. What if everyone else reacted the same way Maddie had when they found out who she was?

Higby clapped his hands to get everyone's attention. "All right. It looks as though everyone is here, so if you would all follow me..." He wove his way through the group of students and headed toward the building. Celia and the others followed him through the doors and marched through the station. Celia caught a glimpse of benches lining the walls and a small ticket counter along one side before they were heading back outside through the front doors. Stepping onto a wide pathway, the group stopped in their tracks as they got their first look at the Renasci Academy.

An enormous structure towered in front of them. Its front doors were two stories high, centered in the front of the building and flanked by smaller doors on either side.

Massive wood beams held up the angled roof, with heavy metal hardware holding them all together. Three granite steps ran the length of the building, leading up to the doors, which were constructed of large wooden planks and detailed with wrought iron fixtures.

"Come along," Higby said, heading up the pathway. The group marched up the path, their speed slowed considerably by the fact that everyone was gawking at the building, heads craning to take in the impressive façade.

"This way, please," Higby said, leading the way through the center doors and into an antechamber that was about ten feet deep and stretched across the front of the building. Another set of doors, though smaller, stood in front of them, and he marched them through the center set of doors. They passed under an overhead walkway, past the foot of the double curved staircases which led up to the second floor, and finally out into the Main Hall.

Every single student in the group stepped through the doors and promptly stopped looking where he or she was going. Celia's mouth dropped open as her eyes traveled to the ceiling and then around the room. Main Hall was immense, with columns made of bundled tree trunks holding up the rafters for the roof. Huge beams like the ones on the outside of the building spanned the ceiling of the hall, which stood at least fifty feet above her head. Doors leading to hallways and rooms lined the side walls, and clusters of sofas and chairs or tables and chairs were scattered around the room.

As Higby directed them through the hall, everyone pointed and commented to their companions about some new thing they had spotted. As they reached halfway through the hall, they spied the end wall, which caused them all to drop their jaws in awe again. Opposite from the front doors stood a wall of windows, spanning from floor to ceiling and framing a view of first the commons and behind that a range of snow-covered mountains. The view was spectacular and seemed like it belonged on a postcard or perhaps even a Christmas card. Pine trees stood as sentries at the end of the grounds, towering over the edges of the buildings nearby but dwarfed by the mountains behind them.

The hall echoed with the noise of students greeting each other after a summer apart. Celia couldn't help but feel a bit overwhelmed by the sheer number of people she saw in that room alone. While she wasn't exactly a wallflower, she hadn't had the best track record when it came to social situations, and she felt a new swarm of butterflies take up residence in her stomach.

As Higby ushered them through a door on the left side of the hall, Celia began to wonder if it had been a wise decision to come to this school. All of these people seemed to know something about this place, and she had never heard of it before she'd met Higby in the book. She didn't *feel* very gifted, and her talents were certainly nothing she'd really been proud of.

The group came to a halt in a small room lined with benches and chairs.

"You'll wait here until the headmaster comes to assign you to your coteries," Higby said. "Each person here has a unique collection of abilities. Your coterie is comprised of those with similar talents, to foster growth among students. While your coterie will be the people you see most often, they are by no means the only ones you should interact with. You will find that though your strongest talents are shared with those in your own coterie, each of you will have gifts that reach beyond the average profile of your coterie."

He gestured to a framed printing on the wall beside him. "This depicts the five coteries here at the school. You can see that they are as follows: Mensaleon, Aquilegia, Tattotauri, Sprachursus, and Corpanthera. If you will all take a seat and wait, I shall go fetch the headmaster." He turned and left the room.

Scuffling followed as everyone found a chair or a spot on a bench, then silence as people looked around the room. After a few moments, hushed voices started talking and then grew louder and louder.

Celia sat off to one side by herself and studied the printing on the wall. Each coterie had the image of an animal beside it; she guessed they were symbols or mascots of some sort. Mensaleon had a purple lion, Aquilegia had a silver eagle, Tattotauri had a red bull, Sprachursus had a green bear, and Corpanthera had a blue panther.

"Hi, Celia!"

She turned to find Maddie sitting beside her. "Hey, Maddie."

"Isn't this exciting?" Maddie clasped her hands together under her chin. "I've been waiting for this day my whole life. My grandmother's talked about this place so much! No one in my family's been in Mensaleon, but I really hope that's where I end up."

"How do they know where we belong?"

"It's all written in the book."

"What book?"

Maddie pointed to a book stand on the opposite wall. "That one."

"How does the book know?"

She shrugged. "The Overseer."

"How does he know?"

"It's... um... well... it's kind of complicated. I guess if you didn't grow up here, you wouldn't really understand."

The door opened again and Higby walked in, followed by six other people. The last man in the line had a bald head except for two patches of hair that made him look like he was wearing earmuffs just above his ears.

"Settle down, ladies and gentlemen," Higby said. He waited a few moments until everyone was silent. "I am pleased to introduce Headmaster Doyen."

The bald man stepped up and shook Higby's hand, then took the spot behind the stand. "I would like to welcome you all to your new home for the next seven years. I'm sure you will all be a valuable part of the community here at Renasci Academy. As Higby has told you, each person will be placed in a coterie, according to the listing here in the book. You will each come up when I call your name, and I will put you with the appropriate dean." He gestured to the five other people standing in a row next to him.

The man closest to the headmaster stepped forward a step and nodded to them. "I am Professor Mesbur, the dean of Tattotauri," he said, and stepped back. Celia thought he looked a little like a professional wrestler, with his huge build and shiny bald head.

The man to his left stepped forward. "I'm Professor Spadaro, dean of Corpanthera." This man was tall and skinny, and he moved as if he had no bones in his body. He had pale blond hair, almost white, and his skin was nearly translucent.

The woman next to him stepped forward as he stepped back. "My name is Professor Legaspi, and I'm the dean of Aquilegia." She had curly hair and wore green rectangular glasses. She looked fairly normal, particularly next to the two previous teachers.

The man next to her took a step forward. "I am Professor Perrin, dean of Sprachursus." Professor Perrin seemed like he should have been an actor or a model. He was quite handsome, and he wore his shirt with the sleeves rolled up to his elbows.

The woman at the end of the row stepped up. "Hello. I'm Professor Twombly, the dean of Mensaleon." She wore brightly colored clothes and large, dangling earrings, which were easy to see with her short red hair.

"Thank you, deans," Headmaster Doyen said, turning back to the book on the stand in front of him. "And now, we will begin."

One by one the students went up to talk with Headmaster Doyen and then walked over to stand with one of the five professors. There seemed to be no particular order to the names being called, so no one had any idea when they were going to be next. Celia wasn't worried at first, but as the group of students still waiting grew smaller and smaller, she wondered when her name would come up. When she was the last student left sitting in a seat, she felt as if she were on display, as everyone waiting on the other side of the room stared at her while the next-to-last student talked with the headmaster. Celia sat on the edge of her seat as the boy in front of her walked over to the Corpanthera group, waiting for the headmaster to finally call her up.

"Deans, if you would all be so kind as to take your students to their new quarters."

Celia's palms grew sweaty. Why hadn't she been called up and placed in a coterie? Were they going to tell her that she didn't belong in any of them and she had to go home? That they'd made a mistake and she really wasn't qualified to be at this school?

Maddie's eyes widened as she noticed that Celia hadn't been called up to talk with the headmaster. Celia shook her head and shrugged as she watched Maddie file out of the room with the rest of the students, leaving her alone with Higby and the headmaster.

"Miss Fincastle," Headmaster Doyen said, turning to her without asking her name. "There seems to be a problem with your coterie assignment."

Celia gulped. "Th-th-there is?"

He nodded. "You see, normally each person's name is listed, followed by the coterie to which they belong. Yours, however... well, it's different."

"How so?" Higby asked, walking over to the stand to peer at the book. "Interesting."

They both looked up at Celia with speculative expressions. She gulped again.

"You see, Miss Fincastle," the headmaster said, "your name has not one coterie listed."

"It...doesn't?" She felt as if she had swallowed a rock. She didn't belong in any of the coteries? Were they going to send her home?

He shook his head. "No. Not one." He paused. "Not two, either. Not three or even four. It appears, Miss Fincastle, that the book believes you are capable of belonging to all five coteries."

"What?" she whispered.

"Yes, Celia, all five," he said quietly, coming to sit in the chair across from her.

"But I..."

"I confess," he said, studying her carefully, "that I have never had this situation arise before. No one has ever been placed in more than one coterie."

"So what do we do now?" Higby asked, stepping around the stand and leaning back on it, his hands in his pockets.

"Well," Doyen said, turning to look at Higby, "I suppose there are two options. We can choose a coterie or..." He turned back to Celia. "...you can choose a coterie."

"I..."

"Headmaster," Higby said, looking at Celia, "perhaps it would help if you could explain the different coteries and what their gifts are. Celia is not familiar with the demesne yet."

The headmaster looked sharply at Higby and then back at Celia. He nodded his head. "Of course." He stood and walked over to the printing on the wall. "First there is Aquilegia. Students gifted at vision abilities fall into this coterie. Things like seeing in the dark or speed-reading are their strengths. Next is Tattotauri. These students have gifts of touch, such as unlocking doors and healing. Then is Sprachursus. Students with the ability to understand languages or communicate with animals fit in this group. Here we have Corpanthera. Students who can do extraordinary physical feats belong to this coterie, such as super-fast motion or other actions that seem to defy the laws of nature. Finally is Mensaleon. This is often the most misunderstood coterie. Students in this group deal with abilities of the mind, and are often proficient at interpreting dreams and visions or cracking codes and solving puzzles."

Celia felt completely overwhelmed. She'd never heard of anyone being able to do any of those things, except maybe in books or movies. How was she supposed to know which one to pick? Why did she have to be the one singled out? Why was nothing ever easy for her?

"Celia?" Higby asked after she sat silent for a moment. "Do you have a coterie you'd like to pick?"

"I don't know how to do any of these things. How can I possibly have that many gifts and not know about them?"

"Everyone is gifted, Celia, but most choose not to believe. Only those who believe are contacted about the school," Higby said.

"So even Aunt Agatha can do some of this?"

"Well, she could at one point. But without use and training, gifts fade, until finally the choice to reject them becomes permanent."

"You mean everyone could come here?"

"Absolutely. If they believed," Headmaster Doyen said. "People have the extraordinary ability to be blind to the magical, miraculous, and amazing, however, and they convince themselves that it isn't real, isn't possible."

"What about kids whose parents don't believe? They never really have the chance."

"Each and every person decides for themselves, regardless of their circumstances. Some, like you, believe despite being raised by those who don't. Some choose to reject everything despite being raised by those who strongly believe. It is a choice that every person makes on their own," said Headmaster Doyen.

Celia looked at her shoes. "Everyone else was told where they belong. How do I know which one I belong in?"

The headmaster walked over to the book. "According to this, you belong in all of them, Miss Fincastle."

"So it really doesn't make any difference which coterie you choose, Celia," Higby said. "Do you have any preference for your coterie? Anyone you'd like to stay with or maybe avoid?"

"The only person I know is Maddie."

"Madelia Hannagan?"

"I-I guess. She just said her name was Maddie."

"It must be her. There's no one else with a similar name," Headmaster Doyen said, looking over the class list. "She's in Mensaleon. Would you like to join that coterie?"

"Um . . . sure, I guess."

"Very well, then. You are now officially a member of the Mensaleon coterie. Ah, and there it is in the book," he said, looking down at the page and then up at Celia, "so everything is now set. Higby, if you would care to show Miss Fincastle to her quarters?"

"Certainly," Higby said, standing up straight. "This way, Celia." Higby ushered her out of the room and into the crowded, noisy hall. "Straight back," he said, waving a hand toward the wall of windows. Celia walked in that direction, glancing around her. None of the other seventh-years were anywhere to be seen.

"Through this doorway, if you please," Higby said, indicating a large set of double doors at the end of the left side of the hall.

Stepping through the doors, Celia found herself in a long hallway, with windows opening onto the commons on one side and a collection of ornate picture frames covering the other. The longest carpet runner that Celia had ever seen ran down the center of the hall, leaving the parquet floor visible only at the very edges. She followed Higby to the end of the hallway, then stepped through the doorway into a wedge-shaped passageway which connected the first building to a second building. The two buildings sat at an unusual angle to each other, but the hallway continued on through the passageway and into the next building. Another wedge-shaped passageway sat between that building and the next, and Higby headed into another building identical to the one they were leaving. Halfway down that hallway, Higby turned away from the windows looking out at the commons and opened the door in front of him. Celia found herself at the bottom of a staircase when she went through the door, and Higby walked around her and started up the stairs.

"The Mensaleon quarters are just up these stairs," he said.

They went up a couple of flights of stairs, and when they finally reached the top, Celia saw a pair of wooden doors at the end of a short hall. The doors had lions carved into them, and two lion statues flanked the doorway, as well.

Higby reached for the door. "Here you are, Celia," he said, holding the door open for her. "Professor Twombly will show you to your room."

Celia caught a glimpse of purple-hued walls but couldn't see much else. Taking a deep breath, she stepped hesitantly toward the door.

Chapter Six

Dorms, Doxa, and Dinner

"Ah, Celia!" Professor Twombly met her as she walked into the room. "Headmaster Doyen just sent me a message that you're joining our coterie. You'll be in room number three, just through that doorway there," she said, indicating a door at the end of a short hallway on the left. "Your belongings arrived just a moment ago. You'll find them in the center of the room. I think the rest of the girls are just picking locations now, so if you hurry, you won't get stuck with whatever's left over."

Celia mumbled, "Thank you," and headed down the hall and through the door.

"Celia!" someone squealed from her left as she entered the room, and she felt someone latch onto her in a hug. "You're in the same coterie!" It was, of course, Maddie. "We're just about to pick our beds. But, here, let me introduce everyone. This is Galena Zwingle and Libby Cresswell. Girls, this is Celia. You know, the one I was telling you about."

All three girls turned to look at Celia with interest. Celia waved at them weakly. "Hi."

"Hey, Celia," Libby said. She had blond hair that fell to her shoulders and a full set of braces on her teeth.

Chapter Six

"Hi," Galena said. She definitely had the characteristics of an Asian, with straight black hair, dark eyes, and very pale skin, although Celia couldn't pinpoint a specific nationality.

"Isn't this room great?" Maddie said, looking around.

The room was a large square with a collection of chairs on an area rug in the center of the room and eight bed units along the walls, each pair creating an L-shape in the corners. The beds were placed up high, like bunk beds, but underneath each bed was a set of drawers and a desk.

Suddenly the door slammed open and smashed against the wall and four older girls strode into the room. "Miss Geleafa!" someone called from the foyer.

"Sorry!" one of the girls called back. She had long blond hair that looked like it had been carefully styled and wore thick eye makeup that made her look like she had two black eyes. "So," she said in a quieter voice. "You must be the new sevvies."

"Uh...sevvies?" Libby said tentatively.

"Yeah. It's what we call the little seventh-years."

"Oh."

"Here's how it works. This is our room. These are our beds," she said, hitching a thumb over her right shoulder to the beds lining the wall facing the commons. "You don't bother us, and we won't bother you."

"Um...okay," Maddie said, shuffling toward the other side of the room.

"Hey, Doxa?" one of the girls near the blond asked.

"What?" she replied.

"Maybe we should ask their names, just so we know who they are."

Doxa shrugged carelessly. "Whatever." She lifted her chin at them. "So who are you?"

The four newcomers looked at each other uneasily. Galena cleared her throat. "I'm Galena."

"Maddie."

"Celia."

"Libby."

Doxa arched one eyebrow and studied them. Finally she rolled her eyes. "I'm Doxa, and this is Katie, Gretchen, and Cy. We're solos — that's what we call first-years — and we don't want to be bothered by all you sevvies." She flicked her hair over her shoulder. Celia thought that all she needed was some bubble gum to pop and she'd complete the picture. "Like I said, you stay over there and we'll all get along fine." She turned on her heel and marched over to the bed in the corner by the door and the other three girls followed.

Celia and the others backed into the opposite corner of the room. "Anyone have a bed they want?" Celia asked.

Everyone shrugged, but Galena said, "I guess I'll take the one by the door."

"I'll grab the one near hers, then" Libby said.

"Fine with me," Maddie said, and Libby and Galena collected their belongings from the pile in the center of the room and headed for their new beds. "You want that one," Maddie asked, gesturing to the bed on the outside wall, "and I'll take this one?"

"Sounds fine to me," Celia said. The further away from the other girls in the room, the better, as far as she was concerned. She and Maddie grabbed their trunks from the center and pulled them toward the corner.

"Where does everything go?" Maddie asked, looking at the bed.

There was a ladder at the end in the corner to climb up onto the bed itself, but other than the drawers on the outside, there didn't seem to be much storage. Celia walked over to the ladder and climbed up onto her bed. There were bookshelves on either side of and in between two large windows by the bed, but it didn't seem like she could hang clothes or put her shoes there.

"Got me," she said as she headed back down the ladder. "Hey, wait. There's a door over here," she said, noticing a door to the side of the ladder. Once her feet were on the floor, she stepped over and opened the door. Looking inside, she was sure her mouth fell open. "No way!" she said, stepping forward.

The door opened to what looked like a large walk-in closet that ran the length of the bed. Celia walked into the space and a light turned on. The wall to her right was covered in ornate purple and gold wallpaper, and the area to the left was hanging space and shelves. "Maddie!" she called.

"Yeah?" Maddie said, stepping to the doorway. "Oh, wow!" she said, stepping inside while looking around. "This is great! Do you think mine's the same?" She ran out of the closet with Celia close on her heels. Pulling open the door next to her own ladder, Maddie squealed with excitement as she found a mirror image version of Celia's closet.

"Do you have a really cool closet under your bed, too?" Libby asked from across the room.

"Yeah!" Celia answered.

"Oh, please!" came a disgusted comment from the other side of the room. "It's just a closet!" Doxa said. "Get over it." She rolled her eyes and shook her head and then marched out of the room, her groupies following behind.

"Can you believe her?" Galena asked when the door had shut behind them.

"Yeah, what a way to welcome the new kids," Libby said, stepping around the edge of her bed. "Oh, look! Hooks and a little bench," she said, pointing at the other end of the bed. Sure enough, each bed had a small bench with storage space underneath at the opposite end from the ladder plus hooks mounted above the bench to hang coats.

The girls quickly unpacked and decided to check out the rest of the coterie rooms. It seemed that everyone else had already unpacked and was relaxing in the lounge. When Celia and the others walked into the room, they saw one big group of people standing around and talking.

"Hey, guys, there's my brother," Galena said, waving at an older boy across the room. "Come say hi, Libby!"

Libby and Galena headed across the room before Celia and Maddie knew what was happening. Celia saw two girls separate themselves from a group and walk towards them. They looked nearly identical, and she would have guessed that they were twins, but while one had dark hair and dark eyes, the other had pale blond hair and gray eyes that were nearly white.

"Hi," the dark-haired one said. "Welcome to Mensaleon."

"Thanks," Celia said. "I'm Celia, and this is Maddie."

"Nice to meet you," the blond one said. "I'm Odette, and this is my sister Odile."

"Hi. Are you twins?" Maddie asked.

They both laughed. "How'd you guess?" Odile said. "We're about as different as night and day, but our parents swear to us that we're twins, so I guess we'll believe them."

Eyeing their long legs and slender figures, Celia asked, "Are you into modeling or something?"

"No, we're both dancers. Ballet," Odette explained.

"We've been dancing for ages," said Odile.

"Our parents told us we might have to cut back on that, though. We're third-years, and they said that our schoolwork is going to get harder this year," Odette said.

"Of course," added Odile, "they've said that every year."

"Did your parents go here?" Odette asked.

"I guess they did," Celia said, recalling Higby's comments about her parents being some of the brightest students at Renasci.

Chapter Six

"You don't know?"

Celia shook her head. "I live with my Aunt Agatha. I don't remember much about my parents."

"Are they... dead?" Odile asked cautiously.

Celia shrugged. "I don't know. No one knows."

A look of understanding came into Odette's pale eyes. "Wait a minute. Celia... are you Celia Fincastle?"

"Ah... yeah." It still felt a little odd to have so many people know her name when she hadn't been anyone out of the ordinary that morning.

"Fincastle? Really?" Odile looked at her again. "Wow. I didn't know you were coming this year."

"Why would you, Deel?" Odette asked her sister with exasperation.

"Well... I just thought... you know..."

"Don't mind her," Odette said to Celia. "I'm sure it must be a little strange having all these people asking questions about you like they've known you their whole lives."

"A little," Celia admitted.

A soft chiming noise filled the room and people rushed excitedly to a box off to one side of the room.

"What's that?" Celia asked.

"It's the mail," Odile said.

Celia caught a glimpse of blue light before everyone tried to grab at something in the box.

"That's mine!"

"Hey, Josh! This is for you."

"Anyone see my box yet?"

And then, "Celia Fincastle!" The room grew deathly quiet for a moment as everyone heard the name, then whispers began.

"Fincastle? Did she say Fincastle?"

"Is Celia Fincastle in our coterie?"

"But I thought..."

"There's something here for Celia Fincastle," the louder voice called again. "Is she here?"

Celia glanced at Maddie, who gave her a sympathetic smile but urged her to go to the front of the room and get her mail. As she started to walk toward the mailbox, she heard the whispers pick up again.

"Is that her?"

"Do you really think so?"

"Wow, she's really here!"

The crowd of people around the mailbox parted in front of her as she walked, and she found herself standing in front of an older girl who held an envelope in her hand.

"Celia?" the girl asked. Celia nodded. "Here's your mail," she said, smiling as she held it out to her. "And welcome to Renasci."

"Thanks." Celia took her envelope and quickly turned and walked back to her group of new friends. "I have mail already? But who would be writing to me?" she asked, trying to ignore the stares from everyone behind her.

"I don't know. Why don't you open it and find out?" Maddie said.

Celia noticed that the envelope was typed out, not handwritten, so she couldn't recognize any handwriting. She opened the envelope and pulled out a typed letter.

Celia,

By the time you read this, I will be off on a cruise with my bridge club. I shall be very busy this year, now that I do not have to stay home with you. I am planning a winter vacation in the Alps, so you shall have to remain at the school

> for the holidays. I have been assured that the people at the school will take care of everything you need, so I do not expect to hear from you until you return for the summer.
>
> Sincerely,
>
> Agatha

Celia's jaw dropped when she read the note. She'd known that Aunt Agatha hadn't been thrilled to have her around, but she hadn't expected something like this, which had to have been sent before Celia had even left for school. And Aunt Agatha was on a cruise? She must have planned it while Celia was still at home, and she had to have left right after Celia had left with Mr. Morven that morning. Sighing, Celia slid the note back in the envelope.

"Who was it from?" asked Maddie.

"Aunt Agatha."

"Already?"

Celia nodded. "Apparently she's enjoying life without me. It looks like I'm spending the entire year here at the school. Including the holidays."

"Oh, that's not so horrible," Odile said. "There are a fair number of kids who stay here for each holiday, and there's lots of stuff to do. It won't be bad at all."

"Hey, I was going to ask you," Odette said suddenly. "Are you guys stuck in the same room with Doxa and her drones?"

"Drones?" Maddie questioned.

"That's what we call her clique."

"They're on the other side of the room," Celia said.

"Oh. Tough luck," Odette said. "Everyone tries to avoid her as much as possible."

"Yeah," Odile said. "Even the girls a year ahead of her were a little scared of her while they were here."

"I guess I can see why," Celia said, thinking about Doxa's speech when they'd first met.

"It's time to head down to the refectory," Professor Twombly called from the doorway.

"What's the refectory?" Celia asked.

"It's like a really big dining room," Odile said.

"Like a cafeteria?"

"What's a cafeteria?"

Celia looked around at the confused faces staring at her. "Never mind," she said.

"Those of you who know where you're going, please go on ahead. Seventh-years, please wait here with me and I'll bring you down."

There was a slight stampede as the majority of people in the room headed for the exit. Soon Celia and Maddie found themselves with Libby, Galena, and four seventh-year boys.

"All right, kids, let's get going," Professor Twombly said. She turned and headed out the door with the group of students following her.

"Oh, good. I'm starved," Maddie said.

They headed down to Main Hall and Professor Twombly led them through a set of large doors on one side. While Celia was expecting another large hall like the one they were leaving, she was surprised when she saw a cozy room filled with tables and fireplaces. There was a long table at the back of the room filled with large bowls of steaming food and platters of meat and rolls.

"Over here, please," Professor Twombly said, guiding them over to a table near the front windows. The tables were large and round and sat eight people at each one. "For tonight, we all sit divided by coterie and year, so all of you seventh-years will sit here. After this, unless you receive other instructions, you may sit wherever and with whomever you'd like." She smiled at them and headed up to another long table at the front of the room reserved for the faculty.

The eight of them slid into their chairs and looked around the room. Celia noticed other tables full of seventh-years, all looking around the way they were.

Headmaster Doyen stood and clapped his hands for attention. Soon the room was quiet and he began to speak. "Welcome, everyone, to another year at Renasci. I hope you all enjoyed your break over the summer and are looking forward to another year of learning." A collective groan rose from the students. Headmaster Doyen smiled. "I see *that* tradition has carried on for another year. There are a few announcements for you, however, I am certain that they will wait until after our meal. Servers, if you will..."

All the students at one table from each coterie jumped to their feet and collected serving dishes off the back table. They spread out through the room and delivered food to each table, then returned to the food table for more dishes. The noise level in the room increased as people started talking and eating, silverware and dishes clinking.

"Oh, wow," Maddie said, serving herself a heap of mashed potatoes. "Roast chicken, mashed potatoes . . . I'm starved."

"I know," Celia said, spooning an equally large serving of potatoes onto her own plate.

There was silence at the table for a few minutes, except for the sounds of eating.

"Hey, Maddie?" Galena finally asked.

"What?" Maddie answered.

"Did your parents know you were coming here?" Galena asked. "You know, before you got the invitation?"

"They were pretty sure." She chewed a bite and swallowed. "I guess I've been doing some really unusual things since I was about three."

"Really?" Celia said. "Like what?"

"My mom always says that I used to read in my room after I was supposed to be in bed."

Libby looked at her. "That's not so unusual."

"It was dark."

Celia did a double-take. "You could read in the dark?"

Maddie nodded. "I guess so."

"Can you still do that?"

She shrugged. "I don't know. I haven't tried in a while."

Celia remembered what Higby had said about gifts fading when people didn't use them, and suddenly the food sitting on her plate looked much less appetizing. As far as she knew, she hadn't ever done anything unusual. If Maddie used to be able to do things and now she wasn't sure if she could do those things anymore, what hope did Celia have that she could do anything at all?

"What about you, Burnsy?" Libby asked the boy sitting to her left.

Burnsy Nesbit had short red hair and a face full of freckles. His cheeks turned bright pink when he realized that everyone was looking at him. "Uh, what?"

"Did you know you had any gifts before you came here?" Libby prompted.

Burnsy looked around the table and seemed to be in distress. "Um, no."

Celia and Maddie glanced at each other. "Hey, Burnsy, I don't think we've met," Maddie said.

"Oh, yeah," Celia said. "You're right. Hi, Burnsy. I'm Celia."

"You're Celia Fincastle, aren't you?" a boy with spiky brown hair said from across the table.

Celia looked around to see the entire table looking at her. *Not again!* she thought. "Um, yes, I am."

Chapter Six

"No way!" said a boy with disheveled blond hair. "Somebody said you were in our coterie, but I thought they were just joking." He said his name was Heath Whitmore, the boy with the spiky hair said his name was Josh Rumbles, and the other boy at the table introduced himself as Kitt Borega.

"Yeah, my parents said they knew the Coridans before they went all crazy and all," Heath said. He sounded like he was a surfer or skateboarder.

"Really?" Maddie said, sounding enthralled. "What were they like?"

"Dude, I don't know. They don't talk about them much."

"Oh." Maddie now sounded really disappointed.

Celia felt a little out of place. It seemed like everyone at the table knew all about what had happened with her parents, but she knew so little about it.

When everyone had eaten their fill, the tables were cleared and everyone filed out to their quarters. It was late and everyone was tired, so no one really talked much as they got ready for bed. Doxa and her friends were nowhere to be seen as Celia climbed up the ladder to her bed. She heard the other girls pull their bed curtains, but she decided to leave hers open and look out the windows for a little while.

"Hey, you."

Celia peered over the edge of her bunk. Her heart sank when she saw Doxa and her posse standing in front of her. "Yeah?"

"You're Celia, right?"

"Yeah."

"Celia, like Celia Fincastle?"

Celia gritted her teeth. "Yeah."

"Huh." Doxa gave her a careless stare. "Just so you know, don't expect any special treatment from anyone in here."

"Fine," Celia said, flopping back down on her bed. "I didn't ask for it."

"Hey!"

Celia propped up on her elbow again.

"I wasn't finished."

"And?"

Doxa sneered at her. "You think you're something special, don't you? You'll learn. You sevvies are nothing here at RAGS."

"Fine." Celia was so tired she could barely keep her head up and they had a busy day scheduled for tomorrow. It was their first full day of classes.

Doxa arched both eyebrows. "Listen, Fincastle. If you're not careful... You'd just better watch your back."

"Uh... okay."

Doxa huffed and flounced back to her bed, leaving her group of friends to follow in her wake.

Celia pulled her curtains closed, no longer enjoying the view out the windows across the room. She stared at the ceiling for a while, thinking about how much had changed in the space of just one day. For a moment she felt hurt that Aunt Agatha had seemed so eager to get rid of her and go on her cruise, but she quickly thought about all of the amazing things that must be awaiting her at Renasci. Her mind brimming with possibilities, she turned over onto her side and quickly fell into a deep sleep.

Chapter Seven
Settling In

Breakfast in the refectory was very different from dinner. There were no servers, no eating as one big group, and, the biggest change from the night before, no assigned seats. The food was served buffet style, and you could sit at whichever table you wanted. Celia was used to Aunt Agatha's breakfasts, which meant that Celia had to fend for herself. She usually just had cold cereal, so she wasn't used to the array of food sitting in front of her. There were piles of pancakes, waffles, bacon, ham, hash brown potatoes, eggs, toast, fruit of every variety, cereal (although Celia walked right past that), and juice. Celia loaded up a plate and turned to find a seat.

"Hey, Celia!" someone called from across the room. While Celia was looking to see who had called her, someone bumped into her from behind, nearly sending her full plate flying and almost spilling her juice.

"Watch where you're going," a voice sneered in her ear. It was Doxa.

"Sorry," Celia said, although she wasn't.

"Get out of my way, sevvie," Doxa said, pushing past her and making Celia off balance again.

Celia watched her saunter away, wishing she could have just dumped her plate of food over Doxa's head. A voice beside her made her jump. "Celia?" She turned to find Maddie next to her elbow. "I saved you a seat over here."

"Thanks, Maddie."

They ended up at a table of seventh-years, with three from Aquilegia, two from Corpanthera, and one from Tattotauri.

"My parents and all my brothers and sisters were in Aquilegia," said a small brown-haired boy with freckles and glasses. "I'm just glad I wasn't the only one in the family who didn't end up in the same coterie."

"My parents were in Corpanthera," said a skinny red-headed girl, "but all my sisters are in Tattotauri, too."

"Could I have everyone's attention?" Headmaster Doyen was standing at the front of the room. "Deans will be handing out schedules during breakfast, except for the seventh-years, who will have an assembly in the auditorium after breakfast. Please remember that classes begin at nine o'clock sharp. Thank you."

"There's an auditorium here?" Celia asked.

A boy with short black hair spoke up from next to Celia. "Yes. It's on the other side of Main Hall from here."

"Really?"

He nodded. "I've studied the floor plans so I know where everything is." He said it simply, not boasting. "It's right underneath the library."

"Oh." Celia sighed. She knew nothing about this school. How was she ever going to find all of her classes and figure out where everything was?

"Want me to show you where the auditorium is after breakfast so you won't get lost?"

"Would you?" Celia asked, relieved.

He shrugged. "Sure."

"Thanks, er, what's your name?"

"Eliot."

"Thanks, Eliot. I'm Celia, by the way."

"I know." He took a drink of milk from his glass. "Everyone's been talking about you."

"I..."

"You're in Mensaleon, right?" When she nodded, he said, "If I hadn't been in Aquilegia, I was hoping I'd be in Mensaleon."

Maddie piped up from the other side of Celia. "I thought I might be in Aquilegia, but I was really hoping I'd be in Mensaleon. So I was really excited when they put me here. I mean, all the Aquilegia gifts are really neat, but the Mensaleon ones are so much better, don't you think?"

Eliot looked a little annoyed. "No. I don't think any gifts are any better than any others. Particularly," he said with a bite to his tone, "since I'm in Aquilegia."

"Oh," Maddie said, nonplussed. "I didn't mean...that is...um..."

"Maddie has a habit of speaking before she thinks," Celia tried to explain.

"I see," Eliot said coolly.

When they had finished eating, Eliot told them he'd meet them in Main Hall in ten minutes. "I don't want to be late, so please be on time," he'd said, so Maddie and Celia hurried to clear their dishes and rushed to meet him.

A few other lost-looking students were wandering around Main Hall, so Maddie and Celia rounded them into one big group and waited for Eliot. When he joined them, they headed off.

He took them through a set of doors on the other side of the hall from the refectory and down a set of stairs. At the bottom, they went down a hallway and through a series of doors and hallways. Celia tried to keep track of it all, but failed miserably after the third turn. Finally, they came into a larger hallway that seemed to be more decorated than the utility hallways they had been in before. Two sets of doors off that hallway led them into the auditorium.

A fair number of students were already there, so everyone split up and found seats. A few minutes later, there was movement in the curtains, and someone stepped out from the wings.

"Attention, students!" Celia was happy to see Mr. Morven on the stage. "You're here to get your class schedule, meet your professors, and collect your textbooks. Seventh-years are not required to buy their own textbooks, but next year and every year after you will be responsible for purchasing your books at the bookstore."

He gestured behind him. "There are five tables set up on the stage. You will form an orderly line, stop at my table first," he said, indicating a table by the stairs leading to the stage, "and then visit each station so the professors can check your schedule and distribute the appropriate textbooks. If everyone will proceed through the stations in a timely manner, we can get this finished quickly and you can get to your first class on time."

Celia and Maddie followed the crush of students and found themselves about halfway back in the line. After a while, they stepped up to Mr. Morven's table.

"Hi, Celia," he said. "Here's your schedule for this year," he said, handing her a piece of paper. "You can follow the line and pick up your books and things."

"Thanks, Mr. Morven." She looked at her schedule while she waited for the people in front of her to finish. Somehow these weren't the classes she was expecting. *Speech? Reading? Art? These sound like classes from my old school!* she thought. Maybe she was missing something.

Maddie came up and stood next to her. "Hey, do we have any classes together?" Maddie asked.

"Does everyone have a different schedule?" Celia asked.

Maddie shrugged. "I don't know. Let me see yours." Celia handed hers over and watched Maddie compare the two pieces of paper. "Wow, it looks like we have all of the same classes."

"Really?" Celia said, taking her schedule back. "That's great!"

The line brought them to the first table, and Celia found herself face to face with Professor Spadaro. She had expected him to have very pale eyes to go with his pale skin and hair, but seeing him up close, Celia discovered that he had vivid peacock-blue eyes.

"Ah, Miss Fincastle," he said when she handed her schedule to him. "So nice to have you at our school." His voice was quiet and smooth, as if he were in a library and was afraid the librarian would walk up at any moment. "Here is the textbook you'll need for class. I hope you will find yourself proficient in the skills of Corpanthera."

Celia thanked him as she took the book, then moved on to the next table.

"Okay, he gives me the creeps," Maddie said when she walked up behind Celia.

"I don't know," Celia said, glancing back at him. "I can't figure out if I should be afraid of him or if he's just quiet."

"Be afraid, Celia. Be afraid," Maddie said.

"Why?"

"Look at him! He's got secret agenda written all over him."

Celia gave her a look. "I think you've been reading too many books or something, Maddie." She stepped up to the next table and found Professor Perrin sitting there. "Hi," she said, handing over her schedule.

"Hello, Miss Fincastle. I've heard so much about you," he said. "I'm looking forward to having you in my classes this year." He sounded warm and friendly, and Celia thought she was really going to like his class. He handed her another book. "Here you go. I anticipate you doing very well in my Sprachursus lessons."

"Thanks, Professor Perrin." Celia headed for the next line.

"Now, *he* is someone I could put up with everyday," Maddie exclaimed when she came over.

Celia laughed. "He's just a teacher, Maddie."

"Wake up, Celia! He looks just like Ed Bornhoft!"

"Who?" Celia thought the name sounded familiar, but she couldn't figure out where she had heard it before.

"Oh, please, Celia, tell me you know who Ed Bornhoft is."

"Um, hello? This is only my second day in the demesne, remember?"

"Oh, yeah. Don't worry, we'll get you caught up in no time. Ed Bornhoft is the best Soccovolle player in the league. And also the cutest!"

Celia vaguely remembered that the magazine she'd purchased at the BUS station had mentioned Ed Bornhoft. But she had no idea what Soccovolle was. "What are you talking about?"

Maddie noticed her bewildered look. "Oh, sorry, I forgot. You've never heard of Soccovolle, right?"

"Ah, that would be a no."

"Oops! Looks like the table's open," Maddie said, pointing over Celia's shoulder.

Celia quickly spun around and saw Professor Twombly waiting for her. "Hello, Celia," she said before Celia even had a chance to hand over her schedule. "I trust you are settling in here at Renasci?"

Celia nodded.

"Excellent! Well, here is the book you'll need for this year."

"Thank you." She marched to the next line and waited to see what Maddie would say next.

Chapter Seven

"I love her earrings, don't you?"

Celia was beginning to think that Maddie had something to say about everything. "To be honest, Maddie, I didn't really pay much attention to them."

"Oh. Well, anyway, I hope we finish up soon, because I really hope I have lots of time to find my first class. I have the worst sense of direction."

"It doesn't seem like it should be that hard to learn our way around," Celia said. "Eliot said he'd studied a map. Maybe you could find a copy?"

"Yeah, maybe, except that I'm even worse when I have a map. Somehow I always get it all turned around and I still get lost."

The next table opened up and Celia headed over to meet Professor Mesbur. He looked a little intimidating, barely fitting on the chair behind the table. Celia handed him her schedule.

"Well, well, I finally get to meet Miss Fincastle," he said, a warm smile on his face. "This is for you," he said, holding out another textbook for her. "I think you'll do just fine in my classes this year." Despite his daunting appearance, he seemed like his personality was the exact opposite, and Celia got the impression of a big, cuddly teddy bear.

Celia piled the book on top of the other three she was already carrying, mumbled a thanks as she picked up the stack, and turned toward the last table. The collection of books in her arms was growing heavy, and Maddie must have felt the same way, because she didn't say much while they waited for their turn at the final stop. Celia was relieved when she could finally set her pile down on the table in front of Professor Legaspi.

"Hi, Celia. It's nice to meet you," she said. Professor Legaspi was the first one who didn't seem to make a big deal out of Celia's presence at the school. "It looks like you have class with me this morning, so here's your book, and I'll see you in a little bit."

"Thank you." Celia took her last book, added it to her stack, and stepped back to wait for Maddie. In a moment, the two of them were headed down the hallway, groaning about the weight of their books.

"We have to hurry so we can get to our first class," Maddie said.

Celia didn't say anything because her mouth was dry and her stomach was a nervous wreck. What happened if she got to class and everyone in there knew what they were doing except her?

Over the next week, Celia felt like she got lost more than she didn't, but somehow she made it to all of her classes. For the first couple of days, she was worried that she might have missed out on something by not growing up in the demesne. However, it didn't take long for Celia to realize that there were lots of other kids who didn't know any more than she did. Even the kids who knew a lot about their gifts had plenty to learn.

While she still didn't understand why the classes were named the way they were, she found each class interesting. Speech class was taught by Professor Perrin, and instead of the public speaking she had been expecting, Celia found that the class covered all sorts of unusual languages and other skills relating to communication. Professor Mesbur's Art class wasn't quite like the paint and papier-mâché Celia had done at her old school, but instead taught the Tattotauri skills of touch and working with one's hands. Her Reading class with Professor Legaspi covered the areas in Aquilegia, and although Celia had feared a literature class, it was full of lessons on the many different ways of using the ability of sight. Logic class was the favorite of many Mensaleons, since it was taught by

Professor Twombly, and challenged all of them to use their minds in completely different ways. Physical Education gave students the chance to stretch their Corpanthera skills with Professor Spadaro, testing their ability to perform physical transformations or feats.

Celia didn't really have a favorite subject yet, and she didn't really feel like any of her classes were easier than the others. Some of the other seventh-years had already mentioned that they were having an easy time with the material in certain classes or were really struggling in another class. To Celia, it just seemed like all of the classes were a challenge.

The hardest thing for Celia, though, was dealing with the fact that her name was Celia Fincastle. At her old school, she had been just another student in the halls, and she could go through the entire day, if not the entire year, without being noticed by anyone other than her teachers and acquaintances. But at Renasci, just the fact that her name was called for attendance made people turn around in their chairs to get a look at her. Every time it happened, Celia felt her cheeks grow warm, and she slouched down in her chair to try to avoid all the stares.

At the end of the first week of classes, Celia was sitting at her desk and flipping through the pages of her textbooks. When she'd first read about Renasci, she'd been excited about the gifts the brochure had talked about. But then she'd heard people talking about the things they could do, and she'd gotten nervous about whether she would be able to do anything at all. Now, she was a combination of both. The things mentioned in her textbooks made her nervous because she didn't think she could do any of them, but she was excited to try and see what she really *could* do.

"Can you believe how much homework we have?" Maddie groaned from her desk. "And this is just the first week!"

Celia laughed. "You're just used to having no homework over the summer, Maddie. It's not that much."

"Maybe you're right." Maddie flipped open a book. "But I don't understand any of this! I mean, really, who in their right mind thinks they can talk to animals or make things disappear?"

"Sort of like reading in the dark?" Celia teased.

Maddie scowled at her. "Okay, so you have a point." She sighed. "I just hope I'm not a dismal failure."

"'Dismal failure'?" Celia asked.

"My parents' favorite phrase."

"Oh." Celia spun around in her chair. "I don't know, I think it could be kind of fun to talk to animals. Imagine what they might have to say." She picked up her Physical Education book. "It's this stuff I'm more worried about."

"Like what?"

"Do they really think I can camouflage myself or squeeze into tiny spaces?"

Maddie shrugged. "Guess so."

"How does this work, anyway?"

"What?"

"Well, let's say I stink at seeing in the dark. Do I have to keep taking classes for seeing in the dark the whole time I'm here?"

Maddie shook her head. "No. I'm pretty sure that we have classes with the heads of each department for seventh year so they can evaluate our skills. You know, see if we have any ability at all."

"Then what?"

"As far as I know, the deans decide what classes we take next year, and, depending on how well we do this year, we might have classes with them or we might get one of the assistants."

"Really?"

She nodded.

"So why do all of these classes sound like something from outside the demesne? Why not give them cool names that really describe what we're doing?"

"I guess it's because there are so many kids here whose parents aren't familiar with the demesne. I heard someone saying that it helps ease them into this stuff if it sounds like classes they had in school."

"Oh."

There was a knock on the door to their room. Since they were the only two in the room, Celia went over and opened the door.

"Hi, Celia." Mr. Morven was standing there with her duffle bag.

"Hi, Mr. Morven. I completely forgot about my duffle bag."

He smiled. "So did I. I saw it under my desk this afternoon, so I thought I'd bring it up. Make sure you put that book in your closet. That's the safest place."

"Thanks," she said, taking it from him. "Why the closet?"

"Because the closets here are fitted with technology that recognizes the person trying to open the door. Your closet will only open if *your* hand is on the door."

"Oh. I didn't know that." She stepped back. "Did you want to come in?"

"Thank you," he said, stepping inside but leaving the door open behind him. He looked across the room. "Hello, Maddie. Have you two settled in here at Renasci?"

"We're getting there," Celia said. "It's taking a little getting used to."

Mr. Morven smiled at them again. "I have it on good authority that you two will have no trouble with your classes this year."

"Really?" Maddie said, standing up from her chair and walking over.

"Absolutely. All of your professors have had nothing but good reports."

"Great!" Maddie said.

"Yeah," said Celia. "Now we can stop worrying about being 'dismal failures.'" She grinned at Maddie.

"Hey!" she cried, holding her hands up in front of her. "It was my parents, not me!"

Mr. Morven laughed as he turned to leave. "Well, there's no fear of that, ladies. No fear at all. In fact..." He stopped in the doorway and turned back to face them. "It would seem that some of your professors think you are some of the best students in your class. I think perhaps you are both in for a surprise when you find out just what you can do." He winked at them as he backed out of the room and closed the door behind him.

Celia walked over to her desk and set her duffle bag on the chair.

"What book was he talking about?" Maddie asked.

"It's something I found in the attic at home," Celia said, pulling it out of the bag.

"Wow! Cool!" Maddie said, running a hand over the cover.

"I know. But I don't know what it says. Mr. Morven said something about it being important to my success, or something like that."

"Huh?"

"I know. There's something going on, but he wouldn't tell me anything. I guess I'll figure it out." She scooped the book up and walked toward her closet. "For now, though, I'm not taking any chances. This is going in my closet."

"Hey," Maddie said when Celia had come back out of her closet. "Do you think it's true that I can't get into your closet and you can't get into mine?"

Celia shrugged. "I don't know. Let's try." No matter how much they tried to get the doors open, it was like they were bolted shut, but both opened easily when they tried their own closet door. "That's really neat," Celia said when they finally gave up trying to get the doors open.

They flopped into the armchairs. "Wasn't it kind of weird with Mr. Morven saying that our professors think we're some of the best students in our classes?"

"I thought so," Celia said. "I mean, there are kids who seem like they know way more than we do, and it's not like we've been really outstanding at anything."

"Maybe he was just trying to be nice."

Celia thought for a moment, then shook her head. "I don't think Mr. Morven is the type to say something without meaning it."

Maddie shrugged. "I don't know. I'm hungry. What time is it?"

"Almost time for dinner, Maddie," Celia said, rolling her eyes. "You're always hungry! Come on, let's go."

Chapter Eight
Confetti and Exams

"I hope there's something good for breakfast," Maddie said as they turned the corner into Main Hall a few weeks later. "I woke up with my stomach growling."

"You're hopeless, Maddie," Celia said.

"AAARGH!" Someone ahead of them screamed and the line stumbled to a stop.

"Hey! What's going on?"

"Let's go, people! I want breakfast."

"What's that?"

Someone pointed up toward the ceiling. All heads swiveled up to see a collection of confetti fluttering down.

"Is that… confetti?" Celia asked.

Maddie shrugged. "Looks like it."

The first few pieces made it down to their level. "Look. They're all little purple lions," Celia said, collecting some in her hand. "Wait. Is that for Mensaleon?"

"Got me."

Someone else screamed and there was a muffled bang from slightly in front of them. A new wave of confetti flew into the air and began drifting down.

"Was that from the flowers on that table?" Celia asked, trying to see around the people in front of her.

Chapter Eight

"Everyone into the refectory, please." Headmaster Doyen was making his way through the crowd of people. "It's just a prank, everyone. Keep moving, please."

In a few minutes, all the students were in the refectory and Headmaster Doyen was standing in front of them. "I want to assure all of you that the exploding confetti flowers are harmless. However, I also assure you that I will find out who is responsible for this and that person, or group of people, will face the consequences of their actions." Everyone murmured, and Headmaster Doyen clapped his hands for attention. "In the meantime, please exercise caution when you are near any flowers. No one should be injured by them, but I don't want you to take any chances.

"In light of these occurrences, all students will be returning to quarters after breakfast and remaining there until further notice. That is NOT," he continued as excited whispers began all over the room, "an announcement that classes will be cancelled. Any class time missed due to this incident will be made up at the end of the day." When groans rose from the students, he said, "You may thank whoever did this for the loss of your free time this evening."

Breakfast was at the same time a lively and subdued affair. Laughter rang out as more flowers exploded and confetti fell like snow, but then everyone remembered that they were going to lose their free time that evening because of the flowers. Rumors and speculations flew about who had pulled such a prank, particularly since it would have required every single flower in the school to be replaced with an exploding one. Surely it had to be a group of people, but who?

Celia headed back to the Mensaleon quarters after she finished eating, although the majority of students were still in the refectory. She wanted to look over a homework assignment one last time before she turned it in. On her way up the stairs, she heard the door at the bottom open and a few people entered the stairway.

"SHHH!" someone whispered. "Make sure there's no one in here."

Celia froze in place, listening.

"I don't hear anything," someone else said.

"Did you tell him?"

"Yeah. Now we just have to get the confetti into her desk before they search it."

Celia's heart was racing. Were these the people behind the confetti flowers? And what were they talking about now?

"Are you sure he believed you?"

"I think so."

"This is going to be great! I can't wait to see the look on her smug little face when she gets hauled off to the headmaster's office." The voice turned falsetto. "But I didn't do it!" There were snickers of laughter.

Celia peered around the edge of the stairs, trying to see who was talking, but all she could see were three pairs of feet.

"Come on, we'd better get back to the refectory before someone notices we're missing."

"I'll get the confetti placed right after breakfast and . . ."

The voices faded as they headed back out the door to the hallway. Celia stepped carefully up the stairs and into the Mensaleon quarters. Some poor innocent person was going to be framed for the confetti flowers. Who knew how much trouble they were going to get into for something they didn't do.

Celia sank into a chair in the middle of the room and waited for Maddie to get back.

Maddie returned a little bit later, laughing with Galena. "That was hilarious! You should have seen the look on his face when the flower exploded confetti all over his suit!" More laughter. "Celia, you missed it! The teachers are all waving their hands over the flowers, trying to get them to explode, but one of them didn't. Headmaster Doyen went to inspect it up close and it blew confetti right in his face!"

Celia smiled halfheartedly. "Sounds funny. Um, Maddie? Can I talk to you?"

"Sure, Celia," she said, her smile fading. "What's wrong?"

"Come here." Celia took her over to her closet and closed the door behind them.

"Why are we in your closet?" Maddie asked.

"Because no one can hear what we're saying in here."

"Oh." Maddie looked around. "What's going on?"

"I overheard some people talking. They're going to frame someone for the flowers."

"What? Who did you hear?"

"I don't know. I didn't see who it was and they were talking in whispers. I couldn't recognize any of the voices."

"What did they say?"

"Something about telling someone and searching someone's desk and they had to get the confetti in before it was searched."

Maddie's eyes grew wide. "You're serious. They're actually going to frame someone else!? Why? Who?"

"I don't know, Maddie! But whoever gets punished for this is not the person who put those flowers out there."

"Girls!" a voice called from outside the closet. Celia and Maddie rushed out of the closet and found Professor Twombly in the middle of the room. Her expression was serious. "Someone has reported that a student from Mensaleon is responsible for this morning's prank. I'm afraid we're going to have to search your belongings."

"What?" Celia said. "Professor, I heard some people saying..."

"Yes, Celia?"

"Well, I don't know who it was, but they said—"

"I'm sorry, Celia, but if you don't know who was speaking, then you probably can't help us at all." She turned to leave the room. "Please remain in this room until someone comes in to search."

It was only after she had left that Celia noticed that everyone else had returned to the room.

"This is so lame," Doxa said, tipping her desk chair onto its back legs. "What a waste of time."

"I know," Cy said, rolling her eyes. "And we were supposed to be looking at dresses for the fall dance." Her voice was whiny as she said this, and she sounded more like she was two years old than seventeen.

"There are dances here?" Maddie asked.

"Duh, yeah," Doxa said, inspecting her fingernails. "But you little sevvies aren't allowed to go."

"But—"

There was a knock on the door, and Headmaster Doyen strode in. "Please stay right where you are, ladies. This shouldn't take long."

A group of teachers came in behind him and they quickly started going through the drawers and shelves in everyone's bed. When the person searching her space paused at a desk drawer, Celia's heart jumped to her throat. Surely not...

Headmaster Doyen was waved over and there was a whispered conversation. The teacher, one Celia didn't recognize, pointed at something in the drawer, shaking his head. Headmaster Doyen bent down to get a closer look, then nodded grimly as he stood up. He turned to Celia. "Would you come here, please?"

Celia's knees were knocking as she stepped closer. "Yes?"

"Can you explain this?" he asked, pointing in her desk drawer.

Chapter Eight

Celia glanced down and felt a knot form in her stomach. Sitting in the bottom of her desk drawer was a collection of the confetti from the exploding flowers. "I...um...I don't know how that got there," she said lamely.

"Miss Fincastle, can you prove that you had nothing to do with those flowers?"

Celia shook her head and looked around. "I-I...honest, I didn't...I wouldn't..."

"But there is confetti in your desk."

Maddie spoke up from behind them. "But that doesn't prove anything, Headmaster Doyen. Everyone has a few pieces of confetti by now." She slid her hand in her pocket and pulled it back out, opening her hand so they could see the confetti sitting on her palm. "I grabbed some off the tables in the refectory before I came upstairs."

"Hmphf," Headmaster Doyen said. "Miss Fincastle, I will expect to see you in my office in fifteen minutes." He turned and headed out the door.

Celia looked at Maddie. "Thanks for trying."

"Oh, it all makes sense, doesn't it," Doxa said, smirking from her chair. "Of course it would be a snotty sevvie who pulls such a dumb prank."

"But I didn't do it!" Celia's mind jolted with a sense of déjà vu. That was the exact phrase she had heard in the stairway. Glancing quickly at Doxa, she thought she saw a faint gleam in her eye before she tossed her hair.

"Students, you will all report to class in ten minutes!" a voice announced.

"Thank goodness!" Doxa huffed. "I'm not staying here with a troublemaker," she said, flouncing out the door.

Celia watched her leave, followed by her posse, and tried to resist the urge to run after her and tackle her to the floor.

"Celia?" Maddie said quietly.

"Yeah?"

"You'd better head down to the headmaster's office. You don't want to be late."

"Right." Celia turned to leave. "Just one question. Where *is* the headmaster's office?"

"Uh..."

"Never mind. I'll ask Professor Twombly."

A few minutes later, Celia found herself sitting in the waiting area outside the headmaster's office, above the refectory on one of the higher floors of the main building. The door opened and she looked up, seeing the smiling face of Higby coming out of the office.

"Don't worry, Celia. I've taken care of everything," he said.

Headmaster Doyen stepped out behind him. "Be that as it may," he said, giving Higby a stern look, "I will be keeping a close eye on you, Miss Fincastle. We do not permit students to behave this way at our school."

"Headmaster, I honestly didn't have anything to do with those flowers."

He folded his arms in front of him. "Without definite proof, I have no choice but to take your word on this one. You are free to go. This time."

"Thank you, sir."

Feeling like she'd just escaped serious punishment, Celia practically skipped down the hallway to her class. She wasn't sure who she'd overheard in the stairway, but they obviously had been talking about framing her, and she had to figure out what was going on before they tried it again.

By the middle of October, the occasional explosion still sent confetti into the air when someone walked past a flower the deans had missed when they checked the school, but things had settled back into some semblance of normal. All of the students (except the seventh-years) were getting ready for the fall dance, and Doxa took every opportunity to point out that she was going and Celia, Maddie, Libby, and Galena were not.

In addition to the dance, everyone was getting ready for the Fall Soccovolle Tournament. The seventh-years in particular were anticipating watching their first official matches. Celia was more excited than most because she had never seen anyone play Soccovolle, and she was curious to see how the game was played and why it was so popular at school.

The fall tournament took place at the midpoint of the semester, so the seventh-years were also getting ready for their first evaluation reports. The students called them ERs, joking that the people who didn't get good marks on their report would be needing the ER when their parents got hold of them. In preparation for the ERs, their professors told all of their classes that they would have evaluations and midterm exams.

This was what Maddie and Celia were talking about at lunch one day when Heath came up and sat at their table. Celia had been pleased to see some familiar faces in her classes, and it turned out that Heath was in all of the same classes with Celia and Maddie. The girls found his surfer dude attitude fun and his sense of humor quirky. Somehow, despite his appearance of carelessness, Heath was the favorite of many of their professors.

"Hey, ladies," he said, sliding a plate of food onto the table next to Celia. He flipped the chair around and straddled it while he pulled a napkin out of his back pocket. "Got a question for you."

"Sure, Heath," Maddie said. "What's up?"

"It's like this. My older brother is on the Corpanthera Soccovolle team, and he wants me to wear his team colors for the tournament."

"But don't you want to support our team?" Celia asked.

"Totally! That's why I need your help." He took a big bite of the sandwich on his plate, then spoke with his mouth full of food. "Mm mmphf fmm hmph—"

Celia waved her hands in front of her. "Heath," she said, laughing, "we can't understand what you're saying!"

He chewed quickly and swallowed. "Merrar," he said, using his word for an apology. He wiped his mouth with his napkin before continuing. "I thought you might have some ideas about how I can wear both colors for the tournament."

Celia and Maddie exchanged a look. "Um, Heath? You *do* remember that Corpanthera's color is blue and Mensaleon's color is purple, right?"

He shrugged. "Yeah, so?"

"Heath! You're going to be the least color-coordinated person in the stands!" Maddie cried.

He shook his head. "Whatever. I don't care about that." He took a drink from his glass. "I want to show my brother that I'm supporting his team and still root for my own coterie." He looked at both of them. "So you got any ideas?"

Celia looked hesitantly at Maddie. "Um, maybe you could wear a scarf or a hat in blue and a purple shirt?"

He nodded his head at her, his eyes wide. "Hey, yeah! That's a good idea. Thanks, Celia. You, too, Maddie." He stood up and flipped the chair back around. "Gotta scat, ladies." He grabbed his plate and drink and headed off across the refectory.

Celia caught Maddie's eye and they giggled. "Can you imagine what he's going to look like?" Celia asked, trying to keep her voice down so the people around them wouldn't hear. "I mean, knowing Heath, he's going to look like a paint factory exploded on him."

Maddie shrugged. "I know that fashion is different in the demesne, but I'm not sure this school is ready for Heath's idea of school spirit!"

"Hi, Celia, Maddie," Eliot said as he sat down at the table with them. "Are you ready for midterms?" Eliot was in a couple of classes with them, and he seemed to be very smart. He didn't show off, but it was obvious to everyone in the class that Eliot was the one who always had the right answer.

Celia blew out a breath. "Are you kidding? I tried to get through the agility course for Physical Education last week and didn't even make it through the first exercise."

"Yeah," Maddie said. "And that vase we were supposed to make for Art class? Mine looked more like a donut."

"I'm just hoping I make it through okay," Celia said. "I really wish they didn't have midterms right before the fall tournament. I'm really looking forward to seeing Soccovolle, but it's hard to get excited when we have exams hanging over our heads."

Eliot frowned at her. "Haven't you seen a game of Soccovolle before?"

Celia shook her head. "I didn't grow up in the demesne, remember?"

A look of understanding flashed in his eyes. "Oh, that's right." He shrugged. "Well, I'm not really into sports, so I'm probably not the best one to talk to about Soccovolle. It's all right, I guess."

The bell rang then, and they hurried off to class. The first few days of the week seemed to creep by, as excitement about the tournament built. By Wednesday afternoon, however, Celia started to get very nervous about her midterms. Her professors had told them all not to worry, that the evaluations were not that important, but no one wanted to get poor marks on their reports.

Celia and Maddie were in their quarters Wednesday evening doing some last-minute cramming for their exams the next day. Across the room, Libby and Galena were doing the same thing.

"Ooh, my head hurts from all this studying," Maddie said, rubbing her eyes.

Celia yawned. "I think I'm at the point that if I don't know it by now, I'm not going to know it for the exam."

"Hey, Celia," Galena called. "Did you guys get through Spadaro's agility course yet?"

Celia groaned. "No. I think it's impossible."

"I know," Libby said. "I can't make it across the balance beam at the start. I know it's supposed to test our physical abilities, but I'm beginning to think I don't have any!"

"Well, I guess it's a good thing we're in Mensaleon, not Corpanthera, huh?" Celia said, closing the textbook on her lap.

"Did you guys have to do Mesbur's vase experiment?" Maddie asked.

"Vase experiment?" Galena asked, frowning in confusion.

"Yeah," Maddie said, rolling her eyes. "We had to try to make a vase in five minutes. Mine looked like I had made a vase in five minutes."

"Five minutes?" Galena said, her eyes wide. "I like pottery, but even I can't make a vase in five minutes. I don't think anyone can do that."

Libby giggled. "Isn't that why we're here?" she said. "I mean, we *are* supposed to be gifted. I'm sure the people who have Tattotauri talents have no problems making vases in five minutes."

"You mean like Celia?" Maddie teased.

"Stop it, please, Maddie."

"You made a vase in five minutes?" Libby asked.

"It's just a stupid vase."

"Hers looked perfect," Maddie said.

"I've never done pottery before, Maddie. I'm sure my vase was far from perfect."

"Then why did Mesbur put it on the shelf in his classroom?"

"I don't know! Maybe... maybe he wanted an example of what not to do."

"Hah! If he wanted that, he'd have put mine up there!"

"Can we just forget about my vase? *Please?*" Celia begged. She saw Libby and Galena looking at her strangely.

"I've gotta get to bed anyway," Galena said, putting her books in her desk drawer. "If I don't get enough sleep, I won't have a chance of doing well on my exams."

Everyone agreed, so they all got ready for bed and pulled their curtains. Celia left the curtains for her window open and looked out at the stars shining brightly in the sky. She hadn't heard from Aunt Agatha since her note the first day. Celia wasn't even sure if Aunt Agatha was home or if she was off on some other cruise or something. Aunt Agatha had always insisted on good grades; anything less than honor roll was simply unacceptable to her. Celia had a nagging thought in the back of her mind that Aunt Agatha might pull her out of Renasci if she didn't get good grades on her ER.

Celia had been as surprised as anyone when she'd made a nearly perfect vase in her Art class. She hoped that it was an indication that she would do well on her midterms and discover that she really was gifted at something.

Yawning, she pulled the curtains closed and drifted off to sleep, wondering what might be on her exams the next day.

"Students, you have ten minutes to finish your exam."

Celia looked up at the clock and wondered how the last two hours had disappeared so quickly. She was taking her last exam, in Logic, and then she could relax and enjoy the Fall Soccovolle Tournament.

Her midterms had been nothing like she expected. Her Reading exam had been a breeze. She wasn't sure if it was the extra studying that she and Maddie had done, but she had finished early and was fairly certain that she had gotten most of the answers right. After the success of her five minute vase, Celia hadn't been too concerned about her Art exam, and she was pretty sure she'd passed with flying colors. Somehow Celia had made it all the way through Professor Spadaro's agility course without any problems, something she hadn't managed before. She still didn't know how that had happened. Professor Perrin had them try to communicate with a parakeet, something they hadn't tried in class before. Celia had been pretty pleased when her parakeet flew across the room and got her pencil, just as she'd asked. Professor Perrin had been impressed.

She just had to get through the last few things on her Logic exam and she would finally be finished. Professor Twombly's exam had been a big challenge. She'd added a few things that they hadn't covered in class, just like Professor Perrin's parakeet test. Celia wasn't sure if she'd decoded the message correctly and she wasn't sure she'd remembered the correct sequence for freezing time, but given that it was Friday afternoon and she was almost finished, she was past the point of worrying.

She quickly scribbled her last few answers and put her paper on Professor Twombly's desk just as the bell rang.

"Whew!" Maddie said, slinging her bag on her shoulder. "I'm glad those are over."

Chapter Eight

"I didn't think they were so bad," Celia said. "Not that I want to repeat them, mind you, but they weren't as bad as I thought they were going to be."

They left the classroom and headed up the stairs toward their quarters. Celia dumped her bag in her closet and kicked off her shoes. Although she was worn out from two days of exams, she couldn't help being excited about the start of the Soccovolle tournament. Maddie had let her borrow a purple sweatshirt to wear for the games, and everyone was talking about the Start of Tournament Banquet.

Celia stepped out of her closet and flopped in one of the chairs. She took a deep breath and let it out slowly, closing her eyes.

"Hey, Celia!"

Her eyes popped back open and she looked toward the door. Odile and Odette were standing in the doorway. "Hi, guys. Come on in."

"How were your exams?" Odette asked as they walked over and sat down in the chairs across from her.

"Not too bad," she admitted. "But I'm glad they're over."

Maddie came out of her closet and took another chair. "Hi, guys."

"Are you getting excited about the tournament?" Odile asked.

Celia nodded. "I've never seen Soccovolle before, so I'm sure I'll be completely lost most of the time, but it sure sounds exciting."

Odile looked at her watch, which Celia noted had a black band, and said, "It's about time for us to head down to the refectory. Are you guys ready?"

Celia sighed. "I guess that means I have to put my shoes back on."

Odile and Odette laughed. "Unfortunately, yes, that's what

it means," Odette said. "Come on. You can sit with us tonight," she said as she pushed to her feet.

They caught up with Heath and Kitt and a couple of Odile and Odette's third-year classmates on their way down the stairs. Once they reached the refectory, they found a table and all sat down.

"Have you heard the rumors?" one of the third-years asked. Odile had introduced him as Rowel.

"What rumors?" Odette asked.

"You mean about the midterms?" the other third year asked. Celia thought he'd said his name was Colton.

Rowel nodded. "Yeah."

"What?" the rest of the table said.

Rowel grinned at them. He leaned back in his chair and linked his fingers behind his head. "Maybe I'll just wait til you hear it yourselves."

"Come on, Rowel," Odile said, rolling her eyes. "Just tell us."

He dropped his arms and leaned forward. "I heard that someone got perfect scores on all their midterms."

The rest of the table stared at him.

"No way, dude," Heath said.

Colton nodded. "That's what I heard, too."

"But..." Kitt said.

"It must have been a first-year," Maddie said.

Rowel shook his head. "Nope. Rumor is that it's a seventh-year."

"Aww," Odile and Odette moaned simultaneously. "I was hoping it was me," Odette said.

"Me, too," said Odile.

"A seventh-year?" Celia asked incredulously. "Are you sure?"

Rowel shrugged. "That's just what I heard. It could just be a rumor, but somehow, I doubt it."

Chapter Eight

Just then, the lights in the refectory dimmed and the sound of trumpet fanfare filled the air. It seemed that the banquet was beginning.

Chapter Nine
The Tournament

A spotlight lit the podium at the front of the room, and everyone quieted as Headmaster Doyen stepped up to speak.

"Welcome, everyone, to the Fall Start of Tournament Banquet. Congratulations on making it through your midterm exams. I am sure that everyone did well during the first half of the semester." There was a smattering of clapping. "Before we begin our feasting, it is tradition that we introduce all of the Soccovolle teams that will be competing this weekend in the tournament." At this, there were cheers and hollers and the room burst into applause. Headmaster Doyen had to speak louder to be heard. "First, let me introduce the Tattotauri team!"

He stepped back from the podium and faced the door as a few more spotlights waved around the room and then focused on the group running into the refectory. They were wearing red shirts and pants and tossing fists into the air as they acknowledged the applause.

Then the spotlights headed back to the podium as Headmaster Doyen said, "And the Aquilegia team!"

The scene replayed, though this time the team wore silvery-gray outfits.

"The Mensaleon team!"

The people sitting around Celia jumped to their feet and the applause was deafening. Celia hurried to stand and caught a glimpse of people wearing purple outfits, but she had a hard time seeing over the taller people in front of her. Finally, they all sat down again.

"The Sprachursus team!"

The green-clad team ran into the room.

"And the Corpanthera team!"

As the blue-clothed players came running into the room, Heath was whistling and cheering while the rest of the people at the table just clapped politely.

The spotlights swiveled back to the podium and Headmaster Doyen. "The schedule for the tournament will be posted in each coterie's lounge. I am certain that everyone will exhibit their most ardent school spirit and cheer on all of the teams this weekend. And now... servers..."

The lights came back up and everyone started talking again.

"Hey, where're all the other seventh-years sitting?" Maddie asked, looking around.

Heath shrugged. "Not sure. Burnsy's been hanging out with the drama club ever since he joined. He's probably with them."

Kitt nodded. "Yeah, I saw him head over to the tables with the rest of them."

"And Libby and Galena are sitting with Galena's brother," Maddie added, nodding to a table to their right.

"What about Josh?"

Everyone looked around. "Got me." "I don't know." "I don't see him."

Celia shrugged and shook her head. "Oh, well. I was just wondering."

The food was piling up on their table, so they all served themselves and starting digging in. After a few moments of silence as they stuffed their mouths with food, Rowel spoke up again. "So do you sevvies have any idea who might have gotten a perfect score on midterms?"

Heath snorted. "Don't look at me, dude."

Kitt laughed. "Yeah, Heath. I'm sure it was you!"

"Hey, man!" Heath looked indignant.

"Sorry, I didn't mean..." Kitt sounded worried.

Heath's face broke into a wide grin. "Aw, I'm just jokin'. No way it's gonna be me."

"Maybe it's Eliot," Celia said, spying him eating at a quiet table of Aquilegia students.

"Could be," Maddie said thoughtfully. "He *is* really smart."

Colton shook his head. "You have to be more than just *smart* to get a perfect score on those midterms. Especially seventh year."

"What do you mean?"

"Seventh year is when they really test you to see if you're gifted enough to really study something," he said, buttering a roll. "They almost expect everyone to fail at least one of the exams because no one ever does well in every class."

"Really?" Kitt sounded relieved. Glancing around the table, Celia noticed that Heath and Maddie looked relieved, too.

Odette nodded. "I remember I completely bombed my Speech exams my seventh year, every single one of them."

"For me it was Art," Odile said.

Rowel grinned. "I stunk at Reading."

Maddie blew out a sigh. "I'm so glad you told me this. I was getting so worried 'cause I can't do Art to save my life!" Everyone at the table laughed, but Celia knew her laughter was halfhearted.

Chapter Nine

She was starting to get an odd feeling about her midterm exams. She hadn't really had any trouble with any of them. Could she be the one who had gotten the perfect score? How was that possible? A couple of months ago, she hadn't even known that anyone could do these things. But then there was the book that had put her in all five coteries... and the parakeet... and the agility course that she'd done flawlessly... And if seventh year was supposed to figure out what your true talents were...

"Celia?" Odette asked, interrupting her thoughts.

She shook her head slightly. "Yeah?"

"Are... you okay? You look kind of funny."

Celia waved it off. "I'm fine. Just kind of drained after taking all those midterms."

"I've always thought that it was really poor planning to have midterms right before the Fall Tournament. And the Spring Tournament is right after next semester's midterms," Odile said, scraping the last bit of chocolate sauce off her dessert plate.

"Better before the tournament than after," Odette said.

Celia tried to push her thoughts aside and enjoy the rest of the evening. By the time they made it back up to quarters, she was completely exhausted. She had just enough energy left to notice that the first Soccovolle match was between Mensaleon and Sprachursus at ten o'clock the next day before she stumbled into her room and collapsed into bed, too tired to think of anything else but sleep.

Saturday morning dawned sunny and cool, the perfect weather for watching the Fall Tournament. At nine-thirty, a whole group of Mensaleon students trekked out to the Soccovolle stadium and found seats in the stands. Celia wasn't sure how she'd missed the stadium before now, but looking back towards the school she noticed that a thick wall of trees blocked the view from the windows. She was now sitting beside Maddie (who was munching on a hot dog from one of the strolling snack vendors) and trying to figure out the game that was about to start.

The Soccovolle field looked a little like a soccer field, but it was square, not rectangular, and seemed much smaller. There was a line marking the center of the field, and each end had a tall, rectangular net with a gold hoop set back from the edge of the field, about shoulder high. The stands ran along the sides of the field, and it seemed like the fans for the two teams had chosen opposite sides of the field, as Celia couldn't find one green shirt on the side they were on, and not one purple shirt lurked in the other stands. A few colors from the other houses were interspersed among the fans, but the vast majority were wearing either purple or green.

"How am I supposed to figure out what's going on?" Celia asked Maddie.

"Well, our team is the one with the purple shirts."

"I got *that*, thank you very much."

"And Sprachursus has the green shirts."

"Ha, ha. Very funny."

Maddie giggled. "Sorry. Okay, the rules are really pretty simple. The object is to get the ball into the goal, that tall rectangle at each end of the field."

"So it's like soccer."

"Well, sort of. See, if the ball is in the air, you can move it down the field by bumping and setting it, like volleyball. Once the ball touches the ground, it has to be played like soccer."

"Oh, I get it: Soccovolle!"

"Exactly. Now, there are seven players on each team: one guard, who guards the goal; three protectors, who play defense; and three attackers, who play offense and score goals."

"I think I understand."

"Each goal is a point, unless you get it through the gold hoop at the back of the goal; that's three points."

"That makes sense." A whistle blew and the players ran onto the field. "Oh, look! The game's starting!"

Celia sat on the edge of her seat as Coach Jeuset-Partie brought the captains to the center of the field. He said something to them, they shook hands, and then prepared for the tip-off. Coach tossed the ball in the air and the game began.

Sprachursus got control of the ball and quickly moved it up the field with their hands. One player made it past the Mensaleon protectors, but he missed the ball when his teammate passed it, and the Mensaleon guard hurried over and booted it to the other end of the field. One of the Mensaleon attackers fielded the ball and let it drop to the ground. The three players in purple shirts at that end of the field whizzed around as they headed for the goal. When they were close, one of the players looked as if he was going to take a shot, but then passed it to his teammate, who slammed it at the guard. The Sprachursus guard tried for a diving catch, but the ball skimmed past her fingertips and flew into the net.

The stands around Celia roared to life as everyone cheered the goal.

When everyone had settled down again, Celia leaned over to ask Maddie a question. "How can these games be fair? Wouldn't some people have an unfair advantage, like being able to jump higher or squeeze through a smaller space?"

Heath, who was sitting behind them, heard her question and leaned forward to answer. "All the players sign an agreement to not use their gifts in the game. It's a binding agreement, so my brother said it makes everyone's gifts somehow unusable while they're on the field." Celia and Maddie were careful not to look at him for fear of bursting out laughing. He was wearing the oddest looking outfit that they had ever seen, with his clothes half blue and half purple. It might have worked if he'd matched the halves together, but his left leg, right side of his torso, left sleeve, and right side of his hat were all blue, while the right leg, left side of his torso, right sleeve, and left side of his hat were purple. He looked a little like a very confused checker board. To make things worse, he was holding a blue pom-pom in his right hand and a purple one in his left.

"Really?"

Heath shrugged. "That's what he said."

"Oh."

They watched the ball speed back and forth across the field for a while before Celia asked Maddie another question. "That ball moves pretty fast. Do the fans ever get hit?"

"Sometimes. But usually you can duck in time."

"Usually?!"

"My parents said I got beaned by a ball when I was five, but I don't remember it." Seeing Celia's look, she laughed. "Honest, I didn't get knocked out or anything..."

Celia nodded her head slowly. "I think I understand now."

"Hey!" She gave Celia a playful shove on the shoulder and they both laughed.

They looked out at the field again. "Hey, is that Josh out there?" Celia asked, squinting at the players on the field.

"Where?"

"Right there. The protector on the far side of the field."

"I can't quite tell. Can anyone see if that's Josh?"

Murmurs went up around them and everyone craned their necks to see the player. A strange feeling came over

Celia as she sat looking intently at the player. *Turn around so I can see your back,* she thought, and gasped quietly when the player did as she wanted. It seemed as though all of her energy was concentrated on what she was trying to do, and the noise around her faded as if she was hearing it from the end of a long tunnel. As she stared at the player who now had his back to her, she felt almost like her eyes were working as a zoom function, magnifying the center of her field of vision. Her heart pounding in her ears, Celia could now see the name on the back of the player's shirt quite clearly. She blinked a few times, but her eyesight didn't return to normal until she closed her eyes and shook her head slightly. The noise of the crowd around her returned suddenly, and she jumped at the unexpected sound.

"Are you all right, Celia?" Maddie asked, a concerned look on her face.

"I'm fine," Celia said carefully. "That's Josh over there. His shirt has his last name on the back, so unless he has a brother or something..." She trailed off at the look on Maddie's face. "What?"

"How do you know what the back of his shirt says?" Maddie hissed quietly at her.

"I... I saw it," Celia confessed.

"From all the way over here? You don't have binoculars or anything!" Maddie eyed her. "Do you?"

"Um..." Celia's gaze slid down to the floor beneath her feet. "No."

"Celia!" Maddie hissed again. "Don't tell me..."

Celia gave her a weak smile. "I guess we know that I'm supposed to be here, huh?"

Maddie flopped back against her seat once more. "I have a feeling that we don't have a clue..."

"What do you mean?"

Maddie shook her head. "It's nothing. I mean, I'll tell you later." She watched the players on the field, but Celia suspected she didn't see what was going on. After a few moments, she sat up straight again and looked across the grass. "So Josh is on the Soccovolle team, huh? I wonder why he didn't tell us?"

Celia shrugged but didn't say anything. She glanced at her watch and then at the game clock. It was getting close to noon and she was starting to get hungry. More than anything, though, she wanted to get away from all of the people around her and just sit by herself for a while so she could figure out what had happened. Surely it wasn't that unusual for her to be able to see across the field, was it? All the Aquilegia students were supposed to be gifted in sight, so somebody else must be able to do the same thing. Growing more annoyed with Maddie and the whole situation, Celia sat and fumed for the rest of the match.

When the final whistle blew, Celia was one of the first people out of her seat and leaving the stadium. She walked quickly toward the school, not slowing when she heard Maddie calling her name.

"Celia! Celia, wait!" Maddie ran up alongside her. "Celia? What's wrong?"

"I don't know, Maddie. You tell me. You seem to know more about what's going on than I do."

"Celia..." Maddie dropped her voice so that Celia could barely hear it. "It's just something that I heard my parents talking about a little while ago. They said something about you... and your parents... and I didn't hear all of it... I just..."

"Would you just tell me, Maddie?"

"Well, they said that they hoped I wouldn't end up in the same year as you because your parents were really good students and you probably would be, too. Something about 'extraordinary gifts' or something. They thought maybe I would look bad compared to you, I guess."

Celia said nothing, but kept up her furious march toward the school.

"Celia, I shouldn't have...I mean, I don't know...they don't know..."

"Just forget it, Maddie."

"No, I'm really sorry. I shouldn't have said anything. I just let my mouth get ahead of my brain again, that's all. Forgive me?"

Celia still said nothing, not slowing down. They reached the doors and she yanked one open and headed for the stairway to the Mensaleon quarters.

"Celia?" Maddie said, hurrying to catch up with her after getting caught in the doorway.

Celia stomped through the next doorway and jogged up the stairs, leaving Maddie behind. She stormed through the doors and into their room, not stopping until she was standing by her bed, breathing hard.

A few moments later, Maddie rushed in, gasping for air. "Celia..." she said, panting, "what...is...wrong?...I'm... sorry...I...said...anything....Will...you...please... forgive...me?"

Celia looked out the window at the line of students coming in from the stadium. She wasn't sure how she felt, but she wasn't angry anymore. "Yeah, I forgive you," she muttered.

"Friends?" Maddie asked, panting a little less than before.

"Yeah."

"What happened?" Maddie asked, walking up next to Celia.

Celia sighed. "Everyone knows everything about me...more than I even know about myself. People keep telling me that I don't understand what's going on, but they won't tell me what's going on. You have no idea how frustrating it is."

"I'm sorry, Celia."

Celia shook her head. "I don't even know anything about my parents. Aunt Agatha never told me anything because she doesn't know anything. And everyone who knew them won't say anything. I don't know what coteries they were in when they were here, or what things they were really good at...I know nothing." She wiped a single tear off her cheek. "It's just not fair. I don't understand why I can make a perfect vase or read a name from across the field. I don't even know if it's normal for people to be able to do things like that. What else can I do that I don't know about?"

"Don't worry about it, Celia. I'm sure that there are plenty of other people who can do lots of the same things that you can do. They just might not be able to do as many things as you can and probably not at your age."

"I don't want to be the odd one out. I just want to fit in."

Maddie chuckled. "Celia, no one fits in here. We're all different."

"I know...it's just...never mind."

Maddie's stomach growled, breaking the tension in the room, and they both laughed.

"Come on," Celia said, pulling her by the hand toward the door. "Let's go get lunch. By the way," she said as they headed through the door, "who won the game?"

By Sunday afternoon, Celia was glad the tournament was coming to a close. She was getting tired of sitting on the hard seats in the stadium and had seen enough Soccovolle for now. Mensaleon had split their matches, winning against Sprachursus but losing to Aquilegia. The final match for the Fall Tournament was between Tattotauri and Aquilegia, so Celia, Maddie, Heath, and Kitt decided to skip the game and relax in the lounge. Conversation soon turned to the perfect score on the midterms as they wondered again who had managed such a remarkable feat.

Celia said little during the discussion, and the feeling she'd had before seemed to have settled in the pit of her stomach. No one else seemed to notice her lack of participation, or at least they didn't comment on it. By the time they headed down for the End of Tournament Banquet, her nerves were frayed.

Everyone was in good spirits at the banquet, although some had begun to realize that the rest of the semester started the next day. The Soccovolle teams were all quite tired, particularly the Sprachursus team, who had played both of their fall games on the same day.

Conversations bounced around Celia but she didn't say much and she only picked at her food. She headed up to bed early, not wanting to talk to anyone, and pulled her curtains. Lying there, looking at the stars coming out in the darkening sky, she thought about what Maddie had said the day before. Again Celia wished she knew something about her parents. Higby had said they had been good students, and Maddie's parents obviously thought the same thing. Did that mean that she, Celia, was the one who had gotten the perfect score on the midterms? Would that mean she would have yet another reason for people to stare at her and whisper behind her back?

Her mind whirled with questions as she looked out the window. Long after the others in the room went to bed, Celia finally fell into a restless sleep, tossing and turning all night.

Chapter Ten

Perfect Scores and Pranks

By Monday, everyone was talking about the student who had gotten the perfect score on the midterm exams. The feeling in the pit of Celia's stomach had grown into a knot, and as breakfast ended and the start of classes crept nearer, a sense of dread came over her. As much as she dragged her feet on the way to her Reading class, she couldn't stop the bell from ringing or Professor Legaspi from calling the class to order.

"Settle down, everyone," she said from the front of the room. After a few moments, everyone quieted and gave her their attention. "I'm sure all of you have heard the rumors that someone got a perfect score on their midterms." Excited murmuring broke out around the room. "Unfortunately," she said over the din, "the rumors were incorrect. I'm sorry to say that no one got a perfect score." A chorus of "aw"s rose from the room.

Celia felt as though a thousand pounds had been lifted off her shoulders. At least she wouldn't be known as the super-genius at school.

Her relief was bolstered by a perfect score on her Reading midterm, which she quietly slid into her folder so no one could see her grade. Even though she wasn't going to get attention for getting a perfect score on *all* the midterms, there was no sense in broadcasting the fact that she had gotten a perfect score on this one exam.

After the announcement about the false rumor, Professor Legaspi had a hard time keeping the class's attention. She must have asked them to quiet down at least fifteen times before the bell rang and everyone jumped to their feet.

"Celia, could I see you for a moment, please?" Professor Legaspi called above the racket.

Celia paused as a few people walked past her, then turned to go up to Professor Legaspi's desk. "What is it?"

Professor Legaspi gathered her books, then looked up at Celia. "Do you have another class right now?"

Celia nodded. "Yeah, I have to get to my Speech class."

"Hmm." She chewed her lip as she scooped up her pile and turned to the door.

"Was there something you wanted to tell me?"

She stopped just inside the doorway and spoke quietly. "I'm sure you heard the rumors about the perfect score, and it's true that no one got a perfect score on all their midterms."

Celia's stomach tightened again. "Yes," she said cautiously, noting the slight emphasis Professor Legaspi placed on the word "all."

"Higby asked me to tell you...but if you have to get to class..." She seemed to waver but then shook her head slightly as if she'd rejected one of the options. "I'll write you a note. Come with me." She turned and walked out the door.

Celia trailed behind as they wove their way through the busy hallways, wondering what Professor Legaspi had to tell her...and had she mentioned Higby? What did he have to do with anything?

They headed through a doorway and up a few flights of stairs. Celia noticed that they were in the building opposite the Mensaleon quarters and thought they might be headed for the Aquilegia quarters. Her suspicion was confirmed when they came up to a set of doors with eagles carved in the panels and two eagle statues standing guard on either side, much like the doors to the Mensaleon quarters.

Professor Legaspi pushed the door open with her shoulder, since her hands were full of books, and held the door open for Celia with her foot. "Come on into my office," she said, letting the door swing shut behind them and turning to the left. She walked up to a door with a frosted pane of glass that obscured the view to the other side and nodded her head at the door. "Would you mind getting the door?" she asked Celia, who quickly grabbed the doorknob and opened the door.

Celia had a quick glimpse of rooms that looked somewhat similar to those in the Mensaleon quarters before she turned to follow her professor, only everything seemed a little bit off since it was all decorated in silver and eagles instead of purple and lions.

Professor Legaspi led the way into the office, stepping behind her desk and dropping her books on one end. "If you could swing the door shut behind you," she said over her shoulder. "There shouldn't be anyone in here right now, but I'd rather not take the chance. Then go ahead and grab a seat."

Celia pushed the door shut and sat down in a silver arm chair on the opposite side of the desk, setting her bag on the floor beside her. She glanced around the office and took in the walls covered in the same wallpaper as her closet, only with silver instead of purple, the huge antique desk piled with books and papers, the numerous bookcases filled with books of all shapes and sizes. The window (complete with silver curtains) looked out into the trees, and Celia thought she caught the shimmer of sunlight on water through the foliage.

"Celia," Professor Legaspi said, sitting down in her chair, "you got a perfect score on your Reading midterm."

Celia nodded, but said nothing. Not that she could have if she had wanted to, due to the lump in her throat that felt like she'd swallowed a grapefruit.

"As I said, Higby asked me to tell you…you got a perfect score on all of your other midterms except one. You missed one point on your Speech exam."

Celia's stomach dropped to her knees. Yes, it was true that no one had gotten a perfect score. She'd missed that by one point. Did it really make a difference?

"Celia?"

She took a deep breath and let out a loud sigh before looking up at Professor Legaspi. "Yes?"

"All of the teachers have been asked to keep this quiet, so no one should find out about this unless you want them to."

Celia looked down at her hands. "Has anyone ever gotten a perfect score on midterms before? Or one point off?"

Professor Legaspi drummed her fingernails on her desk. "I haven't heard of anyone, but this school's been around a long time. I guess you'd have to check the school records somehow to know for sure."

Celia nodded but said nothing.

"It's not such a big deal, you know."

Celia laughed humorlessly. "Then why was everyone in the school talking about it when they thought someone had gotten a perfect score?"

"Okay, so it's not *common*," she admitted. "Celia, this wasn't entirely unexpected."

Celia's head shot up to look at her. "What do you mean?"

Professor Legaspi scratched her head. "Well, your parents…"

"What about them?"

"They…they were exceptionally…talented…students." She leaned back in her chair. "You…definitely take after them."

"How do you know?"

"Your mother was my mentor when we were students at RAGS. She was a second-year when I started here."

"You knew my mother?"

She nodded. "Was very good friends with her, in fact. We stayed in touch after she graduated, right up until..." She looked away.

"Do you know what happened to her?"

Professor Legaspi sighed. "I'm sorry, Celia. I wish I could help."

Celia gazed out the window. "That's okay."

"You're aware that midterms help us assign mentors, right?"

"Uh, no."

Professor Legaspi gave her a sympathetic look. "I'm sorry. I keep forgetting that you've known nothing about the demesne before this summer. If you ever have any questions, please feel free to come and talk to me. I'd be happy to help in any way I can."

"Um, thanks," she mumbled.

"Anyway, based on your midterm scores, I suspect that all of your professors will be requesting a mentor for you from their coterie. I've talked with Higby, and he thinks that might be a little overwhelming for you at this point, so he... *we're* recommending that you be assigned to a staff member in addition to only two student mentors. It's not unusual for students to have two student mentors, as a number of people are gifted in two different areas. We thought it might look strange, however, if you had five student mentors."

"Oh-oh-kay." Celia was a little confused, but tried not to show it.

"Seventh-years will have an assembly in December to introduce the mentor program, so don't worry about anything for right now." She glanced at the clock. "I'd better let you get to class." She pulled a pad of paper out of her top drawer and jotted a note on it. Ripping off the sheet and folding it in half, she looked up at Celia again. "Did you have any other questions, Celia?"

"Well . . . I kind of wondered . . . why is Higby involved in all of this?"

Professor Legaspi paused, as if she were carefully considering her next words. "Higby . . . he has his reasons, Celia, and I'm afraid that's all I can say."

"Oh. All right."

She handed Celia the folded note, saying, "You can give this to Professor Perrin. He shouldn't give you any trouble."

Celia took the note and picked up her bag. "Thanks, Professor Legaspi." She turned to head out the door.

"Hey, Celia?"

With one hand on the doorknob, Celia looked back. Professor Legaspi had a kind smile on her face. "Yes?"

"It's really not so terrible to get good grades on your midterms. I'm sure some of your classmates will be jealous, but you should be proud of your abilities."

Celia nodded, then turned and walked out the door.

Celia had no reason to doubt Professor Legaspi, but she had hoped that maybe someone had made a mistake, confused her exam with someone else's or something. However, as she got each exam back, every grade was exactly what she expected. The only good thing was that all of her professors seemed to realize that any comments would only draw attention to Celia, and they all kept quiet except for a muffled "Good job" or "Nicely done" as they handed her exam to her.

Maddie had no idea about Celia's midterm grades, and Celia was happy to keep it that way for a while. When someone asked her how she had done on her midterms, Celia simply replied, "All right, I guess," and that seemed to satisfy their curiosity.

The seventh-years' ERs were sent out at the end of the week, and Celia wondered what Aunt Agatha would say when she saw Celia's marks. She didn't have to wait long, as no more than three days after the ERs were mailed, a letter came for Celia. It read:

> Celia,
>
> As pleased as I am that you are earning the highest possible marks at school, I simply do not wish to be bothered with the inane details of your education. Please find someone at your school who can act as a temporary guardian while you are away from home so I do not have to be inconvenienced.
>
> Sincerely,
>
> Agatha

Celia tucked the letter in her closet and decided to ask Professor Legaspi about it. Or possibly Higby...She wasn't really sure.

The fall dance came and went, and even though Doxa tried as hard as she could, Celia didn't feel that she had missed out on anything. The Mensaleon seventh-years gathered in the lounge and played a side-splitting game of charades for the evening. Celia didn't think she had ever laughed so hard in her life. From that evening on, it seemed to Celia that they were all better friends than they had been before, and it made it easier to deal with Doxa's attitude.

Chapter Ten

Life settled back into a routine after the dance, and soon everyone was slogging through piles of homework again. Celia talked with Professor Legaspi about Aunt Agatha's request, and she said she would see what she could do.

By the time Thanksgiving rolled around, Celia felt like she was finally getting used to being at Renasci. She could hardly believe that she had been there almost four months already. Her classes were going well, and she found that she was much more interested in the subjects she was studying at her new school than she had been in any of her classes at her old school. It made it much easier to sit down and work her way through piles of homework when she enjoyed the material.

She still hadn't told anyone about her midterm scores, and she was trying to stay out of the limelight in her classes. It wasn't an easy task, as she seemed to be far more adept at learning the new skills than the rest of the people in her year. While the other students in her Speech class were still trying to get their parakeets to fly across the room and back, Celia was teaching hers to tap dance. She had mastered the speed-reading skills in her Reading class long before her classmates, and she read nearly every book in the room twice in the same time that others were still finishing their first book. Professor Twombly told her that she had cracked every code she normally gave to her seventh years, and there was nothing else she could do in her Logic class until they moved on to the next unit. The students in her Art class looked at her a bit suspiciously when they worked on an origami assignment because Celia's desk was full of paper cranes when the rest of them had only managed to fold a couple.

Still, since there were other people in the classes who were also doing well, she didn't seem to attract too much attention. There were only a few people who were in all of her classes, and everyone else seemed to assume that she was only doing exceptionally well in the class they had with her.

Thanksgiving was a festive affair at the school, with fall decorations covering every available surface in Main Hall. The cooks prepared a humongous feast for dinner, complete with turkey, stuffing, mashed potatoes, gravy, corn, sweet potatoes, cranberry sauce, rolls, pumpkin pie, and (Celia's favorite) pecan pie. Everyone ate until they were stuffed, just as the turkeys had been before the meal.

There were no classes scheduled for the following day, and most of the school headed outside to enjoy one of the last warm days before winter swept in. Some of the kids played football, while others tried to figure out why anyone would want to play such a game. Lying in bed that night, Celia thought back to some of the Thanksgiving celebrations she'd had with Aunt Agatha and decided that none of them compared to the one she'd just finished.

A few days after Thanksgiving, Celia was sitting in her Art class, trying not to fall asleep. They were watching a film about something, Celia couldn't remember what, and with the lights off and the curtains pulled, she was having a very hard time keeping her eyes open.

"AARGH!"

Celia jolted upright in her chair, now wide awake.

The noise had come from the classroom next door, and Professor Mesbur hurried out into the hallway to see what was going on. Laughter was now growing louder on the other side of the wall, and the students in Celia's class hurried to peek into the hallway.

"What's going on?" someone asked.

"Can you see anything?"

"What's so funny?"

A few small rubber bouncy balls were dribbling out of the next doorway. It didn't seem like it was that amusing, and they were quickly ushered back into their seats as Professor

Mesbur came back in the room. He headed over to a tall cabinet on the side of the room and carefully opened the door a crack. The door flew out of his hand and all the way open as hundreds of bouncy balls poured into the room.

"AARGH!" Professor Mesbur cried, a perfect imitation of the cry they had heard from next door only moments before.

The balls bounced off the floor, the desks, and anything else in their path, dribbling across the floor or bounding through the room with great leaps. A bunch of them hit Professor Mesbur as he tried to move away from the onslaught of rubber balls.

Celia tried not to laugh, but the sight of so many bouncy balls bouncing through the classroom *was* rather funny, and she started giggling with the rest of the class. In the midst of their laughter, the bell rang, and Professor Mesbur dismissed them, cautioning them to be careful and not trip on any of the bouncy balls.

"Who do you suppose put all those bouncy balls in there?" Maddie asked as she and Celia gathered up their books.

"*Why* would someone put all those bouncy balls in there?" Celia retorted.

Walking through the hallways, it became apparent that the bouncy ball strike was not limited to the classrooms they had just left. Bouncy balls were dribbling out of rooms, rolling all over the halls, and bouncing down the stairs.

"All students must return to quarters IMMEDIATELY," came an announcement through the halls. "Do not report to your next class. Go directly to quarters."

"Sounds fine to me," Celia said, hurrying toward the building housing the Mensaleon quarters. People had started picking up the balls and were now pelting them down the hallways. A few bounced off Celia's head as she ducked around other students and through a few doorways. When she and

Maddie finally reached quarters, they both breathed a sigh of relief.

Celia noticed that a couple of balls fell out of her bag when she dropped it by her desk. Picking one of them up, she froze when she studied it closer. "Oh, no," she groaned.

"What?" Maddie asked.

"Did you look at these?"

"Not really. Why?"

"Look." She held one out for Maddie to see. Printed on the side of the ball was a purple lion.

"Not again," Maddie said.

"There's no way I can get blamed for this one," Celia said.

Doxa and her crew flounced through the door. "I can't believe someone pulled another prank," she said as she dropped her books on her desk. "How could someone be so stupid?" she questioned, looking meaningfully at Celia.

Celia chose not to say anything.

Over the next hour, the Mensaleon quarters were searched again, just like the time before. Celia didn't like the feeling in the pit of her stomach, and her fears were confirmed when Headmaster Doyen was called over to her bed again when the searcher found something in her dresser drawers.

"No way," she heard Maddie whisper as she walked over with great trepidation.

"Miss Fincastle," Headmaster Doyen said sternly, "this is the second time we have found evidence in your possession during our search. What do you have to say for yourself?"

"I . . . I . . ."

"Well? I'm waiting."

"I didn't . . . I wouldn't . . . It wasn't . . . but . . ."

"Miss Fincastle, my patience is wearing thin. I will not tolerate this kind of behavior at my school. Now unless you can come up with a good explanation why these balls are in your drawer—"

Chapter Ten

"Headmaster Doyen?"

Celia looked up quickly at Galena's voice.

"Yes, Miss Zwingle?"

"Can I just say...well, these balls were all over the hallways and the bouncing down the stairs... I guess probably everyone picked up a handful or so, especially the people in Mensaleon. I mean, they *do* have purple lions on them, and..." Celia could tell she was nervous, and probably a little scared to be speaking up in front of the headmaster.

"Yes..."

"Well, it seems to me that nearly everyone has a few balls somewhere in their things. I don't see how you can blame Celia for the whole thing just because you found a few bouncy balls."

Headmaster Doyen took a deep breath. Celia could see his jaw working as he ground his teeth together. "Very well, Miss Fincastle," he bit out angrily. "I see you have gotten off the hook again. But if I find out that you have had anything to do with these pranks..." He left the threat dangling in the air as he stormed out of the room, signaling that the rest of his search team should follow.

"Oh, come on!" Doxa groaned. "You...you..." she sputtered at Celia. "You are despicable! How dare you cause trouble and then get other people to make excuses for you!" She made a sound of disgust and left the room in a huff.

"Thanks, Galena," Celia said after Doxa's posse had left the room after their leader.

"Sure," she said. "It just doesn't seem fair, how you keep getting blamed."

"Well, that was really brave of you to stand up to the headmaster like that," Maddie said, coming over to stand next to Celia.

"Yeah," Libby said. "That guy scares me. I would hate to get in trouble and have him call my parents or something."

"Celia, you really need to stop causing so much trouble." The four girls turned to the doorway at the voice, and saw the four seventh-year boys walking in the room. Kitt was the one who had spoken, but Celia could see the gleam in his eye and knew he was teasing.

"Yeah, dude," Heath said. "If you keep this up, I'll have to stop hanging with you."

"How did you guys hear?" Celia asked.

"Two guesses," Josh said.

"Doxa," all four girls said at once, then burst out laughing.

"Impressive," Heath said.

"Thanks to Galena, I'm not in any trouble yet," Celia said.

"Really?"

Celia saw Galena's face turn pink, but she said, "Yeah, she talked to the headmaster and convinced him that he didn't have enough evidence against me."

"Nice one, Galena," said Kitt.

They stopped talking when they heard an announcement. "All students report to class."

"Oh, man!" Heath said, turning to leave. "Well, at least we got a little time off."

That evening, Celia and Maddie were sitting in the arm chairs at the center of the room, trying to figure out why she had been framed for the two pranks, when one of the other Mensaleon students walked into the room.

"Hey, Celia, a note just came for you," the girl said, holding out a piece of paper for her.

"Oh, thanks, Rebecca," Celia said taking the note from her. Flipping it open, she recognized the writing of the silver-inked words:

Celia,

As a teacher, I am not allowed to

act as your guardian at the school, but I talked with Higby, and he said he would be able to fill in. He'll send a form to your aunt, which will give him permission to sign your ERs and anything else that might come up for the rest of the year. We'll have to fill out the paperwork again each year, but at least you won't have to "inconvenience" your aunt again."

Professor A. Legaspi

"Who's it from?" Maddie asked.

"Professor Legaspi," Celia said, folding it up again.

"What does she want?"

"Nothing. She's just letting me know that Higby will be my temporary guardian so Aunt Agatha won't be bothered."

"Boy, your aunt is really something."

"I know. It's a good thing she doesn't know about the pranks or I'd probably be headed back home right now."

"And wouldn't that be an improvement for this school," Doxa said, coming into the room.

"The best improvement would be if *she* left," Maddie muttered to Celia.

"Did you say something?" Doxa asked.

"No, nothing," Maddie replied.

Doxa looked between Celia and Maddie. "Hmphf."

"Come on, Maddie. Let's head to bed," Celia said, pushing out of the chair.

"Why? A full day of causing trouble catching up to you?" Doxa taunted.

"I didn't do anything, Doxa," Celia said wearily.

"Yeah, I'll just bet you didn't."

"What is your problem?" Maddie asked angrily.

Doxa turned on her. "My *problem* is you dorky sevvies who think it's funny to play stupid pranks that just cause problems. Some of us are trying to finish our last year here at RAGS, and we don't appreciate the interruptions your dumb jokes are creating."

"You don't have any proof that we did anything."

Doxa gave them a sinister-looking smile. "No, not yet, do I?"

"What do you mean by that?" Celia asked.

"I warned you before, Fincastle. You'd better watch your back." Doxa stalked over to her desk, grabbed a notebook, and stormed back out the door.

"Wow, does she have it out for you," Maddie said.

"Yeah, I know. And I can't figure out why. I haven't done anything to her. I just know she's the one trying to frame me for these pranks, but I can't prove it."

"What are you going to do?"

Celia shrugged. "What can I do? No one's going to believe me if I just tell them that Doxa's trying to frame me. I don't have any proof either."

"Still..."

"I'll just try to stay out of her way, that's all, and maybe she'll just leave me alone."

Maddie shook her head. "I really don't think that's going to work."

"Yeah, well, neither do I."

Chapter Eleven
Holidays

The weeks between Thanksgiving and first semester finals seemed to fly past. Christmas decorations appeared around the school the week after Thanksgiving. An immense tree sat in Main Hall, right in the center of the windows looking out at the commons, decorated with ribbons, bows, and lights. The very tip of the tree, capped by a glittering star, nearly brushed the ceiling of the five-story room. Huge boughs of greenery and holly berries were festooned from beam to beam in the hall, and smaller replicas were placed in every hallway in the school.

Hundreds of twinkling colored lights lit up the quarters for the holiday season, and Celia spent many evenings with her curtains open so she could see the soft glow against the ceiling. Smaller trees were placed in every room of the quarters, and no room was left undecorated. On weekends, the lights in Main Hall were dimmed so that the huge room was lit only by the lights on the tree and the hundreds of candles placed around the room. It gave the cavernous space a cozy feeling, and many students spent hours sitting in front of the fireplaces enjoying the atmosphere.

Before Celia even knew it, she was studying furiously for her next set of exams. All her professors were telling them not to worry about these exams either, but semester grades went on permanent records, so everyone wanted to do their best. For Celia, it was a little bit less nerve-racking than midterms because Aunt Agatha wasn't going to see her grades until the end of the year. It would be Higby who had to review her ER and return a signature, and Celia wasn't worried about that at all.

Final exams happened on the last Thursday and Friday before Christmas break. Since most students were heading home for the holidays, there was an added amount of work involved in packing for the trip home. While Celia was a little jealous of the people who were so excited to be seeing their parents and families, she was kind of glad she didn't have to worry about the extra effort.

On the Tuesday before finals, she was sitting in a soft armchair by a fireplace in Main Hall, studying for her Physical Education exam, when she heard someone walk up to her chair. Looking up, she was pleased to see Odile and Odette standing there.

"Hi, Celia," they said in unison.

"Hi." She flipped her book shut, happy for the interruption. "Are you two headed home for the holidays?"

"Yes, and we're so excited! Our Uncle Ezra is coming for a visit," Odette said.

"And we haven't seen him in ages, so it's going to be great," added Odile.

"Sounds like fun."

"Oh, we didn't mean to upset you," Odile said, noting her lackluster response.

"No, actually, we have good news for you," Odette said.

"Really?"

"Yes. We thought it might be an early Christmas present for you," said Odette.

"Um-hm." Odile nodded. "We just heard that Doxa is taking her drones on a ski trip for the holidays."

"Which means she won't be here with you! Isn't that wonderful?"

Celia smiled. "It sounds like a dream come true to me!"

"Well, we won't keep you from studying," Odile said. "Talk to you later!"

Celia watched them walk off, thinking how nice it would be to spend a Christmas without Aunt Agatha or Doxa. She had just opened her book again when Maddie flopped into a nearby chair.

"Celia!" She sounded frantic.

"What?" Celia asked, concerned.

"I just heard that semester finals are twice as hard as midterms! I'm doomed!"

"Being a little dramatic, are we?"

"I barely passed my Art midterm, Celia! There's no way I'm going to pass the final."

"So? Isn't seventh year just supposed to help us figure out what our gifts are so we can take the right classes next year?"

"Yes, but I'll just *die* if I don't pass Art."

"Maddie, you're doing really well in Reading and Logic. Isn't that enough?"

"Well, I guess. I just wanted... never mind. It doesn't matter."

"You just wanted what?"

Maddie dragged the toe of her shoe on the floor. "I just wanted to be good at everything. Not outstanding or anything, just good enough to take classes in everything next year."

"But why would you want to do something you're not good at?"

Maddie shrugged. "I don't know."

Celia thought for a moment. "Well, maybe if you spend

time studying instead of worrying, you'll do better on your exams."

"Hey, that's a good idea. Thanks, Celia!" Celia watched her jump up and hurry off, wondering why her friend would want to give herself extra work if she didn't have to.

By then, people were starting to fill Main Hall before dinner, and the noise level started rising, so Celia headed back up to quarters. She dropped her book on her desk and turned to go back down for dinner, but paused in the hallway when she heard voices in the lounge.

"We have to come up with something else," a girl's voice said.

"I know, but how are we going to make sure that we don't get caught and she does?" a boy's voice said.

"She's so smug," the girl said. "I just want her nailed."

"Let's see what we come up with over break," the boy said. "I'm sure we'll think of something."

Celia stepped quickly back into her room as she heard them walking toward the door and peeked around the doorframe to see if she could tell who had been in the lounge. She saw long blond hair and was pretty certain that had to be Doxa. The boy with her was wearing a blue hooded sweatshirt, but she couldn't see anything that would tell her who it was.

Celia hurried down to the refectory and looked around for Doxa. She saw her sitting at a table with her groupies, but there wasn't anyone around wearing a hooded sweatshirt. Glancing quickly around the rest of the room, she tried to find the person who had been with Doxa in the lounge, but she didn't see anyone wearing a blue sweatshirt of any kind. Disappointed, she grabbed a plate of food and sat down to eat.

"What's wrong, Celia?" Maddie asked.

"I heard two people talking in the lounge when I dropped off my book. It sounded like they were trying to think of another prank that they could blame on me."

"Really?"

"Yeah."

"Who was it?"

"I couldn't see them, just their backs. One of them was Doxa, I'm almost certain. But the other one was a guy wearing a blue sweatshirt, and there's no one here with a blue sweatshirt."

"Oh, too bad."

"I know."

Headmaster Doyen clapped his hands for attention from the podium at the front of the room. "Could everyone please quiet down for a minute? Thank you. I just have one quick announcement for the seventh-years. You will have an assembly in the auditorium just after breakfast tomorrow morning regarding the student mentor program. As the rest of you know, mentors will be assigned the week after Christmas break, so if you are interested in being a student mentor, please let your advisor know. That is all."

"Oh, great," Maddie groaned. "Now we have to try to find the auditorium again!"

Luckily for Celia, Maddie, and all the other students who couldn't remember how to get to the auditorium, Burnsy offered to direct them the next morning. Unlike Eliot, he took them the direct route, going down the stairs next to the front doors, which brought them right into the lobby for the auditorium.

The assembly Wednesday morning was brief and outlined the basics of the student mentor program. Mr. Morven and a few of the other academic advisors explained that the mentor program was to help students further develop their skills by pairing them with a second- or first-year student with similar strengths. There were all sorts of guidelines for the program, including scheduled meetings and evaluations that were submitted to the advisors for review.

Professor Legaspi stopped Celia after class later that morning and asked her to drop by her office that afternoon. Although Celia was trying to fit in some last-minute studying, she took a break just before dinner and headed over to the Aquilegia quarters.

"Hi, Celia," Professor Legaspi said when Celia knocked on the open door. "You can close the door behind you and take a seat. I promise I won't take much of your time." Once Celia was sitting in her chair, Professor Legaspi said, "I just wanted to make sure that you're going to try your best on these semester finals. I don't want you deliberately trying to get lower grades because of last time."

"I...um..." The thought had crossed Celia's mind. She had briefly thought that she could purposely bomb her finals and then she wouldn't have to worry about people finding out about her near-perfect midterms.

"Celia..." Professor Legaspi had a disapproving look on her face. "I certainly hope that you're not considering it. You are remarkably gifted, and if you don't learn to use and develop your gifts...I have no hesitation in saying that your parents would be very disappointed."

"I had thought about it," she admitted. "But I decided that I would rather do my best on the exams and not worry about what other people think."

Relief flooded Professor Legaspi's face. "Wonderful. Well, that was all. Unless you have any questions for me, I'll let you get back to your studying."

"Okay," Celia said slowly. "I'll, um, see you later, then."

"Of course. Good luck on your exams." She was already

busy with some paperwork and didn't seem to notice when Celia left the room.

Her semester final exams *were* harder than her midterms. Professor Spadaro had a huge boulder that he wanted them to lift with only one finger. Celia could only get it to hover an inch or so off the floor, but at least she was able to set it back down without dropping it. Professor Perrin had them listen to a recording in a language that none of them had ever heard before. He wanted them to translate the words, but Celia felt like she was just guessing and making things up.

Professor Mesbur had a small locked chest that he wanted them to open. Celia thought she heard something move in the lock when she tried, but the lid wouldn't open. Professor Twombly wanted them to move a pencil across her desk without touching it. Celia nearly laughed when she heard the directions, because she didn't think it was possible, but she gave it a try. The pencil didn't make it across the desk, but it did roll off the edge, although Celia wasn't sure if she made it move or if the desk was just uneven.

The only exam Celia thought she might have done all right on was Professor Legaspi's. She had a picture on the wall and asked them to write down anything that they saw in the picture, obvious or hidden. Celia was pretty worn out by the time she took that exam, but she thought she might have seen some things in the picture, although after she handed in her paper, she thought maybe she had just been imagining things.

The hallways were chaos after the final bell rang on Friday. Everyone was in a hurry to get their things together and make it out to the BUS before it left. Celia, who didn't have to go anywhere, took her time getting back to quarters, and sat relaxing in a chair while everyone scurried around her. No one from her room was staying at the school for the break, so she would have the entire room to herself.

Libby and Galena were ready first and they wished Celia a merry Christmas as they headed out the door. Maddie was still in her closet packing, while Doxa and her drones were all trying to decide what color jacket they should wear on the ski slopes.

"Oh, what difference does it make?" Maddie muttered when she finally heard what they were discussing.

"Excuse me?" Doxa said. "Oh, like you would understand."

"Hey, just leave her alone," Celia said. "Can we please not be nasty right before Christmas?"

Doxa snorted in disgust. "Why do you care? It's not like it bothers you. No, you're everyone's favorite. Teacher's pet, headmaster's pet . . . school pet."

"Ha. Not hardly."

"Right. Too bad you'll be stuck here all by yourself for the holidays, while we're off having fun at the ski lodge."

"If you're staying in the lodge the whole time, then why do you care what color your jacket is?" Maddie asked, rolling her eyes.

Doxa sauntered over to her. "Jealous?"

"Of you? You wish."

"Uh-huh."

"Guys, I mean it," Celia said. "I really don't want to be cleaning blood off the floors when you leave."

"I am *so* glad I'm not stuck here with you for two weeks," Doxa said, flouncing back to her half-packed bag. "What a nightmare *that* would be."

Maddie took a deep breath, but turned to Celia instead of saying anything to Doxa. "I'm off, Celia. Have a good holiday, okay? I'll see you when I get back."

"Okay, Maddie. You, too. Say hello to all of your family for me." She hugged Maddie and watched as she headed out the door.

Chapter Eleven

"Oh, how sweet." Celia tried to ignore the sneering voice. "Come on, you guys. Let's get out of here before I get sick."

Celia watched in silence as the residents of the other side of the room all filed out the door, and she breathed a huge sigh of relief when they vanished from sight. She leaned back in the chair and closed her eyes, enjoying the peace and quiet.

"Celia!"

She jumped at the noise and sat up straight, her heart pounding in her chest. "Heath, you scared me!"

"Merrar."

"Are you staying here over break?"

"Yeah. It was either this or go stay with my great-aunt Mildred. Every time I visit her, she spends the whole time pinching my cheeks and telling me I need to 'stop wearing such scruffy clothes and cut my hair.'" He said the last in falsetto voice, and Celia couldn't help but giggle.

"Who else is staying here?"

"Couple of kids. There are about ten of us, I guess. C'mon and meet 'em."

"Okay." Celia pushed to her feet and followed Heath to the lounge. Even though she'd made more friends here at Renasci than she had at her old school, she was still a little nervous around people she didn't know. It was especially unsettling that everyone seemed to know who she was when she didn't know any of them.

"Hey, guys!" Heath said, stepping through the door. "Here's the last member of our Christmas crew."

"Hi, Celia." "Hey, Celia." "Come join our group."

"Hi, everyone," Celia said, sinking onto the edge of a chair.

"Well, I guess we don't have to introduce Celia," Heath said. "Do you know everyone?" he asked her. When she shook her head, the group went around in a circle and introduced themselves.

"Hi, Celia, I'm Matt, second-year."

"I'm Rebecca, fourth-year. I think we've met before, but..."

"Hey, I'm Emmalene, fourth-year, too."

"Blaine, first-year."

"Victoria, fifth-year."

"Max, sixth-year."

"Jass, second-year."

"Maybell, sixth-year."

"Awesome," Heath said. "Now we all know each other."

And so began the best two weeks that Celia could remember in a long time. All of the Mensaleon students who had stayed at the school were very friendly, and they all quickly became friends. They spent evenings playing board games or watching movies in the lounge, and soon the other students staying at the school were asking to join them during their activities.

There were only about thirty students staying over for Christmas, which meant there were more Mensaleon students staying than any other coterie. Mealtimes became a big group affair, with tables pushed together so that they ate as a crowd. Only Professor Legaspi and one of the academic advisors remained at the school with the students, and they were included in all the group meals, as well.

Snow began to fall just after lunch on Christmas Eve. It hadn't stopped by the time Celia went to bed that evening, and on Christmas morning, the ground outside had a thick covering of white. When Celia woke up, she noticed that a small pile of presents were sitting under the tree in her room. Scurrying down the ladder, she shrugged into her robe and dropped to the floor by the tree.

"Hey, Celia! Come out here!"

Celia hurried to the lounge and found the rest of the Mensaleon students sitting with their presents around them. She ran back, collected her small stack, and carried them into the lounge. For the first time she could remember, Celia's Christmas morning was a festive, lighthearted celebration, as they took turns opening presents, talking and laughing with each other.

Aunt Agatha gave Celia a stack of note cards, which Celia was certain she was supposed to use right away to send Aunt Agatha a thank-you note. Maddie gave her a pen with purple feathers on the end, and Celia was happy to find that it wrote in purple ink, too. Heath gave her a small key chain with an odd figure dangling from the ring.

"It's an imago," he said. "It's supposed to be good luck, I guess."

Celia thanked him but wasn't sure she wanted to carry something that ugly around with her, good luck or not.

Odile and Odette gave her a pair of gloves trimmed with lace at the edge, which Celia thought were very delicate and pretty.

After lunch, many of the students who had stayed at the school headed outside for a big snowball fight. Heath dragged Celia outside with him, but she had the last laugh when her snowball landed right in his face.

Christmas dinner was a fabulous meal, and everyone ate more than they should have. After the meal, everyone gathered in Main Hall and sang Christmas carols around the tree.

On New Year's Eve, the whole gang congregated in Main Hall to count down to midnight. As the clock struck twelve, everyone cried out, "Happy New Year!" and tossed confetti and streamers in the air. More snowball fights occurred over the next few days, and soon everyone realized that Christmas break was winding down.

The Friday before the end of break, Professor Legaspi caught up with Celia in the Mensaleon quarters.

"Hi, Celia," she said, sticking her head in the room. "Got a minute?"

"Sure," Celia said, closing the book she had been reading. Ever since Professor Legaspi had taught them speed-reading, Celia just couldn't stop reading. She could finish a book in no time flat, and was always looking for something new to read.

Professor Legaspi closed the door behind her and sat down in one of the armchairs by Celia. "Celia... I don't know how to tell you this, but... this time you actually did it."

"Huh?"

"Your semester finals... you got a perfect score."

"Are you kidding?" Celia thought she must be joking. There was no way she could have gotten a perfect score on those exams. Nobody could have. "That's impossible."

"No, it's not, because that's exactly what you did."

"But... I couldn't lift Professor Spadaro's boulder very far... and my pencil... and the locked box didn't even open... and your picture... and I had *no* idea what that person was saying... Professor Legaspi, you don't understand. I just guessed on half that stuff. I had no idea what I was doing!"

"Celia, seventh-year exams are not to see how much you have learned. They are tests to see how much you are capable of. You didn't have to perform everything we asked of you to get a perfect score. You only had to slightly succeed, and you were the only one who managed to do even a small fraction of every task that was set before you. And the fact that you had no idea what you were doing only proves that you have raw talent."

"But..."

"You saw things in that picture I put on the wall that no one could see if they were not gifted in sight. Minute, miniscule details that no average person could see, you noticed. You saw hidden images that no one else in your class picked up on."

"I don't even know what I did! It didn't seem like I was doing anything but looking at the picture. At the fall tournament..."

"What?"

"Well, I read the name off one of the shirts from across the field. It was really weird, like I was looking through a camera or something. And all the noise around me just seemed to fade away."

Professor Legaspi smiled at her. "That's how it starts."

"But it wasn't like that during the exam."

"No. The more you use and develop your talents, the stronger they become, and the easier it is to use them. You reach a point where you're not even aware that you're using your unusual abilities."

"And the other exams? We weren't supposed to be able to do any of those things, either?"

"Not exactly. We use your seventh year to teach you the basic skills for each area of abilities. Seventh-year exams are meant to challenge your abilities so we can identify which areas are your strongest and therefore should be your focus for the remaining six years. You'll have another set of similar exams at the end of third year to narrow down your focus even more."

"Oh."

"Except in your case, it appears that you won't be focusing on anything."

Celia had the fleeting thought that Maddie was *not* going to be happy to hear that. "So what happens now?"

"I'm not really sure. I've never had a student in this situation before." She glanced at Celia. "One thing I am fairly certain of, however, is that this isn't likely to stay a secret. Someone will let it slip, because it is a rather remarkable accomplishment."

"Oh, great."

"I know you've had a lot of attention on you already, but my suggestion would be to just get it over with and hope it blows over quickly. The more you try to hide it, the more rumors will fly out of control."

"I guess."

"It's up to you, of course."

She left her to decide, but all Celia wanted to do was forget any of it was even happening. By the time Sunday rolled around, she concluded that she might as well at least tell Maddie. Doxa and her crew arrived first, and Celia tried to pretend they weren't there. When Maddie walked in, Celia saw Doxa sigh and roll her eyes.

"Hi, Celia! How was your break?"

"Great! How was yours?"

"Not bad." Maddie dumped her stuff in her closet. "I'll unpack later."

Celia walked over to the corner between their two beds. "Hey, Maddie, I've got something to tell you."

"Sure. What is it?"

"Well, it's about our semester finals. Um, Professor Legaspi came and talked to me over break. She, uh, she said that... well, she told me I got a perfect score."

Maddie's mouth dropped open. "No way!"

Celia shrugged. "That's what she said."

"A perfect score? Hey, wait a minute. Did you get a perfect score on midterms, too?"

"No."

Her eyes narrowed. "What *did* you get on midterms, Celia?"

Celia looked down at her feet. "I, uh, missed one point on my Speech exam."

Maddie nodded slowly. "I see."

Celia studied her. "What do you mean?"

"You didn't tell me." She sounded hurt.

"I'm sorry, Maddie. I thought... well, I thought you might get jealous."

Maddie sighed and looked away. "Yeah, I suppose I would have."

"Would have? But not now?"

She shook her head. "I talked to my parents. It turns out that they didn't know how classes work here. They thought I would be a 'dismal failure' if I didn't pass all of my exams this year. Now that they know how it works, they just want me to do well in the classes that I enjoy the most."

"So you don't care that I got a perfect score?"

"*You* got a perfect score!?" Both Celia and Maddie jumped at the sound of Doxa's voice screeching next to them. She had apparently wandered over while they were talking. "Oh, isn't that just *perfect*."

"A perfect score?" Katie asked incredulously.

"No way," Cy said.

"No one can get a perfect score on seventh-year exams," Gretchen piped up. "Besides, they said that was just a rumor going around."

"Spill it, Fincastle," Doxa said, setting one hand on her hip.

"Why should I tell you anything?"

Doxa looked at her with revulsion. "You're lying."

"No, she's not," Maddie spat.

Doxa studied Celia. "You're not lying, are you? I can't believe it! Of all the luck...Now you'll be even more of a teacher's pet! Ugh! Wait until I tell everyone."

"No, wait!" Celia cried, but Doxa didn't hear because she was too busy hurrying out of the room to tell everyone she saw her new piece of juicy gossip.

"Hang on tight, Maddie," Celia murmured. "Because I have a feeling it's about to become a wild ride."

Chapter Twelve
Mentors

By dinnertime on Sunday, everyone in Mensaleon knew about Celia's semester exam scores, and most of them had stopped by her room to congratulate her. Celia tried to wait until the last possible minute to head down to dinner, hoping to avoid everyone and just blend into the crowd, but as they made their way to the refectory, nearly everyone around them was pointing and whispering, just as they had the first few weeks of school. She slunk into the room and slouched into a seat, hoping people would just leave her alone, but soon the entire room was whispering and everyone was craning to see her.

Blaine, who she'd learned over break was a bit of a prankster, gave her an amused look as he rose to his feet. Celia watched him, trying to figure out what he was doing, and then wished the floor would open up and swallow her when he started clapping. "Woo-hoo, Celia!" he called. Soon everyone was standing and clapping, and Celia just wanted to crawl under the table.

"All right, all right," Headmaster Doyen called from the front of the room. "That is enough, thank you. Servers, please."

"Blaine!" Celia cried over the noise of everyone taking their seats again.

"Sorry, Celia, but I figured that if everyone was going to be looking at you, they might as well get it over with. Besides," he grinned, "I wanted to see what color your face would turn."

"You're impossible!"

Maddie eyed her while the servers brought food to the table. "So..." she said once everyone was loading up their plates. "Who's Blaine?"

"He's just a first-year who stayed at the school for Christmas break, that's all."

"Wow. Seems like I missed everything over the holidays."

"Maddie! There was a group of us that stayed here, and we just spent a lot of time together. We're sort of like... brothers and sisters, I guess." Celia poured herself a glass of milk. "I've never had brothers or sisters. It's kind of nice." She made a face. "Well, except when they embarrass me like that."

"Welcome to siblings, Miss Fincastle," Maddie said, rolling her eyes. "Mine are nothing but pests."

During the next few days, nearly every person passing Celia in the hallway either congratulated her on her exam scores or whispered behind their hand to their friends. More people did the former than the latter, so Celia guessed that was a good sign.

They got their exams back on Monday and Tuesday, and, sure enough, Celia got perfect scores on all her exams. It felt a little bit better to not have to hide her grades, as everyone already knew what she had gotten. By the end of Tuesday, however, she was getting a little tired of having so much attention, and she just wanted to relax in her quarters for the evening. When she walked into the room, she nearly groaned aloud when she saw Doxa sitting at her own desk.

"Well, well. If it isn't little miss perfect."

"Hello, Doxa," she said unenthusiastically.

"Had enough of everyone falling all over themselves to talk with the great and mighty Celia Fincastle?"

Celia raised an eyebrow at her. "Well, no one would have known if you hadn't told them."

"Of course they would have, sevvie. Everyone knows about you."

Celia shrugged. "Not my problem."

"Not yet. But wait until they know all about the other side, the side that causes trouble and kisses up to the headmaster."

"Ha! Boy, are you wrong. Headmaster Doyen would like nothing better than to..."

"Than to what?"

"Than to... uh..." Celia had been about to say "nail me," but then she remembered that was the phrase she had heard Doxa use in the lounge before Christmas. "Uh...catch the person who pulled those pranks."

Doxa smirked at her as if she knew what Celia had been about to say. "Oh, I'm sure he will. And when he does, I'll be there to watch you get what you deserve."

"Fine, Doxa," Celia muttered, walking over and climbing up into her bed. Doxa kept tossing insults at her as she pulled the curtains, but when Celia had shut the last curtain around the bed, she noticed that she couldn't hear Doxa anymore. Curious, she lifted the edge of one of the curtains and heard Doxa still ranting away, but when she let the curtain fall back down, the noise stopped. *Yes!* she thought. *Peace and quiet!*

She did all of her homework on her bed that evening and didn't hear a peep of anything else going on in the room. She had to leave her cave to get ready for bed, but she hurried as fast as she could and managed to avoid running into Doxa. She was so exhausted from the past two days that she quickly fell asleep.

Chapter Twelve

On Wednesday, the seventh-years started getting called down to Mr. Morven's office to receive their student mentor assignments. Celia's note told her to stop by just before lunch, so she got a hall pass from Professor Perrin and headed to the administrative wing.

Mr. Morven's door was open, but she knocked anyway. He glanced up from his writing. "Oh, hello, Celia. Come on in and grab a seat. I'm just about... finished," he said, punctuating his statement by dotting his pen on the paper. He closed the folder and moved it to the side of his desk, then turned his attention to her. "So I hear you had quite the first semester."

Celia smiled weakly. "I guess you could say that."

He winked at her. "Some people would be very pleased to be doing so well in school."

"I am... it's just..."

"Kind of hard to get so much attention?"

She nodded.

"Well, keep your chin up. I'm sure things will get better. In the meantime, you're here to discuss your student mentor assignment." He fingered through another pile on his desk and pulled out a folder. "Based on your exam scores..." He scanned the paper in front of him. "... well, all your professors have recommended a mentor from their coterie. However, I met with Higby and Professor Legaspi, and they're suggesting we assign you only two."

"Do you guys have a meeting about me every week or something?" Celia mumbled under her breath.

"I'm sorry," Mr. Morven said, leaning forward in his chair. "Did you say something?"

Celia felt her cheeks go red as she dropped her eyes to study her shoes. "No, it was nothing. Sorry."

"Okay. Well, since you *are* in Mensaleon, the most obvious choice for one of your mentors would be someone from your own coterie. In fact, it would be rather peculiar if you *didn't* have a mentor in Mensaleon. As for the other one, I talked with some of the other advisors and I think we've found a good match for you. There's a student in Corpanthera who also does quite well in the gifts of touch, so it will cover two areas in one. How does that sound?"

"Um... okay."

"Great. Professor Legaspi also offered to be a faculty mentor for you, in addition, obviously, to Professor Twombly. You won't have the scheduled meetings with them, of course, but they will be available to help you with anything, should you need it."

"All right."

Mr. Morven opened his desk drawer and pulled out an index card. "Okay," he said, writing some information on the card and handing it to Celia. She noticed that he had written a rather large amount in such a short period of time, but she didn't comment on it. "These are your two student mentors, then. They should be in touch with you by the end of the week to set up your first meeting."

"Okay."

"Do you have any questions?"

Celia shook her head. "I don't think so."

He smiled at her. "All right, then. Keep up the good work, Celia."

"Thank you."

It was time for lunch when Celia left Mr. Morven's office, so she headed down to the refectory. On her way, she glanced at the two names Mr. Morven had written on the card. She didn't think she knew a Merriweather Lenox or a Neel Winokur, but maybe she had met them and just forgotten their names. Maddie had saved her a seat, but everyone was already eating when she sat down with her plate.

Chapter Twelve

"Celia!" someone called just as she took her first bite. She glanced around and saw a smiling girl coming her way. She had long, wavy, red hair and it seemed like every inch of her pale skin was covered with freckles. "Hi, Celia," she said, stopping by the table. "I'm Merry; Merriweather, actually, but everyone calls me Merry. I just found out I'm your mentor!"

"Oh, hi, Merry," Celia said after she had swallowed her food. "Yeah, I just talked to Mr. Morven and he gave me your name."

"I'm so excited! Can you meet me tonight in the lounge?"

"Sure."

"Okay, great! See you later."

"Yeah, see you." As Celia watched her walk away, she thought it was very appropriate that her name was "Merry" because it seemed like she never stopped smiling. After meeting her, Celia remembered seeing her with Jass, who had been one of the Christmas crew.

"Don't you feel sorry for the poor person who got stuck with Doxa as a mentor?" Maddie mused aloud from next to Celia.

"Oh, that would be horrible!" Celia thought for a moment. "But don't you have to sign up to be a mentor?"

"Only for first-years. All second-years have to serve as mentors."

"That means some poor sixth-year got stuck with Doxa last year. How awful!" Celia took a drink, then turned to Maddie again. "When do you go up to meet with Mr. Morven?"

"Later this afternoon. I just hope I don't get stuck with someone really terrible."

"You mean like Doxa?"

"Oh, please don't say that! It'd be just my luck!"

That evening, Celia met Merry in the lounge. The bubbly second-year had staked out a corner of the room, and was, as usual, in a cheerful mood.

"Hi, Celia! Sit down."

"Hi, Merry."

"I guess we should start by getting to know each other a little, so I'll start. I have an older sister and a younger brother. My parents run a cute little coffee shop and bakery. I love watching Soccovolle but I stink at playing it, and my favorite class in seventh year was Logic. How about you?"

Celia felt a little overwhelmed. "Well... I'm guessing that you probably know as much about me as I know about myself."

Merry laughed. "You're probably right! Isn't it so weird how everyone knows your name and everything? I think that would just be a little creepy to me."

"Um, yeah, I guess it is at times."

"Well, tell me about yourself, anyway."

"Okay. I don't have any brothers or sisters. I know almost nothing about my parents. Um, I've never played Soccovolle because I'd never heard of it before I came here, and I don't think I have a favorite class. I like all of them."

Merry laughed again. "Well, since you got a perfect score on your exams, I'd say you probably *do* like all of them." She pulled a piece of paper out of the folder on her lap. "The sheet says we're supposed to discuss any concerns you have about your schoolwork. Is there anything you're having trouble with?"

Celia shook her head. "No, other than I can't figure out how I managed to do so well on my exams."

Merry raised her eyebrows. "Really? Well, it's not so unusual for seventh-years to not be aware of what they can really do. My friends and I thought we were going to be kicked out of school for having lousy grades, but we turned out okay. I'm sure you'll figure it out soon."

They chatted for a few more minutes before Max came up and interrupted them. "Sorry, girls, but this just came for

Celia," he said, handing her a piece of paper.

"Oh, thanks, Max."

"Sure," he said, walking away again.

"Who's it from?" Merry asked, her eyes wide with curiosity.

Celia flipped it open and scanned the message. "Oh, it's from my other mentor. He just wants to set up a time to meet."

Merry looked surprised. "You have two mentors?"

"Um, yeah. Since I did so well on my exams, they assigned me two mentors." She looked over at Merry. "That's not a problem, is it?"

"Oh, my goodness, no! I mean, I'm just terrible at some of the other gifts. What coterie is your other mentor in?"

"He's in Corpanthera."

"Oh, no, I wouldn't be any help for you in that at *all.*" Merry glanced at her watch. "Oh, it's getting late and I have a ton of homework to finish tonight. Do you mind if we call it an evening?"

"No, that's fine."

"Okay, great! Now, I just need you to sign my sheet here," she said, pointing to a line on the bottom of her paper, "and I have to sign yours, too." They both scribbled their names on the papers. "And then we just have to fill out the rest of the information and hand it in to our advisors."

"Okay."

"I'm so glad I get to be your mentor, Celia. I'm just so excited! It should be a lot of fun. Now if you need anything, you just let me know, all right?"

"Sure."

"Okay. I'll see you later, then. Good night."

Celia headed into her room and found Maddie reading at her desk. "Hey, Celia. How was your meeting with Merry?"

"She's very... happy."

Maddie giggled. "And?"

Celia shrugged. "And she's really nice. It sounds like she could be a big help with some of my Logic homework. She's just really... enthusiastic. That's all."

"Well, better that than someone like..." She nodded her head toward Doxa's bed.

"True."

"How about your other mentor?"

"He sent me a note. I'm supposed to let him know when I can meet him."

"'He'? Wow, that's unusual. They usually pair girls with girls."

"How do you know so much about this school, Maddie?"

She shrugged. "I talk to a lot of people. And my grandmother went here."

"Really? But not your parents?"

"No. My mom doesn't really talk about it much. Something with my grandfather, I guess, but I'm not sure."

"Hmm."

Maddie yawned, which made Celia yawn. "I guess we'd better head to bed, huh?"

"Guess so. Night, Maddie."

"Night, Celia. Sweet dreams."

Celia met Neel in the library on Friday afternoon, since it was one of her favorite places in the school. The library at Renasci spanned two floors on the opposite side of Main Hall from the refectory, but the high ceilings made Celia suspect that it actually took up more like four floors. As far as Celia could figure, it was upstairs from the auditorium. There were spiral staircases and rows and rows of bookshelves. The room had a musty old book smell to it, and lots of corners set aside for reading and studying. Celia's favorite spot was on the second floor at the far end, where there was a window seat where you could almost see the lake through the trees. It was so far out of the way that people rarely bothered her, and it was almost always empty.

For this meeting, however, Celia had chosen one of the meeting rooms. The librarian, Mrs. Romanaclef, greeted Celia when she stepped through the door, and then opened up one of the meeting rooms for her.

Neel showed up precisely on time, and Celia was a little surprised by him. For some reason, she had been expecting a burly jock of some sort, but he was about as far away from that as you could get. He had short black hair that was spiky on top and dark brown eyes that were almost black. He seemed to move effortlessly, and every motion was fluid and graceful. He was neither short nor tall, just average height, which kept him from being stocky or lanky.

"Hello, Celia Fincastle!" he heralded as he stepped through the door to the meeting room.

"Um...hi," Celia said.

He flopped into the chair across the table from her. "I've heard a lot about you," he said, dropping his bag on the floor next to him. "It's such an honor to meet you."

"Uh...thanks. You, too."

"I bet you get that a lot, huh?"

"Well..." Celia shrugged.

"So I hear you got a perfect score on your exams."

"Yeah."

Neel pulled a folder out of his bag and flipped through papers until he found the sheet for student mentor meetings. "I'm not sure how much help I'm going to be for you, but I guess we'll see." He scanned the sheet. "Is there anything you need help with?"

Celia shook her head. "No, not right now. Unless ..."

"What?"

Celia shrugged. "It's just... I share a room with Doxa, and she's kind of hard to get along with."

Neel rolled his eyes at her. "I hear ya. She can be... difficult."

"You know her?"

Neel tucked his pen behind his right ear. "I've had a few classes with her over the years. Just ignore her. She'll get over it."

"You think so?"

"Trust me, kid. Doxa's just a bunch of hot air." He leaned back in his chair and propped his feet up on the corner of the table. "She's probably just jealous 'cause everyone pays attention to you. Don't worry about it."

Over the next half hour, Celia and Neel went through the same process that Celia had done with Merry. Although Neel seemed very laid back, a little like Heath, Celia noticed an intense light in his eyes, as if he was watching everything that went on around him and filing it away for some future use. By the end of the meeting, Celia felt quite comfortable around him, laughing at his jokes and rolling her eyes at his good-natured teasing.

After they wrapped up, Celia gathered her things and headed back to her quarters.

"Hey, Celia," Maddie said when she entered the room. "How was your meeting?"

"Great!" she exclaimed. "Neel's pretty cool. He seems like a great guy."

"Neel?" Doxa said from across the room. "Are you talking about Neel Winokur?"

"Yeah. Why?" Celia replied.

"How do you know Neel?"

"He's one of my student mentors. Why?"

Doxa had an odd look on her face. "Is he, now? Interesting."

"What are you talking about?"

Doxa rolled her eyes. "Don't get so suspicious, sevvie. It's just that Neel's kind of...arrogant, I guess. I suppose it's fitting, isn't it? That they pair you with someone else who thinks they're the greatest thing to ever happen to this school."

"Hey!"

"Oh, please, don't try to deny it," Doxa scoffed. "I don't want to hear it."

"That's unfair!" Maddie piped up. "You're the one who was eavesdropping on our conversation. If you don't like Celia, just keep it to yourself, would you?"

"I'd love to," Doxa sneered, "but she just won't go away, you know?"

"I don't know what your problem is, Doxa, but—"

"My problem is *you*, Fincastle. And sooner or later you're going to learn that you're not all you think you are." The menacing look on Doxa's face and the tone of her voice sent chills down Celia's spine. "I have a feeling it's going to be sooner, sevvie, and I'm going to enjoy that day."

Celia tried hard to focus on her schoolwork during the next few months, but it wasn't an easy task. Between meetings with both of her mentors and trying to figure out what Doxa was up to, Celia found her mind wandering in the brief time she had for homework. Although she would have preferred to work in the library, she figured it might be smarter to work in her room so she could overhear anything Doxa might say.

Snow covered the campus most days during January, and many snowball fights took place on the commons. A few wayward snowballs hit the windows, but it seemed that the teachers conveniently looked the other way when it happened.

To keep everyone from getting cabin fever, each coterie held a decorating competition in quarters. Professor Twombly provided supplies and each room vied for the titles of Best Decorations and Most Creative. Some of the other Mensaleon students came up with some outstanding ideas, but Celia's room ended up looking pretty pathetic. Doxa didn't like any of the ideas that the seventh-years came up with and refused to work with them for decorating, so they ended up dividing the room and decorating each half separately.

Celia and the other seventh-years chose a beach theme and put up palm trees, tiki torches, coconuts, and brightly-colored leis. Everyone said that their side of the room looked great and that they might have won the competition if not for Doxa's side of the room. Doxa and her posse had decorated their half in a Japanese tea room style, but it ended up looking like a halfhearted attempt and really didn't fit well with the beach theme on the other side of the room.

The winners of the decorating competition in the Mensaleon quarters were the second- and third-year boys, who picked a fireworks theme, complete with chasing lights and a soundtrack; they swept both awards.

January quickly gave way to February, and soon Celia and the other seventh-year girls were hearing about the spring dance that they wouldn't be allowed to attend. Doxa only grew more annoyed when they showed little interest in the dance, other than anticipating another round of charades in the lounge.

Valentine's Day brought a new distraction, in the form of candy-grams. The seventh-year Mensaleon students teamed together and made sure they all got at least one apiece, but that didn't stop Doxa from bragging about the ones she had received.

Chapter Twelve

As February drew to a close, Celia's teachers began to mention their next exams, the spring midterms, happening in March. To try to avoid falling behind and having to cram, Celia and her other seventh-year roommates decided to head to the library for a study session after dinner one evening. A few hours later, they walked back into their room and stumbled to a stop. Things were spread all over the corner by Doxa's bed.

"What's going on?" Libby asked.

"I don't know," Celia said.

"I'll tell you what's going on," Doxa said, stepping out from her closet. "My book is missing. I need it to finish a very important paper. I left it right there on my desk, and now it's gone."

"Very important, huh?" Maddie whispered into Celia's ear. "What's it about, the over-use of eye shadow?"

"Stop it!" Celia hissed, trying not to laugh.

"You think this is funny, Fincastle?" Doxa asked, moving closer to tower over her.

"Uh, no, of course not."

"Good. Because it's not. Someone stole my book, and I want it back."

"You don't think one of us took it?" Celia asked incredulously.

"Well, it wasn't one of my friends, so that narrows it down to one of you."

"Come on, Doxa. Anyone could have come in here and taken a book off your desk."

"No, they couldn't. No one can come into this room unless one of us is in here, except the staff members. They can't make it past the doorway."

"Really?"

Doxa wore a smug smile. "So either one of you stole my book, or you let someone in here who stole my book."

"Why would we do that?" Maddie asked.

"How would I know? Far be it from me to try to figure out how the mind of a sevvie works."

"Come on, guys," Celia said, waving them over to their side of the room. "Just ignore her."

"Hey!"

Celia turned back to Doxa. "What now?"

"I want my book back."

"I don't have it."

"Well, someone does."

"Great. When you find out who, let us know."

"Why, you!"

"Oh, just leave me alone!"

"Just make me!"

"I didn't do anything to you!"

"You stole my book!"

"No, I didn't!"

"LADIES!" They both jumped at the sound of Professor Twombly yelling from the doorway. "That is enough yelling! What is all this commotion about?"

"She stole my book, Professor."

"No, I didn't. I've never even seen her book."

"Miss Geleafa, do you have proof that she stole your book?"

"Well, no. But it was on my desk, and I just know she'd steal it just to sabotage me so I won't be able to graduate."

"Miss Fincastle, do you know where her book is?"

"No, Professor Twombly. I don't even know what book she's missing."

Professor Twombly sighed. "Ladies, you need to figure out how to get along and stop fighting. Doxa, without any evidence, I don't see how you can conclude that Celia stole your book. And both of you need to start treating each other with some respect. Now I don't want to have to hear you yelling again, understood?"

"Yes, Professor Twombly," they chorused.

"Very well." She spun on her heel and left the room.

"This isn't over!" Doxa hissed in Celia's ear. Celia had an ominous feeling that it wasn't. Not by a long shot.

Chapter Thirteen
Accusations and Rumors

March blew in with a fierce windstorm that rattled windows and shook walls. Celia woke up in the middle of the night to the sound of branches and leaves hitting the windows by her bed. By morning, the windstorm had given way to a heavy rainstorm, which lasted for three days. It didn't bother Celia, who spent as much time as possible at the window seat in the library, watching the rain and studying. Anything to avoid running into Doxa.

On Monday morning, Celia noticed that Maddie was acting a little strange, but thought maybe midterm nerves had started a little early.

"You okay, Maddie?" she asked her at breakfast, noticing that Maddie had only picked at her food.

"What? Oh, uh, no, I'm fine."

"Are you sure? You seem...I don't know, funny, I guess."

Maddie sighed. "Celia—" The bell cut her off.

"Oops. We'd better get to class. Tell me on the way?" Celia asked, scooping up her stuff.

"I...Sure."

They dropped off their dishes and headed toward their first class. Celia thought people were giving her funny looks in the hallway, but then wondered if all of the studying was starting to get to her, too. But were people whispering, too?

"Hey, look! It's Steal-ia, the thief!" someone called. Taunting laughter followed.

"What are they talking about?" Celia whispered to Maddie.

"Celia . . ."

"What? What's going on?"

"Doxa found her book on your bed," Maddie said.

"What!? That's impossible. I didn't take it."

"*I* know that! But she must have told everyone you did."

"But I didn't take her book. How did it get on my bed?"

"It's not like people can't get into our room, Celia. We share it with six other girls."

Celia's temper began to boil. "I just don't understand. Why is she doing this to me?" She marched down the hallway, Maddie hurrying to keep up, and into their Reading class. Slamming her books down on the desk, she sank into the chair and sighed.

"Celia?" Professor Legaspi asked, giving her a concerned look.

"Sorry, Professor Legaspi. I didn't mean to make so much noise."

"Is something wrong?"

"Kind of."

The bell rang, so she said, "Come talk to me after class, okay?"

"Okay."

Celia fumed her way through the class, noticing the glances that some of her classmates sent her way. By the time the bell rang to dismiss class, she was more than happy to see everyone leave the room.

"What's going on?" Professor Legaspi asked when the last student had left the room.

Celia sighed and looked out the classroom window. "Doxa lost a book and she told everyone that I stole it from her."

"And I assume you didn't."

"Of course I didn't!"

Professor Legaspi nodded silently.

"I just don't understand why this is happening!"

Professor Legaspi looked at her sharply. "There are things going on here that you know nothing about, Celia. You need to be careful."

"Things like what?"

She glanced at the doorway. "I can't tell you here. I'm not even sure I should tell you at all. But seeing as it has to do with you... Come to my office tonight, just after dinner. I can tell you some, but it's not my place to tell you all of it. That must be someone else's decision." She started gathering her books and papers.

"What do you mean?"

"I know this doesn't make any sense to you, and it's frustrating when you don't understand." She looked her in the eye. "Celia, promise me that you won't do anything rash. It is very important that you keep alert. Be careful about who you trust. Everything is not always what it seems."

"Why does everyone keep saying that?"

"Because in the demesne, just as in the normal world, there are forces at work that no one can see. Sometimes they work for good, but sometimes they work for evil. It takes a discerning eye to tell one from the other."

"I don't understand. What does that have to do with me?"

"More than you realize, and probably more than you think. I can't say more now. Remember: my office after dinner." With that she turned and hurried out the door, leaving Celia standing in confusion.

For the rest of the day, Celia tried to figure out what Professor Legaspi might tell her, but no matter how hard she stretched her brain, she couldn't see how any of the pieces fit together. It probably wasn't the best time for her attention to be wandering from her classes, as all her professors were doing review for their exams at the end of the week.

In Professor Spadaro's Physical Education class, they were working in pairs on balance exercises, and Celia had been teamed up with Kevin Fackler, a short, skinny Tattotauri seventh-year with braces. They were supposed to be balancing on one foot on a skinny pedestal, but every time Celia took her turn, she kept falling off and running into Kevin.

"I'm *so* sorry," she said when she smacked Kevin's arm on her tenth fall.

"Don't worry about it," he said sullenly.

"This shouldn't be this hard!" she exclaimed, jamming the pedestal upright once more.

"Tell me about it," he groaned morosely. "I'm never going to make it past this year."

Celia patted his arm awkwardly. "Don't worry. I don't think they kick people out after seventh-year."

He shook his head. "I don't know. I can't even ask my mentor for help 'cause he quit."

"He *quit*?"

Kevin nodded glumly. "I guess his grades weren't doing so well, so he asked to be excused from the mentor program."

"Oh, no. What are you going to do?"

He shrugged. "I guess they're going to try to find someone else to volunteer."

"I'm so sorry," Celia said. Suddenly her own problems didn't seem so horrible.

Professor Spadaro clapped his hands and called, "All right, everyone. Time to pack it up!"

"Boy, what a day," Celia said, collapsing into a chair next to Maddie in the refectory at dinnertime.

"It wasn't *that* bad," Maddie said, looking at her askance. "I know. I was there, remember? What made your day so bad?"

Celia glanced around, and seeing everyone nearby involved in other conversations, she leaned over to Maddie and spoke quietly. "Professor Legaspi wants to talk to me after dinner. It sounds really important."

"Really?"

"She said something about 'forces you can't see' and how they can be for good or evil."

"Really!?" Maddie's eyes were huge.

"Shhh!" Celia glanced around again. "Maybe I'll get some information and I can finally figure out what everyone is talking about."

"What do you mean?"

"It's just some stuff that Mr. Morven and Professor Legaspi and…well, you have said. It's like there's something going on with me that I don't know about, and no one will tell me."

"You mean like with that book in your closet?"

"Exactly. So maybe Professor Legaspi will tell me what's going on."

"Maybe." Maddie didn't sound convinced.

"What?"

"It's just…if they…whoever's involved…wanted you to know what was *really* going on, wouldn't they have told you by now?"

Celia's spirits sank. "You're right."

"But that doesn't mean you won't find something out tonight," Maddie said quickly.

"Yeah, maybe."

"Look, Celia. I don't know what's going on any more than you do. For all I know, Professor Legaspi might tell you everything you wanted to know."

Celia nodded, but didn't say anything. During dinner, Maddie tried to cheer her up again and get her excited about talking with Professor Legaspi, but it didn't work much.

After dinner, she walked slowly toward the Aquilegia quarters for her meeting with Professor Legaspi. She was just about to head up the stairs when she heard a door open a few floors above her, followed by quick footsteps.

"Did you get it?" someone said quietly.

"I think so."

"You *think* so?"

"I heard footsteps. So I grabbed and ran."

Celia heard footsteps on the stairs, so she carefully eased around behind the stairs and hid in the shadows.

"Let's get out of here."

They said nothing more as they hurried down the stairs and rushed past Celia's hiding spot. She noted that there were two people, one slightly taller than the other. She tried to see who it was, but they were heading away from her again. All she could see was short dark hair on the taller one and long blond hair on the shorter of the two. As they pushed through the door, the taller one glanced back to make sure the other one had made it through the doorway. Celia shrank further back into the shadows to make sure they didn't see her, but she squinted to try to see better.

The door clicked shut after them and Celia stepped shakily out of her hiding spot. She walked carefully up the stairs, trying to figure out who she'd seen. The blond one had to be Doxa, no doubt about that. But the other one? Was it the same person who had been with Doxa the last time, the one with the blue hooded sweatshirt?

She headed into the Aquilegia quarters, returning the greetings of a few of the people she came across. Professor Legaspi's office was dark, but she knocked on the door anyway and found it slightly ajar. Pushing it open, she switched the light on and stepped inside. “Professor Legaspi?” she asked.

When she heard no answer, she left the door open and sat down in one of the silver chairs.

“Hey, Celia,” someone said from the doorway. When she turned, Celia saw Eliot standing there.

“Hi, Eliot.”

“What are you doing here?” he asked, leaning against the doorframe and crossing his arms.

“I have a meeting with Professor Legaspi, but I guess she’s not here yet.”

“Hm,” he said, looking around the office. “That’s odd. She doesn’t usually leave her office unlocked when she’s not here.”

“The door was open when I knocked on it. So I just came in and took a seat.”

“Don’t worry, Celia. We don’t learn how to unlock doors until at least fifth year, so I know you didn’t break in or anything. It just seems out of character for Professor Legaspi, that’s all. Maybe she’s been too busy with midterms.”

“Oh, don’t remind me,” Celia groaned. “I have so much studying to do yet!”

“I don’t think you have anything to worry about.”

“That doesn’t mean I don’t have to study.”

“Hi, Eliot, Celia,” Professor Legaspi said, coming up behind him. He stepped aside and let her enter the office.

“I was just keeping Celia company until you got here, Professor Legaspi. I’ll go now.”

“All right. Thanks, Eliot.” Professor Legaspi closed the door behind him and then walked around her desk.

“The door opened when I knocked on it, Professor, so I just came inside to wait.”

She frowned. “Hm. I thought I closed that behind me, but maybe I didn’t get it closed all the way.” She sat down in the chair and looked at Celia. "I wanted to give you a word of warning, Celia. Between the rumors and the other events so far this year . . . "

"I swear I haven't done anything."

"I didn't say you had," she said, "But I must insist that you walk very carefully around school. Certain people cannot be trusted and there are things going on that you don't understand."

"So why doesn't someone just tell me?"

She sighed again. "It's not that simple. The situation is very . . . complicated. There's so much that you don't know, that you're not ready to hear. I know it must be very frustrating, but please believe me when I say that it's better this way for now."

"So what am I supposed to do?"

"Just keep your eyes open and try to stay out of trouble."

"But I haven't done anything! I *am* staying out of trouble, and it's not helping me any!"

"I know, Celia. I'm sure everything will be straightened out soon." She drummed her fingers on the desk. "Some people are worried that someone will try something now that you're here."

"Who? Try something like what?" Celia was totally confused.

"There are certain people who do not want you to succeed. They would like nothing more than to see you fail."

"At school?"

She shook her head. "No, this has much bigger implications than just passing classes at school. It has to do with what you have been called to do."

Celia felt like Professor Legaspi was talking in a foreign language that she didn't understand. "I don't know what you're talking about."

"I know you don't. And I can't say a whole lot about it. I... Well, it's just not my place to say anything. But I can warn you that there are people using their gifts for evil purposes, and it isn't always clear who they might be."

"How am I supposed to know who that is?"

"You'll just have to learn, Celia. It's not something that comes easily."

Celia thought of Doxa. "Somehow I think it's more obvious in some people than in others."

"Have you noticed anything that makes you suspicious?"

Celia sighed. "I heard something on my way up here."

"What?"

"There were two people in the stairway. One of them said something about grabbing something."

"Do you know who it was?"

Celia shook her head. "No, not for sure. I have a guess, but I can't prove it."

"This isn't the first time you've heard something, is it?" Celia shook her head again. "I really wish I could do something, but without any solid proof, there's nothing we can do."

"I know."

Professor Legaspi smiled at her. "Don't give up, Celia. The year's almost over."

"Yeah, I know."

"Okay, well, keep your eyes and ears open and let me know if you see anything that might help identify those people you heard."

"All right," Celia said, standing up. "Good night."

"Good night, Celia."

Although the rain had stopped by Tuesday morning, the skies stayed cloudy for the next week. Between the gloomy weather and the upcoming exams, the mood at the school shifted and people began getting uptight and antsy about their exams. On the Wednesday before midterms, Celia was sitting with the other Mensaleon seventh-year girls in the refectory at lunchtime when Heath came up to sit with them.

"Hey, ladies," he said, spinning his chair around and taking a seat.

"Hi, Heath," Celia said.

"Do you think they'll find the person who took it?"

The girls looked at him as if he'd just dropped out of the sky. "What are you talking about?" Libby asked.

"Haven't you guys heard?" Kitt said, coming up behind Heath and setting his plate down on the table.

"No," Maddie said. "We've been holed up in the library all morning."

"Word is that someone stole an answer key from one of the teachers."

"What?" Celia's mind whirled. "How could they do that?"

Heath shrugged. "Beats me. But whoever did it is in mega trouble."

"Oh, no, not again!" Celia moaned, dropping her head into her hand.

"Relax, Celia. No one's going to believe that you stole an answer key. Not after your perfect semester exams," said Kitt.

"You don't understand," Celia said. "Doxa's got it in for me. She's going to make it look like I did it, even though I didn't."

"What do you mean?" Heath asked.

"It's a long story," Maddie said, "but to make it short, Doxa doesn't like Celia and we think she's been behind a lot of the things that Celia's been framed for this year."

"Really?"

Celia nodded glumly. "Like that book she says I stole off her desk."

"Oh, come on," Kitt said. "You'd never do something like that."

"Thanks, Kitt. But Doxa thinks I'm the worst human being on the planet."

"Yeah, that's Celia," Heath quipped.

As the whole table laughed, Celia found her mood lifting slightly, and by the end of the meal she had almost forgotten to be worried about what Doxa was going to do next.

The whole school was buzzing all afternoon about the missing answer key, although none of the teachers or deans would say anything about it. Celia had her own suspicions, and tried hard to shake off the feeling that she had seen the people responsible and that they would somehow manage to make it look like she had been the culprit.

That evening, Celia had a meeting with Neel in Main Hall. She got there early and sat around listening to all of the speculation running around about who would have taken an answer key and whether someone had been trying to cheat on their midterms or not.

"Good evening, Miss Fincastle," Neel said, coming up beside her. "My apologies for being late."

"Oh, no problem." She watched him slide into a seat. "Have you heard all the rumors?"

He raised an eyebrow as he grinned at her. "Which ones? The 'someone took the answer key' rumor, or the 'Celia stole a book' rumor?"

"Well, both, I guess. But I was talking about the answer key. You don't believe I stole Doxa's book, do you?"

He leaned back in the chair and crossed one leg over the other. With his elbows on the armrests, he tented his fingers in front of him and perused her face with a mock frown and an impish gleam in his eye. "Now let me think. Would Miss Celia Fincastle be likely to steal a book? Yes, yes, I can see it now. Of course that seems like something she would do."

"Neel!"

He laughed. "Of course you wouldn't steal a book," he said, fiddling with his shoelaces. "Why would you need to?" He pulled his folder out of his bag. "Now, was there anything you needed help with before midterms?"

Celia grinned at him. "Believe it or not, I'm actually ahead of schedule. My roommates and I started studying last week."

Neel gasped loudly and placed his hand on his chest. "No! Studying early!? Oh, no, that just won't do."

Celia's eyes bugged as her grin faded. "What?"

Neel laughed as he waved his hand. "I'm just kidding, Celia. That's great. You must not be a normal kid, though. No one ever starts studying early."

Celia shrugged. "I just didn't want to be spending all night studying like everyone else does."

"Good thinking." He tapped his pen on his leg. "Listen, after midterms, your professors are going to really start piling on the homework. If you need my help on anything, just let me know. I'd be happy to check your homework for mistakes or help you study for finals, if you want."

"Thanks, Neel. I just might take you up on that."

The next morning at breakfast, Headmaster Doyen stood at the podium and called for attention. "As you all have probably heard," he said after the room had quieted, "one of the teachers' answer keys was stolen earlier this week." Murmuring went up around the room. "I certainly hope that no one at Renasci Academy would participate in any kind of cheating, so I anticipate that the theft was accidental. However, if any of you have any information about the missing answer key, I urge you to talk to any member of the faculty or staff. In the meantime, I wish all of you success on your exams, and I know we're all looking forward to the Spring Tournament this weekend."

A cheer went up around the room at his final words, but then everyone turned back to their meal and the room quieted to a normal noise level again. Celia sat with the rest of the Mensaleon seventh-years, eating a breakfast of eggs and toast.

"I hope our exams aren't too tough," Libby said, picking at her cereal.

"Does it matter?" Josh asked from beside her. "As far as I can tell, you can't fail seventh-year exams. They're just using them to figure out what gifts we have so they can pick our classes for next year."

Heath nudged his arm. "Dude, so we should try to fail all of them so we don't have to take so many classes next year!" Everyone at the table laughed at that.

"But what happens if they decide you aren't gifted at anything?" Galena asked Heath.

He looked shocked. "Oh, I didn't think of that." Everyone laughed again.

"Hey, Josh," Kitt said, "how do you think our Soccovolle team is going to do?"

"Oh, man, the team is doing great!" Josh sounded excited. "Even though we couldn't practice outside 'cause of all the rain, we're still playing really well."

"Do you think we can win the whole tournament?"

"I think we have a pretty good chance."

"Okay, you're going to have to excuse those of us who have no idea what you're talking about," Galena said. "What do you mean, 'win the whole tournament'?" Celia was glad she wasn't the only one who didn't understand.

"The results from the Fall and Spring Tournaments are combined. Whichever team has the best record wins the year's tournament," Josh explained.

"What does that mean?"

"The winning team plays in the Summer Tournament."

"Really? Wow," Libby said.

Josh nodded. "It's really cool to be able to play in the Summer Tournament, because it's the best teams from around the country."

"Are there other schools, then?" Celia asked.

"Yeah, and bunches of them around the world, too."

"I didn't know that."

The bell rang and they all scurried into action. Midterms started promptly at nine, so they hurried to their first class, ready to face whatever their professors had planned for them.

Celia was pleasantly surprised by her spring midterms. Compared to the semester finals, the midterms seemed rather easy. Professor Perrin just asked them to repeat the sounds that he played for them from a recording. Celia was glad that he had set up a sound-proof recording booth for them because she felt a little silly making all the weird-sounding noises from the recording. She nearly missed a few of the sounds because of her giggles, which she couldn't stop when she heard some of the noises and her repetitions of them. Professor Spadaro's Physical Education midterm had been a timed obstacle course race, but it ended up feeling a lot like field day at Celia's old school. Instead of the traditional events that Celia might have expected, Professor Spadaro had picked some more unusual things, such as a super-skinny balance beam and weighted potato sacks. Celia had never laughed so hard during an exam in her life. The whole class had enjoyed cheering each other through the course and really didn't pay any attention to the stopwatch Professor Spadaro had in his hand.

Professor Twombly's midterm had been more traditional, if anything at Renasci could be considered traditional. She had given them a written exam, which covered a lot of the things they had studied during the year, such as cracking codes and the process for interpreting dreams, which they had studied but never practiced. Professor Legaspi lined them up and had them enter a doorway one at a time, with no idea what they were walking into. Celia was a little unnerved when she found herself closed in a pitch-black room with no light, but discovered after a few seconds that her eyes seemed to adjust and she had no trouble reading the instructions on the table in front of her, which directed her to take a single page out of the notebook in front of her and simply write her name on the page. She squinted when she stepped out the opposite door, but by the time she handed her paper to Professor Legaspi, her eyes had readjusted to the bright light in the classroom again.

Professor Mesbur handed them a pile of paper, telling them to start copying their textbook by hand and to write as much as they possibly could in the time allotted for their exam. Celia was glad her Art exam was her last exam, because when the bell finally rang, she felt like her hand was going to fall off, she'd written so much. She gathered all her sheets of writing and handed them to Professor Mesbur, a little surprised at how much she had been able to copy during the exam.

With an extra bounce in her step because of the easy exams, Celia headed off to her quarters to get ready for the spring tournament. It looked like the weather was finally taking a turn for the better, and Celia couldn't wait to get outside and enjoy the break from schoolwork. Nothing was going to ruin this weekend, not even the missing answer key rumors.

Chapter Fourteen

More Purple Feathers

On Saturday morning, everyone was anxious to get outside after spending so many days inside the school. The sun was shining and the temperatures had warmed up, which made for perfect tournament weather. Well, for the fans, at least.

The melting snow and rainstorms had turned the Soccovolle field into a giant mud pit, and it was obvious after the first few minutes of the first match that the tournament was going to be more of a mud bath than anything else.

Celia, still feeling stuffed from the Start of Tournament Banquet the night before, laughed along with the rest of the fans at the antics of the players on the field. The players looked a lot like bad ice skaters, slipping, sliding, and falling in the patches of mud covering the field. By halftime, Celia was glad she and Maddie had picked seats at the top of the stands, because the people in the front few rows were splattered with mud. They both laughed when they saw Doxa with mud all over her face and hair, although they ducked down behind the people in front of them so Doxa wouldn't see them.

By the end of the day Saturday, everyone was glad to be heading back into the school. The players were looking forward to showers to clean all the mud off, and the fans were looking forward to warming up, as the temperature had dropped in the middle of the night match and left everyone shivering.

Spirits were high in the Mensaleon quarters, as their team had won their match against Corpanthera. If they won their next match against Tattotauri, then Mensaleon would be the overall winner of the Soccovolle tournament. Conversations in the lounge buzzed with excitement about the possibility.

"Hey, Josh!" someone called across the room to where Josh was huddled in front of the fireplace. "Nice goal this afternoon." Josh had scored the game-winning goal against Corpanthera, at the expense of his game jersey, which ended up completely covered with mud.

"Hey, thanks," he said.

"Man, my brother was *not* happy," Heath commented.

"Sorry," Josh said, not sounding it at all.

"Did you see that mud fight after the second game?" someone asked, and voices erupted all over the room with comments about the flying mud and the mess it had made.

Although everyone was excited, exhaustion soon overtook them and they headed off to bed. Celia noticed that the first-years already had their curtains closed, and she chuckled at the memory of Doxa with mud smeared all over her face. Celia dropped onto her bed and fell asleep instantly, not moving once the entire night.

The next morning, Celia woke up early and opened her curtains. No one else was up yet, so she sat reading a book until the others stirred.

"Hey, Celia," Maddie said, rubbing her eyes as she pushed her curtains back.

"Hi, Maddie." Libby and Galena were up soon after, and everyone on the other side of the room seemed to get up at exactly the same time.

Chapter Fourteen

Libby yawned and stretched, then climbed down her ladder and put on her bathrobe. The first-years were whispering about something, gathered together at one of the windows looking out on the commons.

"What are you guys looking at?" Galena finally asked.

"The commons," Katie said.

"What's so interesting about the commons?" Libby asked, walking over to the window. "Oh . . . my . . . goodness," she said, staring out the window.

"Did the school prankster strike again?" Maddie asked, running over.

"Looks like it," Doxa said.

"What'd they do this time?" Celia asked, pulling her robe on over her pajamas as she walked to the window. "Oh, my . . . "

The coterie mascot statues that stood in the commons were the target this time. The lion for Mensaleon was untouched, but the other four had been painted purple and dressed in lion costumes, complete with big, feathery, purple manes. Celia thought fleetingly that they looked a little like they were wearing her purple chicken hat.

"Oh, the headmaster is going to flip," Maddie said.

Before anyone could say anything else, Professor Twombly called all the students in the coterie to the lounge. She looked either very grim or extremely angry, Celia thought as she shuffled in behind the rest of the girls from her room.

Professor Twombly looked solemnly around at all of them. "As some of you are already aware, someone painted the mascots purple and dressed them in lion outfits during the night." There were small gasps and a few snickers around the room. "Given the circumstances, *again*," she said, sounding quite annoyed, "the headmaster has asked that all of you remain in your quarters until further notice. Breakfast will be brought up from the refectory." She glared at all of them. "I must say, I am quite disappointed that one or more of you have disgraced the Mensaleon name yet again." Celia thought Professor Twombly looked at her just a moment longer than everyone else. "I certainly hope that this…this…rash of prank-pulling will come to a quick end." She didn't say it, but her words seemed to suggest an "or else."

Everyone filed back to their rooms. Everyone, that is, except Doxa and her drones. Celia heard her mutter, "Like I'm going to sit with a bunch of sevvies all morning," as she turned the other way and headed for one of the boys' rooms.

The rest of the girls in the room sat in the chairs in the center of the room.

"Who do you think did it?" Galena asked, her eyes wide.

"Got me," Maddie said.

"Me, too, but I know who's going to get blamed for it," Celia muttered.

"Come on, Celia. You don't know that. Besides, you said the same thing about that missing answer key, and that didn't happen," Libby said.

"Oh, yeah? I've been blamed for every single prank that's happened this year. I haven't had anything to do with any of them, but nobody believes me."

"We believe you," Maddie said.

Breakfast arrived and everyone grabbed some food. When they finished, Headmaster Doyen and his crew arrived to search the dorms again. Celia stood in the center of the room with the three other girls while they combed through the room. As Professor Twombly left the room, she told them to get dressed and head to the Soccovolle match.

The whole school was talking about the mascot statues, and some of the people in the other coteries were giving the Mensaleon students ugly looks. Most of the students just laughed about it, but it made for some uncomfortable moments during the first game, which was Corpanthera's match against Sprachursus.

A few hours later, just after lunch and right before the final match of the year, Mensaleon's match against Tattotauri, Celia was summoned to the headmaster's office. A sinking feeling in her stomach, Celia followed the student aide through the halls. She knew what was coming.

She was whisked into the office as soon as she arrived. Headmaster Doyen was sitting behind his desk, dressed in his usual suit and tie instead of the casual clothes the rest of the staff wore on the weekends.

"Miss Fincastle," he said, sounding grim. "There have been some disturbing accusations by some of the other people in your coterie."

"I'm sure."

"They told me that you're the one responsible for the statues in the commons."

"But I didn't!"

He looked at her sharply. "I cannot simply take your word on this, Miss Fincastle. I warned you before that you were under suspicion because of all the other incidents."

"But I . . . "

He held up a hand to stop her. "When the deans searched the Mensaleon dorms, they found purple paint drops on your shoes. That fact, combined with the previous evidence suggesting your guilt in other pranks, leads me to conclude that this was your doing. I must say that we have never had these kinds of problems on this level before. An odd prank or two, but nothing so calculated and never one person consistently."

"Headmaster, I didn't—"

"Miss Fincastle, I am quite certain that you will continue to deny any wrongdoing. However, your actions cannot go unpunished. Therefore, in lieu of the end of tournament banquet, you will be cleaning all the purple paint off of the statues. Understood?"

Celia thought about pleading innocence one last time, but decided that nothing was going to help her when the headmaster was obviously convinced that she was guilty. A knock on the door made them both look up.

"Come in," Headmaster Doyen said.

Higby walked into the room, glanced at Celia, and gave Headmaster Doyen a hard look. "Do you honestly think that Celia is capable of something like this?" Higby asked.

"Well, Higby, I have no way of knowing."

"If you will recall our conversation prior to the start of the year..."

Celia looked between them, trying to figure out what was going on.

"I am well aware of your position on the matter, Higby. But I have a school to run, and I cannot tolerate such behavior. Those statues must be cleaned and the guilty person should be responsible."

"But you have no proof that she did it."

"There is paint on her shoes. I believe that is evidence enough. Why else would she have paint on her shoes? The punishment stands."

"You are making a poor decision based on circumstantial evidence, Headmaster."

"It is my decision to make, Higby. Regardless," Headmaster Doyen said icily, looking at Higby and then shifting his gaze to Celia, "I will not stand for this kind of behavior, Miss Fincastle. Do I make myself clear?"

Celia nodded.

"Come along, Celia." Higby had a hard glint in his eyes as he looked at Headmaster Doyen. "Does she have permission to receive assistance with her punishment?"

"If someone else wishes to miss the banquet and help her with her task, I will not stop them."

"Good day, Headmaster."

Higby ushered her out of the headmaster's office and into the hall. Celia almost had to run to keep up with his rapid strides as he stormed toward the Mensaleon dorms.

"Um, Higby?"

"Yes?"

"What were you talking about, something about a conversation before school started?"

"It needn't concern you, Celia," he said, casting a glance her way. "Just something I had hoped the headmaster would understand."

"Oh."

When they reached the door to the dorm, Higby held it open and followed her into the lounge. "Celia, I must warn you..."

"What?"

"I believe that if you are not careful, whoever is doing this to you is going to achieve exactly what they intended."

"What do you mean?"

Higby glanced around to be sure no one was listening to them before continuing. "I am fairly certain that someone wants you out of this school."

"Why?"

"It's far too complicated to go into now, but I must impress upon you that you try very hard to stay out of trouble. "

"But I haven't done anything at all!"

"I know that. And I am certain that we will find the person behind all of this. But until then, you must do everything possible to avoid anything that might even look suspicious. Do you understand?"

Celia nodded.

Higby sighed. "I had hoped your first year here would be easy, however... Well, no matter. We'll get to the bottom of this." He pushed to his feet. "Keep up the good work, Celia."

"I will."

"Oh, and if you can't find anyone to help you clean those statues, I will come give you a hand. I'll also bring up some food for you when you've finished, seeing as you can't go to the banquet."

"Thanks, Higby."

He smiled at her. "You're welcome."

He headed out of the lounge and Celia trudged to the dorm room. Maddie was sitting in one of the chairs in the center of the room.

"Well?"

"He didn't believe me," Celia said, flopping into the chair next to her. "Someone put paint on my shoes. He's making me clean the statues instead of going to the banquet."

"You're kidding!"

"I wish I was."

"I'll help you," Maddie said quickly.

"But you'll miss the banquet, too."

"It won't be much fun without you there."

"Thanks."

"Hey, what are friends for?"

The final match was due to begin at any moment, so they hurried out to the stadium. Sliding into the only seats they could find, the two girls were soon wrapped up in the excitement of the game. It was a close match, going down to the last few seconds. Every time one team scored, the other team quickly tied it up again. As the time on the clock ticked down, Mensaleon got control of the ball and moved it down the field. Celia saw Josh bump the ball to his teammate, who spiked it toward the goal. There was a hush in the stands as everyone waited to see if it would get past the Tattotauri guard. The buzzer sounded as time expired, and the crowd gasped as the guard brushed the ball with his fingertips, but he couldn't quite get to the ball in time, and it slid past his hands and into the goal.

The stands erupted with cheers as the Mensaleon team celebrated on the field. The Tattotauri team walked off dejectedly, and Celia noticed that the Corpanthera students didn't look so happy, either. They had won their match against Sprachursus, and Mensaleon's win against Tattotauri had put them in a tie with Corpanthera, but since Mensaleon had won the match between the two teams, they were declared the overall winner.

Later that day, Celia and Maddie lugged buckets of water out to the commons to start cleaning the statues. They were halfway through the first one when people started heading to the refectory for the banquet. People pointed and laughed at them and some made comments.

"Just ignore them, Celia," Maddie said, concentrating on getting purple off the panther's ear.

"But it's so unfair. I didn't do this. And neither did you."

Maddie shrugged. "I know. But what's done is done, so we might as well just keep going."

A little while later Higby came striding across the grass. "Good evening, ladies."

"Hi, Higby," Maddie said, now scrubbing the bear's paw.

Celia looked up at him and nearly laughed. Instead of his usual suit, he was wearing red and yellow plaid pants, a green and orange striped shirt, and bright blue shoes. "Hi, Higby. Um, nice outfit."

"I thought I'd come give you girls a hand with this, and I didn't want to ruin my good clothes." He winked at her. "Besides, if everyone wants to stare at something out here, it might as well be my hideous attire and not the innocent people toiling away because of someone else's practical joke."

The trio worked until sunset, and Celia scrubbed off the last bit of purple paint just as the sun dipped behind the mountains.

"Thanks, Higby," Celia said, collecting the buckets and sponges. "You, too, Maddie."

Maddie shrugged. "Like I said before, what are friends for?"

Higby picked up the buckets. "I'll get these put away for you. You two can run along to your quarters and head to bed. There should be a sandwich waiting for each of you. Everyone else should be there soon."

They were so tired, they headed straight to their room. Celia took a shower, and wandered around the room as she combed her hair. She looked out the window by Doxa's bed at the commons and the now sparkling clean mascot statues. Someone had framed her for this prank, too, but who would keep doing this to her? If Higby was right and someone wanted her out of the school, what were they going to do next? How was she going to prove that she wasn't the one pulling all these pranks?

Sighing, Celia turned away from the window. Her gaze fell to the bench at the end of Doxa's bed and she let out a gasp. "Maddie!" she cried. "Come here!"

Maddie rushed over. "What is it?"

"Look!" Celia said, pointing to the storage space under the bench. Doxa had a couple of pairs of shoes lined up. The pair on the left, dingy white canvas sneakers, had drops of purple paint on them.

Chapter Fourteen

"I *knew* she was behind all of this," Celia said furiously the next morning on the way down to the refectory for breakfast. "But how am I going to prove it?" She marched through a doorway. "It's so unfair. I got blamed for the statues just for having paint on my shoes, when Doxa had the same paint on her shoes! Why didn't she get caught?"

Maddie hurried along beside her. "Celia, if Higby's right and someone *is* trying to get you kicked out of school, then you have to be extra careful around Doxa."

"I *know* that, but I can't avoid her! She's in the same room. There's no way I can stay out of her way."

"Well," Maddie said as they rounded the corner into Main Hall, "just keep your eyes and ears open and see if you can figure out what she's up to."

Their professors handed back their midterms that day, and Celia wasn't surprised to find out that she had gotten perfect scores again. What *did* surprise her was how many people had gotten poor scores on their exams. She'd thought that everyone else had found the midterms as easy as she had, but apparently she had been in a small minority. It seemed that many people had struggled with Professor Legaspi's pitch-black room and Professor Perrin's sounds.

No one was particularly surprised by Celia's scores this time, seeing as she had done so well on her previous exams. A few people congratulated her throughout the day, but it was nothing like the fuss after semester finals.

That evening, Celia and Maddie were working on homework in their room. Maddie asked to look at Celia's notes for her Speech class, so Celia handed her the folder. She looked up quickly when she heard Maddie gasp.

"What?" Celia asked. Maddie held out the folder for Celia to see.

There, in the middle of Celia's folder, was the missing answer key.

"No way," Maddie breathed.

"How..."

"You!" Both Celia and Maddie spun around in their chairs when they heard Doxa's voice. "You're the one who took the answer key! I knew it!" she crowed. Before Celia could say anything, Doxa spun around and rushed out the door.

Within minutes, Headmaster Doyen, Professor Legaspi, and Professor Twombly were all in the room. After shooing everyone else out and closing the door, they turned to Celia. She couldn't figure out why Professor Legaspi was there, but thought maybe she had been asked to come because she was Celia's faculty mentor.

"Well, Miss Fincastle. We meet again," Headmaster Doyen said, his hands behind his back as he rocked on his feet. "I suppose you have some great excuse this time?"

"I..."

"Celia," Professor Legaspi said, holding up the answer key, "where did you get my answer key?"

Celia's heart sank. It had been Professor Legaspi's answer key? Did she think that Celia would steal from her mentor? "It was in my folder. But I didn't take it! Honest. I don't know how it got there!"

"And I guess we're supposed to believe that?" Headmaster Doyen said nastily.

"Celia, I trusted you," Professor Legaspi said with a hard glint in her eyes. "How could you do this?"

"I didn't!"

"Then why was it your folder?"

"Someone else must have put it there. I swear I didn't do it!" Celia looked at Professor Legaspi, trying to get her to believe what she was saying.

"Why on earth would someone else have put it in your folder?" Headmaster Doyen asked.

Celia saw something flash in Professor Legaspi's eyes before it was quickly shuttered. She broke eye contact with Celia to look down at the answer key. "I don't understand," she muttered.

"What is it?"

She looked up at the headmaster. "Well, this answer key is for my fourth-year class. It would have done Celia no good whatsoever. I don't see why she would have taken it."

"She must have taken that one to cover the fact that she had looked at the seventh-year answers."

"I don't know..." Professor Legaspi wandered over to the window.

Professor Twombly had been leaning against one of the armchairs, but now she straightened up. "I must say, Celia...this year has not gotten you off to a great start at Renasci." Celia decided that nothing she said would change their minds, so she kept silent. "You have done nothing but tarnish the coterie since you got here."

"That's not true! What about my exam scores?"

"Miss Fincastle!" Headmaster Doyen blustered. "Given the recent events, I assure you that no one will believe you earned those marks honestly."

"Headmaster," Professor Legaspi said, coming over to them again, "this isn't adding up to me. My seventh-year midterm had no answer key. There was no way Celia could have cheated on it."

Headmaster Doyen looked irate. "Nevertheless, this girl had the stolen answer key in her possession!"

"True..." Professor Legaspi caught Celia's eye, and Celia thought she saw a look of warning in her eyes.

"Miss Fincastle, we have no choice but to mark your scores as the product of cheating. If this continues, you will face severe consequences. Do you understand?"

Celia opened her mouth to defend herself once more, but stopped when she looked at Professor Legaspi and simply nodded.

"Very well. I am very disappointed in you, young lady. Your behavior has been inexcusable. I certainly hope that you will make better decisions in the future."

Headmaster Doyen and Professor Twombly filed out the door, leaving Celia with Professor Legaspi.

"Someone is framing me, professor," Celia said.

"I know, Celia. I believe you. But you can't make the headmaster any more upset with you at the moment. I promise that we will figure out what's going on and get this all cleared up. In the meantime, just lie low for a while, okay?"

Celia nodded glumly. Professor Legaspi patted her arm and then left the room. Maddie, Libby, and Galena hurried in.

"What happened?" Maddie asked.

"I got in trouble, of course."

"Did you take it?" Galena asked, her eyes wide.

"No! Besides, the answer key was for a fourth-year exam. There was no way to cheat on our exam."

"I didn't think so," Galena said. "But everyone else is going to think you did."

"But why would I take something that I don't even need?" Celia asked no one in particular. "It doesn't make sense."

"It's 'cause you're a thief and a cheater," Doxa said, coming in and sitting down at her desk. "And now everyone is going to know it. I wouldn't be surprised if you get expelled."

"Expelled!?" Celia cried.

Doxa sniffed. "I told you to watch your back."

"*You're* doing this to me?"

"I didn't say that."

"Why else would you tell me that?"

Doxa looked at her with revulsion. "Because you're a

sevvie who thinks she deserves special treatment just because her name is Celia Fincastle. I don't like snobs."

"I haven't asked for any special treatment!"

"You don't have to," Doxa said coolly, turning her back. "You get it anyway."

Celia made a sound of frustration as she marched over to her bed. She climbed up her ladder and onto her bed and pulled all of her curtains shut except the ones for her windows. She hugged her knees as she sat looking out at the fading sky.

A little while later, Maddie stuck her head through the curtains at the end of Celia's bed. "Celia? Can I come up here?"

"Sure, Maddie."

Maddie scurried onto Celia's bed and closed the curtains behind her. "Don't listen to her, Celia. She's just jealous."

"I don't care what she is. I just want her to leave me alone."

"I know. Just...don't give up. I'm sure everything will work out."

"Yeah, and I'll go home to Aunt Agatha."

"Celia, that's not going to happen."

"How do you know, Maddie? Doxa wants me expelled, and she's going to get it if I can't figure out how to stop her!"

"There's no way you're going to get expelled," Maddie said, shaking her head. "There are too many people who would stop that from happening."

Celia sighed. "I don't know."

"Trust me on this one."

"I'm just going to go to bed and hope this all goes away by tomorrow," Celia said.

"Okay. Good night, Celia."

"Good night." Celia watched Maddie climb down the ladder, then sighed deeply when she was alone in her soundproofed bed. She cried herself to sleep that night, wishing all her problems would just disappear.

More Purple Feathers

People were whispering behind Celia's back the next day, but Celia honestly didn't care what they thought. She guessed the whole school probably knew what had happened, and she just didn't feel like defending herself to people who took someone else's word over hers. She had meetings with her student mentors, who both tried to cheer her up, but she was beyond caring. She asked them to check over her homework assignments, but didn't feel like talking with them much.

By the end of the following week, the whispers had died down some, and Celia thought the whole ordeal was finally winding down, but she was wrong. On Friday afternoon, she was called to Professor Perrin's office just before dinner.

"You wanted to see me?" Celia asked, stepping through the door when Professor Perrin told her to come in.

"Yes, Celia. I'm afraid..."

Celia's stomach clenched. "What?"

"Well, the paper you handed in yesterday was exactly the same as another student's paper. I'm afraid that it looks like one of you has been cheating, and given the past few weeks, the evidence points toward you."

Chapter Fifteen
A Trap Is Set

Celia felt all the blood drain from her face. This couldn't be happening. "I . . ."

"Can you prove that you wrote this paper?" Professor Perrin held up her assignment.

Celia's mouth worked, but no sound came out.

"I'm sorry, Celia," he said, looking disappointed, "but unless you can give me an explanation, I have no choice but to give you a zero on this assignment."

"Lee, do you have—" Professor Legaspi walked around the corner and into the office. She stopped short when she saw Celia sitting there. "Oops. I'm sorry. I didn't know you had someone in here." She glanced at Celia. "Hi, Celia." When Celia sat numbly in her chair without saying anything, Professor Legaspi asked, "What's going on?"

"Come on in and close the door, Anne," Professor Perrin said. After Professor Legaspi sat down in the chair beside Celia, he said, "I've just informed Celia that her last assignment is exactly the same as another student's paper. I'm required to give her a zero on it if she can't give me an explanation."

"Oh, surely you don't think Celia would be cheating on her homework!" Professor Legaspi exclaimed.

Professor Perrin shrugged. "She won't say anything in her defense, and given the past events..." He winced. "It seems a logical conclusion."

Professor Legaspi pressed her lips into a thin line. "I see." She glanced over at Celia. "Is there anything you want to say, Celia?"

"I...I wrote that paper, Professor Perrin. Honest."

He shook his head sadly. "I'm sorry, Celia, but without more evidence, my hands are tied. I have to report this to the headmaster."

"Very well," Professor Legaspi said sharply as she stood. "Would you come with me to my office, Celia?"

Celia nodded, still feeling numb as she got to her feet and followed Professor Legaspi to her office. Once inside, she collapsed into a chair as Professor Legaspi closed the door.

"Celia, this is serious," she said, leaning against her desk.

"I know," Celia said. "But no one's going to believe I wrote that paper."

"Do you know anyone who would have copied that paper from you?"

Celia searched her mind, but the only person she could come up with who would be capable of doing something like this was Doxa, and she was pretty sure that Doxa wouldn't have any contact with any other seventh-years. "Not that I can come up with."

"Professor Perrin isn't allowed to reveal the other student's name to you, so we're out of luck on that one." She looked around the office, thinking. "I'll see what I can find out." She pinned Celia with her gaze once more. "There's a three strikes rule at this school, Celia. If you're caught cheating three times, you will be expelled."

Celia nodded, her mouth too dry to speak.

"I know you have no reason to cheat on your schoolwork, but you'll have to watch your every move so that this doesn't happen again. Understood?" When Celia nodded again, she said, "Go ahead to dinner for now. I'm sure we'll get this all straightened out soon."

As Celia headed down to the refectory, she thought that everyone kept telling her that, but things were getting worse instead of better. She didn't mention anything to her friends at dinner, and said little during the meal. She knew Maddie was wondering what was up, but she managed to avoid her for the evening.

Instead of sleeping in the next morning, Celia awoke early and headed down to breakfast. Only a small handful of students were in the refectory at that time on a Saturday, and she was surprised to see Heath among them.

"Yo, Celia!" he said, coming to sit next to her. "Um ... yeah, listen. You said you got Neel Winokur as one of your mentors, right?" When she nodded, he said, "Well, I asked my brother about him and he said you, like, have to totally watch him."

"What do you mean?"

Heath shrugged one shoulder. "Don't know. He wouldn't say anything else."

"Nothing? Why not?"

"I told you. I don't know. But ..."

"What?"

"Nothin'. Just be careful, okay?" Celia watched him as he left the table, totally confused. Neel was a great guy, not anyone sneaky. Why would she have to watch him? She thought about the cheating accusation and briefly considered that Neel might be involved, but just as quickly dismissed the thought. There was no way Neel would do something like that. After all, he was her mentor.

Celia spent most of the day in the library, trying to avoid everyone. She had a book in front of her but didn't manage to make it through even a single page. Instead of reading, she kept thinking about her assignment and who might have copied it. She didn't like the thought, but aside from Doxa, the only people she could think that would have been able to copy her assignment were the other girls in her room. Maddie wouldn't copy her paper, but maybe Libby or Galena would.

Disgusted and depressed by the thought, Celia stayed away from everyone for the evening and headed to bed early. She really hoped she was wrong in her suspicions, but she couldn't come up with any other explanation. And that meant that one of the other girls in her room wanted her out of Renasci just as much as Doxa did.

By Monday morning, it seemed news of Celia's cheating had somehow spread throughout the school. The whispering that had died down last week returned in full force, only this time accompanied by taunting comments and rude remarks.

"Oh, look. There goes the cheat," someone said in the hallway. "Watch out, she'll steal your work so she can get perfect scores."

"Yeah, perfectly dishonest!" Laughter followed.

"Hey, Celia!" someone else called. "I was just wondering, have you done any of your own work this year?"

"Of course she hasn't," someone replied. "It's easier to just copy someone else's!"

Celia lowered her head and walked quickly to the refectory, but it wasn't much better there. She ate as fast as she could, trying to ignore the comments flying around her. As soon as she finished, she left the room and headed to her first class.

Her classmates made comments until her professors quieted them down, and Celia sank as low as possible in her chair to try to avoid their disapproving glares. By the end of the day, she wanted to go to her room and have a good, long cry. As she dropped her bag on the floor by her desk, Maddie walked in the room.

"Long day?" she asked sympathetically.

"You don't know the half of it," Celia muttered.

Maddie grimaced. "I was there for most of it." She set her own bag down by her desk. "What are you going to do?"

"What *can* I do, Maddie? No one's going to believe anything I say. They all think I cheated."

"Do you know who copied your paper?"

Celia shook her head. "They can't tell me."

"That stinks."

"What difference would it make?" she muttered. "It wouldn't change anything."

"Yeah, but at least then you might be able to figure out who's framing you and how to stop them."

Libby and Galena walked into the room, glanced at Celia, and scurried to their corner of the room, whispering to each other.

"See?" Celia said. She climbed up on her bed and began pulling the curtains.

"Are you heading down for dinner?" Maddie asked, a worried look on her face.

Celia shook her head. "I'm not hungry. I'm just going to stay here."

"Okay." Maddie sounded uncertain. "I'm sure we'll figure this out, Celia."

"Yeah, but by then it might be too late."

The next few days weren't any easier for Celia, and she learned quickly who her real friends were. Only Maddie and Heath believed her when she said she hadn't cheated, so she spent more time with them. On Thursday, she had a meeting with Merry, who wasn't her normal, bubbly self. She had heard the rumors, too, and felt that Celia had taken advantage of the help Merry had offered. The meeting was awkward and stilted, and for the first time, Celia was glad when they wrapped up early.

As Celia headed to her Friday meeting with Neel, she prepared herself for the worst, expecting the same sort of treatment she had received from Merry.

"Oh, no! It's Celia!" Neel deadpanned as she walked up to his table in Main Hall. "I'd better watch out, or she might steal my paper!"

Celia glared at him as she sat down across from him.

"Ooh, ouch," he said. "I was just joking. If looks could kill, I'd be a dead man."

Celia sighed. "Sorry, Neel. I'm not really in a joking mood."

"Hey, I understand. I'm sorry everyone's giving you such a hard time."

"Thanks."

He fiddled with his pen, tapping it on the table and twirling it with his fingers. "What happened?"

Celia sighed. "Someone must have copied my paper for my Speech class and turned it in as their own. I swear I wrote that paper, but Professor Perrin doesn't believe me."

"That stinks."

"Tell me about it."

"Listen, I know we were supposed to meet for half an hour, but I've got this huge assignment that I really need to work on. Do you mind if we cut this short, like, really short?"

Celia shrugged. "That's fine."

"Did you want me to look over your homework?"

"Would you? You were right when you said they'd really be piling on the homework. Are you sure you have time for it?"

Neel waved a hand. "No problem. If you don't mind, I'll just take it with me and get to it this weekend. Can you meet me here on Monday so I can get it back to you?"

Celia hesitated. Heath's comments about Neel ran through her mind, and she wondered if she should trust Neel with her assignment. What if he really was involved? She'd be handing her work off to the person causing all her problems.

Neel noticed her hesitation. "Hey, I understand. I don't blame you for not trusting me. If I were you, I wouldn't trust anybody, either. We'll just meet some other time."

Celia shook her head. "No, that's okay. Here," she said, holding out her assignment. "Last time it was my Speech paper, and you didn't even look at that one, so I honestly don't believe that you did anything."

"Thanks for trusting me," Neel said, taking her paper and tucking it in his folder. "I've never found any mistakes on your Phys Ed or Art papers, so I'm sure this one won't be any different, but I'll look it over, just in case."

"Okay. Thanks, Neel."

He stuffed his folder back in his bag and slid the strap onto his shoulder. "I've gotta get going, but I'll catch up with you soon. Hang in there, okay?"

"I'll try," Celia said, watching him stand up. He gave her a jaunty wave and headed off across the room. Celia thought about staying in Main Hall, but she noticed a lot of the people around her glancing at her and whispering to their friends, so she headed back to her room. Unfortunately, when she stepped through the door, she saw Doxa sitting with her posse in the chairs in the center of the room.

"Oh, great," she muttered, heading over to her bed.

"Hey, Fincastle," Doxa said.

Celia rolled her eyes before turning around to face her. "What do you want?"

"I was just wondering..." Doxa said airily, twirling a lock of hair around her finger. "Did you get in trouble for cheating?"

Celia glared at her. "Why?"

"Just wondering when you're heading home." Now Doxa sounded more like herself.

"I'm not," Celia ground out.

"Not yet," Doxa said with a smug smile.

Celia narrowed her eyes. "How'd you do it, Doxa?"

Doxa wore an innocent look. "Do what? Shouldn't I be asking you that question?"

"Look," Celia snapped, "I know you're behind all of this."

"*Moi*?" Doxa asked, touching a hand to her chest.

"Yes, you. Whatever you have planned in your evil little mind, just...just forget about it, would you?"

Doxa laughed, then rolled her eyes. "Listen, sevvie. You're the one in trouble for cheating, not me. So if anyone needs to watch their step around here, it's you, not me." She pushed to her feet and looked at her drones. "Ladies, let's head somewhere else. This room is beginning to smell like a cheater." She flicked her hair behind her shoulder and headed for the door. Celia might have thought it funny, the way the other three girls copied her actions exactly as they followed her out the door, but she wasn't in a laughing mood at the moment.

As far as she could figure, someone must have taken her paper off of her desk or out of her bag and copied it. If that was the case, then she needed to make sure she didn't leave any of her stuff sitting around where other people could get to it. Glancing down at her bag, she decided her closet was the safest place to keep her things, so she tossed her bag inside before grabbing a book off her shelf and sitting down to read.

When Libby and Galena came in the room later, they didn't say anything to Celia. The camaraderie they had developed had disappeared when the rumors started flying, and although Celia was upset that they actually believed the rumors instead of taking her side, she was more upset that she had lost the friendship of so many people at school.

Sighing, she headed to bed, pulling the curtains around her bed and staring out the window. She never expected her time at Renasci to be like this. She'd thought maybe she would have trouble making friends or possibly have a hard time with the schoolwork, but she never imagined being framed for pranks, accused of cheating, and having the whole school turn against her. At least at her old school, where no one knew who she was, she could go through the day without anyone paying attention to her. Here, where everyone knew who she was before she even set foot in the door, she had no chance of that happening.

It took Celia a long time to fall asleep, and when she did, she had nightmares about Doxa, Professor Perrin, big, fat zeros on her papers, purple, feathery lions, and lots of jeering kids, all laughing and pointing at her.

"Sorry, Maddie," Celia said on Monday afternoon, "but I can't work on my homework with you. It's not that I don't trust you, it's just that with everyone else here in the room, I can't take the chance that someone will copy my work. It's just too risky."

Maddie's face fell, but she nodded. "I understand. Well, I guess I'll see you later, then."

"Hey, Maddie?"

"Yeah?"

"Thanks." Celia lifted one shoulder in a shrug. "You know, for sticking with me. I know it hasn't been easy for you either."

Maddie gave her a small smile. "Sure, Celia. What are friends for?"

Celia gave her a quick hug, then grabbed her bag out of her closet and headed out of the room. Before she could reach the main door, Odile and Odette stopped her.

"Hey, Celia," Odette said tentatively.

"Hi."

"Listen . . ." Odette started.

"We thought about it and decided that things just don't add up," Odile finished.

Celia said nothing, but looked back and forth between them.

"We don't believe that you would cheat on your schoolwork, and we're hoping you'll forgive us for listening to the rumors," Odette said.

Celia looked at their anxious expressions, and saw that they were telling the truth. "Yeah, I forgive you."

They both blew out a sigh of relief. "We're really sorry," Odile said. "But everyone was saying . . . well, it doesn't matter what they were saying, because we don't believe them anyway."

"Thanks, guys," Celia said.

"If you need anything, Celia," Odette said, "just ask, okay?"

"Sure."

"Okay. We'll see you around."

Celia headed off to the library, her steps a little bit lighter. At least a few people were coming over to her side. She spent the rest of the week working on homework in the library and making sure that she didn't leave her work sitting where anyone could find it. She kept her papers carefully hidden during class, and covered her answers when anyone came past her desk.

By the middle of the following week, Celia felt fairly certain that she had given no one the opportunity to steal her work. She handed in her assignments, including a long paper for her Physical Education class, confident that she would get credit for her work and hoping that some of the whispers and jokes would finally die down.

At dinner that evening, she sat with Maddie, Heath, Odile, and Odette, and finally felt relaxed for the first time in almost a month. She hadn't heard anything from any of her professors, and she was hoping it stayed that way. Although no one else filled the remaining seats at their table, the five of them had a very enjoyable meal, talking and laughing the way they had earlier in the year.

Celia's good mood stayed the next day, as she still hadn't heard anything from any of her professors about copied work. She got most of her homework back without comment from her professors, and she was starting to think her efforts to keep her work hidden had paid off.

But on Friday morning, Celia was summoned to the headmaster's office, and as soon as she saw the student aide standing with the note requesting that she report immediately, she knew something else had gone horribly wrong. As she followed the aide through the hallways, her feet felt like lead and her stomach felt like it was sitting in her throat.

She took a seat in the waiting area and saw through the window that Professors Twombly, Legaspi, and Spadaro were currently talking with the headmaster. She sat nervously in the chair until the door opened and Professor Spadaro walked out.

"You can go in," he told Celia, then left the room.

Celia stood with shaky knees and walked into the headmaster's office.

"Please sit down," Headmaster Doyen said, gesturing to the chair Professor Spadaro had vacated.

Celia sat into the seat, glancing at Professor Legaspi, who gave her a tight smile.

"Celia," Professor Legaspi said, "your assignment for Professor Spadaro was an exact duplicate of one of your classmate's."

Celia nodded, hearing the words as if through a fog.

"Do you have anything to say for yourself?" Headmaster Doyen asked.

Celia shook her head. "I wrote my own paper, and that's all I can say."

Headmaster Doyen crossed his arms over his chest and glared at her reproachfully. "Miss Fincastle, this is the second time in less than a month that you have handed in work that is an exact copy of another student's homework. Effective immediately, you will be placed on academic probation. Your work will be carefully monitored and any questionable actions will result in immediate expulsion. Do you understand?"

Celia nodded dejectedly.

"Good. I am placing you under the supervision of your two faculty mentors," he said, turning to Professors Twombly and Legaspi. "I assume that they understand the seriousness of this situation and are aware that any unacceptable action on their part will result in their dismissal." Both women nodded gravely. "Very well." He turned his sharp gaze back to Celia. "I hope I do not have to see you in my office again, Miss Fincastle. You may all leave."

The three filed into the hallway, where Professor Twombly said simply, "My office." They marched through the hallways, a gloomy procession, until they were sitting in the purple office in the Mensaleon quarters.

"Celia, I am extremely disappointed in you," Professor Twombly said. "I cannot believe that a student in my coterie would stoop to cheating."

"But I didn't!"

"Celia," Professor Legaspi said, "would you please go wait in your room for a few minutes? I'd like to talk to Professor Twombly."

Celia left the room, but walked slowly toward her room, trying to hear their conversation.

"Do you honestly believe Celia would cheat on her schoolwork?" Professor Legaspi asked.

"I wish there was some other explanation, but all the evidence points to her."

"That girl got a perfect score on her semester finals, Bridgette! You know as well as I do that there was no way to cheat on those exams. Why in the world would she need to cheat?"

"I don't know. Maybe she just got overwhelmed by all the homework and looked for the easy way out."

"You know Celia. Does that seem like something she would do?"

"No," Professor Twombly admitted. "But if she hasn't been cheating, then what's going on?"

"We told…beginning of the year…high alert…" Their voices were starting to fade as Celia got closer to her room. "…someone at the school…trying to…"

Celia sat in one of the chairs facing the doorway, her mind completely blank. She had no idea what was going on, and didn't figure any of it would really matter if she got expelled. As she sat waiting for someone to come get her, she was surprised to see both Higby and Mr. Morven walk past the doorway and into Professor Twombly's office.

She couldn't wait outside her room without being caught when someone came looking for her, and she couldn't hear anything from inside the room, so she just waited, staring at the ceiling. After what seemed like an hour, she heard Professor Twombly's office door open, and she sat up again. She saw Mr. Morven and Higby walk past again, but neither one said anything to her.

Professor Legaspi came into the room and sat down in the chair next to Celia. Her expression was grim. "Celia, I know Higby told you about his concern that someone is trying to get you kicked out of the school." Celia nodded. "We don't think the student involved in this is the one behind that, but we're going to try to come up with a way to catch the person responsible. If you come up with any ideas, please tell me right away." She sighed. "I know this has been very hard for you, and I promise that we *will* get this cleared up. I don't honestly think you'll be expelled, but I don't think we can take any chances. If you think of *anything*, even if it seems unimportant, let me know, okay?"

Celia nodded. She could tell her about Doxa, and all the conversations she overheard, and the warning that Heath gave her from his brother, and her suspicions about Libby and Galena...but everyone had said before that without proof, they couldn't do anything.

"All right," Professor Legaspi said. "We'd better get you back to class."

It seemed to Celia that things couldn't get much worse, and in some ways that was a good thing. No one seemed surprised that Celia had been caught cheating again, so they didn't make a big deal about it.

Every meal became a brainstorming session for Celia and her four remaining friends. They searched their brains for any possible explanation or idea that might catch Doxa framing Celia, but no one could come up with anything.

It wasn't until Reading class the next week that Celia had her great idea. She was so excited about her thought that she could hardly wait for lunch that day to run it past the rest of them. Everyone thought it was a good idea, too, so she set up a meeting with Professor Legaspi that evening.

"So what did you come up with?" Professor Legaspi asked when Celia closed the office door behind her.

"I figured out that the assignments that get copied are the longer essays, not the shorter homework assignments. The first one was my Speech paper, then my Physical Education paper."

"Okay."

"So the next big assignment I have is for your class, Reading."

"Right. I just handed that out today."

"Well, I thought maybe I should write two papers. I'll finish them early and give one of them to you. The other one I'll leave sitting around the way I normally do, and then when, or if, someone hands in a duplicate of *that* paper, we'll be able to prove that I didn't copy their paper."

"And if I have the copy of the paper that you're not handing in for a grade... You know, I think it might work." Professor Legaspi nodded. "At the very least, we should be able to convince Headmaster Doyen to question the other student and clear your name." She frowned slightly. "Can you finish two papers that quickly?"

Celia nodded. "I think so."

"Well, Celia, it's worth a try. Good thinking. Let me know as soon as you finish writing those papers, okay?"

"Okay."

Celia worked every spare minute she had to finish two papers that covered the same topic but weren't the same paper. Between her speed-reading skills and her newly-discovered speed-writing skills (thanks to Professor Mesbur's midterm exam), she finished both papers by Sunday evening. She gave both papers to Professor Legaspi and kept a copy of one of them in her folder. She eyed every person she came in contact with over the next week, trying to see if they would take the bait of her fake assignment. She left it sitting on her desk for an entire day, giving Doxa plenty of time to take it and copy it. On Friday, she took it to her Reading class and handed it in, her heart pounding. She carefully avoided Professor Legaspi's gaze, in case someone else was watching, and then sat down to begin her waiting game.

She heard nothing all day, and by lunch she was quite antsy.

"Have you heard anything?" Maddie whispered to her in the refectory.

"No, not yet."

It was almost funny, how Heath, Odile, and Odette repeated the same conversation as they came to the table. Celia tried not to show her impatience, but found herself drumming her fingers on any flat surface nearby: the table, her leg, her notebook...

Somehow she made it through her afternoon classes, although she spent most of her time watching the doorway for an aide to call her to the headmaster's office. When the bell rang at the end of her last class, she was disappointed that nothing had happened yet.

After dinner, which was almost a repeat of lunch, Celia and Maddie headed to their room, still waiting to hear something. Celia spent most of the evening pacing the room, her mind going through all the things that might have gone wrong. What if no one copied her paper this time? What if the headmaster didn't believe them? What if the other student could come up with a good story and the headmaster believed it?

Finally, around seven o'clock, Celia heard Professor Legaspi talking to Professor Twombly. A few moments later, she stuck her head around the door. "Celia, I need you to come with me to the headmaster's office," she said.

Chapter Sixteen
Busted

Celia's heart pounded in her ears as she followed Professor Legaspi through the hallway. "Who was it?" she asked.

Professor Legaspi shook her head. "We can't talk about it here," she said, looking straight ahead.

"Oh." Nothing more was said as they headed to the headmaster's office. When they walked into the waiting area, Professor Legaspi told her to take a seat in one of the chairs, and she knocked on the office door and walked in.

Celia could see a boy sitting in one of the chairs facing the headmaster's desk, but she couldn't tell who it was. Headmaster Doyen looked very displeased, as if he had eaten something that hadn't agreed with his stomach. Professor Legaspi gestured with her hands, tapping the desk and pointing toward Celia through the window. When Headmaster Doyen nodded, she came to the door and asked Celia to come into the office.

The short walk from the waiting area into the office felt like it was a million miles long. Celia couldn't tell anything from Professor Legaspi's expression; she didn't smile at Celia or anything. Looking past Professor Legaspi, Celia saw

Headmaster Doyen looking at her with what looked like doubt and impatience on his face. Nervous again, Celia stepped into the office and turned to take a seat in the remaining chair.

"Kevin!?" Celia stopped in her tracks and stared at the boy with wide eyes and a dropped jaw. The skinny boy from her Physical Education class was sitting in the other chair, his face pale and his own eyes wide with fear.

"I take it you two know each other," Headmaster Doyen said.

"Um, yeah, we're in the same Physical Education class," Celia said, sinking onto the edge of the chair next to Kevin's. When the headmaster looked at Kevin, his head bobbed up and down quickly.

"I see." Headmaster Doyen looked between the two of them, then turned to Professor Legaspi. "And you think you can prove Miss Fincastle's innocence?" He didn't sound convinced.

"Absolutely." Professor Legaspi's voice rang with confidence, a confidence Celia wasn't feeling at the moment.

"And just how do you propose to do that?"

Professor Legaspi pointed to the two papers that were sitting on the desk in front of the headmaster. "As you can see, those two papers are identical, except for the names at the top of them."

The headmaster nodded. "Yes, but that doesn't prove who copied the paper and who originally wrote it."

"That's true. However," Professor Legaspi said, handing him another paper, "this is the paper that Celia handed in for her grade. The other paper was bait for the people who have been framing her all year."

The headmaster's eyebrows rose high on his forehead. "And just how would you know that?"

"Celia gave me both of these papers almost a week before they were due. There would be no reason for anyone else to write their paper that quickly so that Celia could copy it, and I am convinced that she did the work on both of these papers." Professor Legaspi folded her arms in front of her.

Headmaster Doyen studied the three papers in front of him, then looked up at Celia. "You wrote both of these papers in . . . how much time?" he asked Professor Legaspi.

"Three days," she said curtly.

"Three days . . . " He looked back at Celia. "And how can a seventh-year student write two papers in such a short amount of time?"

"I . . . Professor Legaspi covered speed-reading earlier this year, and . . . well, Professor Mesbur's spring midterm was on speed-writing, so . . . "

"Headmaster," Professor Legaspi said, "you will find that Celia is an exceptionally gifted student."

"I see." He looked over at Kevin. "And what do you have to say about all of this?"

Kevin blinked rapidly. "I-I . . . I don't have any idea what's going on."

Headmaster Doyen frowned at him. "You aren't aware that your papers have been exact copies of Miss Fincastle's?"

Kevin looked over at Celia with shock in his eyes. "They were? What . . . how . . . ?"

The headmaster was looking increasingly agitated as the discussion went on. "Mister Fackler," he said, holding out one of the papers, "would you look at this paper, please, and tell me if this is the paper you wrote?"

Kevin took the paper and started reading, his eyes somehow growing wider as he read. "N-no, sir. I didn't write this."

"Did you copy it from Miss Fincastle?"

"No, sir! I wouldn't do something like that!"

Headmaster Doyen nodded slowly, then turned to

Professor Legaspi. "So how did Mister Fackler end up handing in those papers?"

"Someone must have done something to Kevin's papers, but I'm afraid I don't know who," she said.

Headmaster Doyen turned back to Kevin. "Did anyone else have access to your assignments before you handed them in?"

Kevin blinked again. "I-I don't know. M-maybe."

"Do you know who?"

"M-my m-mentor has been checking my assignments for mistakes. I g-guess it could have been him."

"Did you look at your papers after your mentor handed them back to you? Before you turned them in?"

"I-I guess not. H-he said they looked fine, so I just handed them in."

Headmaster Doyen looked furious. "Professor Legaspi," he said, tapping a paper clip on the desktop, "would you please ask Thomas to call Mister Fackler's mentor to the office?"

"Certainly." Professor Legaspi turned and left the room, and the other three sat in silence for a few moments.

"Um, Headmaster?" Celia finally said tentatively.

"Yes?"

"Um, should I . . . leave . . . or something?"

A muscle worked in his jaw. "No, Miss Fincastle. If you are correct in saying that someone has been framing you all year, you have the right to be here and find out who has been doing this and why. I would prefer that you stay."

"Um . . . okay."

Professor Legaspi came back in the room. "He's on his way."

"Thank you."

Celia wasn't sure who Kevin's mentor was, but she was certain it must be one of Doxa's friends. She hoped whoever it was would name Doxa as the guilty party, and now that her fear was dying down, she was starting to get excited at the idea of Doxa finally getting in trouble for everything she had done to Celia.

Mr. Morven stuck his head in the door a few moments later. "He's here."

"Send him in," Headmaster Doyen said tersely. "Miss Fincastle, if you would be so kind as to stand over there for the moment..." He gestured to the other side of Kevin's chair. Celia nodded and slid out of her seat as Kevin's mentor walked in the door.

Celia glanced over, then did a double-take when she saw who sauntered into the office. Neel Winokur stood with a defiant look on his face, completely different from the person Celia had seen all semester.

"Mister Winokur," Headmaster Doyen said in a curt and less-than-welcoming greeting. "Please take a seat." He waited while Neel shrugged carelessly and slouched in the chair with a bored expression on his face. "What can you tell me about Mister Fackler's assignments, Mister Winokur?"

"What do you want to know?" Neel drawled.

The headmaster frowned. "Anything you know," he said, a threatening note entering his voice.

Neel lifted one eyebrow at him. "Kevin just asked me for some help with his homework. Isn't that what mentors are supposed to do?"

"Yes, they are, but they are not supposed to replace a student's papers with copies of another student's papers!"

Neel didn't look surprised at the comment. He looked almost...devious. Celia couldn't believe what was happening. Neel, the same person she had been meeting with all semester...stealing her papers and giving them to Kevin?

"Mister Winokur!" the headmaster bellowed. "You took advantage of the student mentor program!"

Neel rolled his eyes. "It's so lame, and those kids are so gullible."

Headmaster Doyen breathed in so hard his nostrils flared. "Are you admitting that you stole Miss Fincastle's papers and gave them to Mister Fackler as his own?"

Neel said nothing, but stared at the headmaster with narrowed eyes.

"Um, headmaster?" Celia said quietly.

He snapped his head around to her. "Yes, Miss Fincastle?"

"Well, it's just...some of the papers that were copied weren't ones I had Neel check over. How did those happen?"

"Good question," Headmaster Doyen said, looking back at Neel. "What about those?"

Neel smirked at Celia. "You have a really great roommate."

Celia narrowed her eyes at him.

"Miss Fincastle?" the headmaster asked. "Do you know who he's talking about?"

"Doxa." Celia said the name like it was a disgusting food she had been forced to taste.

Headmaster Doyen rubbed his forehead. "Professor Legaspi," he said wearily, "I'm afraid this is going to be a long evening. Would you wait in the office with Mister Winokur while I call a few people down here?"

"Absolutely."

"Miss Fincastle, Mister Fackler, I would rather you wait in the other room," he said, rising to his feet and motioning them toward the door. Kevin walked shakily past Neel and into the waiting area, and Celia refused to look at Neel as she headed past him. "Both of you, please take a seat. This might take a while."

The next few minutes were a blur of activity, as Headmaster Doyen went back and forth between his own office and the other administrative offices. Professor Mesbur showed up and tried to calm Kevin down, and then Professor Spadaro walked in, his lips pressed into a thin line. Higby and Mr. Morven came in just before Professor Twombly arrived with Doxa in tow. Headmaster Doyen called Professors Spadaro and Twombly into the office and then asked Doxa to come in.

Celia couldn't hear what was being said, as Professor Legaspi had pulled the door mostly closed, but she could see through the window how irate the headmaster was becoming. The group in the waiting area was silent, except for Kevin's shallow, rapid breathing. Celia felt sorry for him, he looked so scared.

After a while the headmaster called Celia, Kevin, and Professors Legaspi and Mesbur into his office. It was a bit cramped with so many people in the room, and Celia was glad that Neel and Doxa were on the other side of the room from her.

"Mister Fackler," Headmaster Doyen said, "you are aware that cheating is a very serious offense?"

The terrified student literally shook in his shoes. "I-I was j-just g-getting some h-help from my m-mentor," he squeaked.

"And you admit that you were responsible for Mister Fackler's involvement in this, Mister Winokur?"

"Of course I did it," Neel said angrily. "She should have expected it," he said, glaring at Celia.

"What?" Celia asked, confused.

Neel gave her a calculating grin and said smoothly, "So the next princep doesn't know… "

"That's enough!" Professor Legaspi said quickly.

"And you?" Headmaster Doyen asked Doxa.

Doxa flipped her hair and glared at Celia. "She deserved it."

Headmaster Doyen looked furious. "Enough! Never, in all my years, have I seen such blatant insolence, such calculated cruelty against another student." He pushed to his feet and buttoned his jacket. "Professor Spadaro, could you keep an eye on these two while I take care of Miss Fincastle and Mister Fackler?"

"Of course."

The headmaster ushered Celia and Kevin into the waiting area outside the office where Higby and Mr. Morven were waiting. Professors Legaspi, Twombly, and Mesbur followed behind them.

Headmaster Doyen turned to Kevin. "Mister Fackler, I expect you to redo the assignments in question, but you won't receive any punishment for your actions."

"Thank you, sir. Of course, sir."

Headmaster Doyen nodded once. "Very well. Professor Mesbur, if you would escort Mister Fackler back to quarters, and assure him that there will be no permanent record of this in his file."

"Certainly. Come along, Kevin." He held the door open as Kevin walked through on shaky legs.

Headmaster Doyen turned to Celia. "Ahem... Well, Miss Fincastle... it seems I owe you... an apology." His face glowed red, and although Celia tried hard not to gloat, she couldn't help but feel immense satisfaction at his discomfort. "I will remove all of the incidents from your record and release you from probation immediately."

"Thank you, Headmaster Doyen," Celia said with a politeness she didn't feel. She glanced over at Higby and saw a glimmer of pride in his eye as he nodded at her.

"Yes, well... you are free to go back to your quarters, Miss Fincastle. Ah... keep up the good work."

She nodded and slipped out the door. She had just started down the hallway when Professor Legaspi's voice stopped her.

"Celia?"

She spun around and saw Professor Legaspi's head leaning out the door. "Yeah?"

"Come to my office after breakfast tomorrow and we'll explain everything."

"Okay."

Celia practically skipped through the hallways. When she made it to the Mensaleon quarters, she was surprised to see that it was close to ten o'clock. As she pushed open the carved wooden door, she saw Odette's face peering out from the lounge. A few seconds later, she found herself seated on one of the sofas in the lounge, with Odile, Odette, Maddie, and Heath all looking at her expectantly.

"Well?" Maddie said. "What happened?"

"Did it work?" Odette asked.

Celia grinned. "It worked." Her grin faded as she looked at Heath. "Your brother was right," she told him.

"Neel!?" Maddie asked incredulously.

Celia nodded. "But Doxa was part of it, too."

"Are they gonna get in trouble?" Heath asked.

She shrugged. "I don't know. I guess so. They sent me back here, so I don't know."

They all looked disappointed.

"But Headmaster Doyen said he's going to clear my record, and I'm not on academic probation anymore."

"Hey, that's great!" Odile said.

"Professor Legaspi told me to stop by her office tomorrow, so maybe I'll find out more then."

Heath gave a big yawn. "Merrar. I think I'd better hit the sack."

Odile looked at her watch. "Yeah, me, too. We've got a late night tomorrow."

"You do?" Celia asked, confused. "Why?"

"Earth to Celia!" Odette said, laughing. "Tomorrow night's the school play. You have been out of it!"

"Sorry. I've had a lot on my mind."

"That's okay. We forgive you," said Odile.

"Yeah, but Burnsy won't if you miss the play. He's got the lead," Maddie said.

"Burnsy!?" Celia tried to picture the shy redhead acting on stage.

Maddie shrugged. "I guess he's different when he's performing."

"We'll see." Celia yawned. "Boy, I'm really tired all of a sudden. I guess we'd better go to bed."

Doxa wasn't back by the time Celia went to sleep, and she wasn't in the room when Celia woke up the next morning. She woke up late, though, getting her first good night's sleep in a long time, so she wasn't sure if Doxa had returned to the room for the night or not.

The sun was shining brightly, a reflection of Celia's cheery mood, and she noticed the birds chirping outside her window. Smiling to herself, she dressed and headed down to the refectory, where everyone else was already eating.

Celia and Maddie had a good laugh at Doxa's drones, who looked like lost little children, sitting there without their leader. She was pretty sure one of them had been part of the exploding confetti flower prank, but since they had probably been forced to help, maybe they wouldn't get into too much trouble.

Rumors were flying at breakfast, as word about a big to-do in the headmaster's office spread through the student body. No one was really sure what had happened, but everyone kept giving Celia speculative looks, as if they somehow knew she must have been involved. Celia tried to eat quickly, and as soon as she saw Professor Legaspi head for the door, she quickly cleared her dishes and set out for Aquilegia's quarters.

On the way, Mr. Morven passed her in the hallway and gave her a big smile. "Good morning, Celia," he said cheerfully.

"Good morning, Mr. Morven," she said, returning his smile.

"Nice job," he said quietly before heading on down the hall.

The silver-colored quarters were deserted when she stepped through the door, and her footsteps echoed on the floor as she walked over to Professor Legaspi's office. She knocked on the door and when she heard, "Come in," she pushed the door open and walked in.

Higby was sitting in one of the silver chairs and Professor Legaspi was sitting behind her desk. Both had dark circles under their eyes, but Celia thought Professor Legaspi didn't look as tense as she had the past few weeks.

"Hi, Higby," she said, sitting down in the remaining chair.

"Hello, Celia. How are you this morning?"

Celia grinned. "Great!" They both smiled at her. "So, what's going to happen to Neel and Doxa?"

Professor Legaspi's smile faded. "When Headmaster Doyen confronted them with the evidence, they confessed to everything. It looks like they're going to miss graduation," she said.

"What will they do?"

"Headmaster Doyen's giving them the opportunity to finish their schoolwork and get a diploma, but he's not letting them stay at the school."

"Oh."

"Celia, did you know or suspect Neel was involved in any of this?"

"Well, Heath told me his brother had warned him about Neel, but I didn't really believe him. It just didn't seem like Neel."

"Really," Higby said thoughtfully. He exchanged a look with Professor Legaspi.

"What's going on?" Celia asked.

Higby shook his head. "Ah, my dear, it's nothing for you to worry about. It's just that no one else ever suspected Mister Winokur, so it is quite interesting that your friend's brother would have singled him out."

"Why?"

"Well, it would seem that Neel has a connection with the Coridan family."

"Who?"

"The Coridans," Professor Legaspi said. "If you'll remember, Mr. Morven told you a bit about the Overseer, your family, and the Coridans on the BUS at the start of the year."

"Oh, yeah."

"And apparently Neel was involved with the Coridans, in particular, Casimir Coridan."

"Who?" Celia felt a little stupid, repeating questions, but she didn't have any idea what they were talking about.

"Casimir Coridan wanted to be chosen as the Overseer's princep, but the Overseer chose your family again instead," Professor Legaspi explained.

"And Neel?"

"I guess Neel's mother is a cousin of Casimir," Higby said.

"And no one knew?"

Professor Legaspi shook her head. "No, not until last night. They've kept their connection well-hidden, at least until now. Apparently Neel's parents disagree with the way Casimir has behaved and have tried to keep their family ties hidden. Unfortunately, Neel found out and contacted Casimir without his parents' knowledge."

"Are there a lot of them, the Coridans?"

Higby thought for a moment. "No, not really, but the few remaining are very powerful, and they, shall we say, win friends and influence people. And not in the most polite ways,

I might add." He picked a piece of lint off his pants. "I'm sure you'll hear more about them, Celia, but you needn't worry about them now."

"So if Doxa was involved, too..."

"Well," Professor Legaspi said, "Doxa and Neel have been friends for a few years now, and when she complained to Neel about being in the same room as you, he asked for her help in trying to get you expelled. They nearly succeeded."

"I don't understand. Why was it so important that I get kicked out of school?"

Professor Legaspi smiled at her. "Without proper training, you can never learn to use your gifts to their highest potential, something Casimir was likely counting on."

"Why?"

"Because a weak princep is easier to remove from power, and Casimir would dearly like to be princep," Higby said.

"But why is he so worried about me? I'm not so important."

"Celia, your parents..." Higby swallowed and then continued. "They were chosen as the Overseer's princeps, with the stated intent that you would be the next in line for the position. The Coridans and their allies believe they should be the Overseer's princeps, and will stop at nothing to gain that power."

"What do the Overseer's princeps *do*?"

"The Overseer chooses princeps to sort of interpret between himself and the people in our demesne, and those princeps are given the responsibility of leadership within the demesne. It is up to the princeps to maintain order and peace in the demesne."

"And *I* have to do that?"

"Oh, my goodness, not yet, my dear."

"You'll have plenty of time to worry about that later, Celia. You cannot take the position of princep until you are sixteen, and even then there is a remarkably long process that must be followed," Professor Legaspi said.

"So... what happens next?"

"Well, there's very little that Casimir can do while you're here at school. And he likely doesn't dare show his face anywhere in the demesne where people might recognize him, as he's been a highly-sought-after individual ever since your parents' disappearance."

"Was he... did he..." Celia wasn't sure how to phrase her question. Fortunately, Higby understood what she was asking.

"No one knows what happened that day, Celia. There was very little evidence to work from in your family's quarters, and other than you, no one saw anything. Given the events that occurred before, the entire Coridan family was under suspicion, but no one knew where they had gone, either."

"What do you mean, 'events'?"

Higby glanced at his watch. "I'm terribly sorry, Celia, but this will have to wait for some other time. I have another appointment I must get to."

"Oh."

"Perhaps there will be time before the end of the year to discuss this some more," he said, standing and placing a hand on her shoulder. "As your guardian for the school year, I am very impressed with the way you handled yourself with the whole situation, and I am quite pleased with your performance in your classes at Renasci. Well done, Celia." He patted her shoulder and then headed out the door with a cheery wave at them.

"He was quite honored that you allowed him to be your guardian," Professor Legaspi said. "Not many people have the opportunity to work so closely with the Overseer's princep."

"But I'm not..."

Professor Legaspi held up a hand. "I know you're not *officially* princep yet, Celia, but the Overseer did specifically mention you when he chose your family. I have no doubt that when the time comes, you will be ready for the responsibility."

Celia said nothing and dropped her gaze to study the chair Higby had just vacated. It seemed that everyone was expecting her to do something that she wasn't sure she could or even wanted to do.

"In the meantime, Miss Fincastle," Professor Legaspi said, standing up and giving her a smile, "you have plenty of time to think it over and make a decision, so you don't have to worry about it now. You should just focus on finishing the school year without having to worry about being framed for any pranks or cheating, and enjoy the end of the year activities." She walked around the desk and leaned back on it.

"Yeah, I'm sure it will be loads of fun with everyone thinking I'm a cheater," Celia said quietly.

"I believe the headmaster was going to make an announcement in the refectory just after we left, and the deans have been permitted to inform the students in their coteries. You'll probably find people have a very different opinion of you after that."

"Really?"

"Really." She glanced at her watch. "And now, I believe we both should head off and enjoy our weekend. I hear one of your fellow Mensaleon students will be playing the lead."

Celia headed out of the Aquilegia quarters a few moments later and into the hallway lit by bright sunshine. She went down the stairs and headed for the commons, deciding to take the outside route to the Mensaleon quarters since it was such a nice day.

"Hey, Celia, nice going," someone said as she stepped out the door.

"Yeah," another person said, "I guess we should have believed you instead of Neel and Doxa."

"Oh, um, thanks," Celia replied, feeling her cheeks turn red.

A few other people said something similar as she made her way through the commons and up the stairs to the Mensaleon quarters. Doxa's friends were all sitting at their desks, looking like they had no idea what they were supposed to do. Celia wondered if they had ever thought for themselves or if they had just let Doxa order them around all the time.

Maddie dragged her outside, telling her that she'd spent too much time in the library over the past few months, and she found that a group of Mensaleon students had decided to play a friendly game of Soccovolle. It seemed Professor Twombly had sent word around the coterie about Celia and what had happened the previous night, and the students in Celia's coterie, at least, had decided she wasn't so bad after all.

They had a few too many players on the field, and some of them, like Celia, had never played before. Others had played many times but still were pathetic at getting the ball to go where they wanted. But since there were only a few weeks left in the school year, no one seemed to care that they were breaking the rules of the game left and right.

After a few hours of playing, they were all exhausted, so they headed back inside. Celia decided that while it was a lot of fun playing Soccovolle, she wasn't very good at it.

"Hey, that was a pretty good bump, Celia," Josh said as they came up to the school.

"The *only* good move I made all day," she retorted.

"Well . . ."

"I know I'm terrible at it, Josh."

"No, not really," he insisted. "You just need a little practice."

"So says the Soccovolle superstar," she teased. "Weren't you the only seventh-year on a school team this year?"

"Yeah, but . . . " He rubbed the back of his neck as he stared at the ground.

"But nothing. If it weren't for you, our coterie would never have won the Soccovolle tournament," Celia said. "Have you heard where you're playing this summer?"

"Yeah, it's such a mush! Can you believe the Summer Tournament is gonna be in Florida!? That's where *I* live! I don't get to go anywhere." He kicked at a weed growing near the pathway.

It took Celia a moment to remember what his first phrase meant, since she still hadn't quite gotten all of the slang they used in the demesne, even after almost a year at school. "Oh, that's too bad," Celia said. "I've never been to Florida. But, hey, at least you still get to play in the tournament, right?"

"Yeah, I guess."

Everyone was so tired after running around all morning that they spent the afternoon in quarters, either relaxing or talking and playing games in the lounge. Doxa's posse was still a little confused, and they seemed to look around like they had never realized there were so many other people in the coterie.

The refectory was filled with excitement about the school play that evening, and Celia noticed that Burnsy looked quite nervous. He was so quiet and shy, she hoped he would do all right on stage.

The school play at Renasci was a fancy affair, where everyone dressed in nice clothes and behaved as if they were going to a royal palace instead of just heading down to the auditorium. Students served as ushers, everyone was given a program, and there were snack carts in the lobby, in case anyone wanted to munch on something during the show.

The students in the drama club had obviously put a lot of work into the play. It was written by the students, and they were in charge of nearly every aspect of the performance.

Celia was surprised at how good the play really was; compared to the plays at her old school, this one was fantastic.

By intermission, everyone was raving about Burnsy playing the lead. Despite how uncomfortable he was with attention, he seemed to come alive on stage, and it was like they were looking at a different person.

At the end of the play, the audience gave the cast a standing ovation, and the auditorium filled with cheers and applause, the loudest coming from the Mensaleon students for Burnsy.

Celia heard Heath holler, "Way to go, Burnsy!"

"Woo-hoo!" "Yeah!" "All right!" "Encore!"

After a few minutes, the house lights came up again and everyone started to file out of the auditorium. Celia noticed that people were still pointing at her and whispering, but she hoped they were starting to learn the truth.

Back in their quarters, some of the Mensaleon students, with the help of Professor Twombly, had set up a celebration for Burnsy. It took him a little while to get out of costume and help tidy up the auditorium, but when he came in and saw the cake and balloons, his face turned bright red, even though he was grinning from ear to ear.

Although it was already late and the people who had played Soccovolle that morning were dead tired, everyone enjoyed the party and stayed in the lounge almost until midnight. When Celia finally collapsed in her bed, she fell asleep without even closing the curtains on her windows.

Chapter Seventeen
The ALPHAs

The last few weeks of the semester were a welcome change from the previous ones for Celia. Between the headmaster's announcement at breakfast and the deans talking to their coteries, word had spread quickly about Celia's innocence. On Monday, all of Celia's classmates clustered around her seat, peppering her with questions about Neel, Doxa, and how she had helped catch them. Celia figured that it wasn't her place to talk about Neel or Doxa, so she tried to explain what had happened without telling too much about their involvement.

After a few classes, it got a little tedious, and Celia was glad her professors stepped in and asked everyone to leave her alone and take their seats. In the hallways, people were back to smiling and greeting her cheerfully as they went past, instead of the whispers she had seen recently. Although sometimes Celia would have preferred people just ignore her, it was nice to get polite reactions again, rather than the suspicious accusations.

The last week of school brought a combination of dread, relief, and sadness for the seventh-years. Dread because everyone kept telling them that the final exams were the hardest of the year, relief because it meant their schoolwork would finally be finished, and sadness because the school year was coming to an end and everyone would be going home soon.

Final exams were not at all what Celia expected, although she wasn't surprised, since nothing at RAGS was what she expected. After all the rumors and speculation, Celia figured her professors would give them lengthy written exams, full of hard questions requiring long answers.

What actually happened was in some ways easier, in other ways harder. On Monday of the last week of school, the deans handed out notes to all of the seventh-years. Celia looked at hers when she got it:

CELIA FINCASTLE

Seventh-year students will report to the gymnasium at their designated time for combined final exams. Please bring a sharp pencil and be prepared for anything. Your time is:

10:30 A.M. FRIDAY

If you arrive late, you will not be given an extension to make up for the missed time, and all students will be graded the same, regardless of time available or used. It is strongly suggested that you arrive promptly.

For the rest of the week, all of Celia's professors reviewed the material they had covered during the year, saying nothing specific about the final exams. They told everyone that the exam changed every year, so they wouldn't be able to ask the older students about the exam, not that it stopped some of them from trying. Celia and Maddie laughed at Heath and Kitt, who asked every single student they met what their seventh-year finals had been like. Despite the fact that the students in different years all had different exams, the two boys still asked and then tried to figure out if there was some sort of pattern that they could use to predict what their own exam would be like.

Thursday was a rather odd day. All the other classes had to take their final exams as usual, but the seventh-years had nothing to do until their allotted time for their individual exam. They didn't have to go to classes or be anywhere specific at any particular time, which Celia thought was both good and bad. It was nice to be able to sit around and relax a bit, but the thought of the final exam hung over her head like a dark cloud, and she felt like she had to study for most of the day.

When Galena returned, the first Mensaleon student to take the final, all the others crowded around her to ask questions.

"I'm sorry, everyone, but they told me not to talk about it until after the exams are all finished," she said.

"Aw, man!" Heath groaned. "That stinks."

"You guys are impossible!" Maddie chuckled.

"You can't even give us a little hint?" Kitt asked.

Galena laughed. "I wish I could, but I really don't think that would be a good idea," she said.

"Besides, everyone," Celia said, "the exams are supposed to determine what our gifts are, so it wouldn't do you much good to get help on things that you might not be gifted at."

Josh sighed. "Way to go, Celia. You had to remind us that there's no way to get help on our exams."

"Sorry, guys, but you'd be better off spending your time studying."

Maddie groaned. "Celia! You sound like my parents!" Everyone laughed at that, but they all headed back to their books.

On Friday, Celia screeched to a halt in front of the gym at 10:15, then took a few deep breaths to calm her rattled nerves. She double-checked her pencil; she'd chosen a mechanical pencil rather than a traditional one, but she wanted to make sure she wasn't going to need a new piece of lead and that she hadn't lost her eraser. Drumming her fingers against her leg, she paced the hallway, glancing at the clock on the wall every minute and trying to remember everything she had learned that year.

At 10:27, the door swung out and Mr. Morven stepped into the hallway. "Hi, Celia," he said quietly. "They're almost ready in there. You have your pencil?" When Celia held hers up, he said, "Good." He smiled at her. "Don't worry. I'm sure you'll do fine."

Celia gave him a weak smile, then tapped her pencil against her leg. She couldn't believe how nervous she was.

At exactly 10:30, Mr. Morven pushed the door open and gestured for her to head through. Her legs shook as she stepped through the door and her heart jumped to her throat when she heard loud bangs and shouts from somewhere in the gym.

Mr. Morven held his hand out to the right and said, "Follow the signs that way and start your exam. Good luck."

She nodded and walked around a few corners and into a room made from partitions. It was dimly lit, with a single table in the center. A clear light bulb and a note sat on the table. Celia picked up the note and read:

Complete this feat, you'll be all right
Because you will have lots of light.
Your hands alone you'll have to use,
And fifteen minutes, win or lose.
If you can get this bulb to glow,

Chapter Seventeen

Then you'll show how much you know.
We wish you all the best of luck;
Just call out "Help!" if you get stuck.

Celia set the note down. Were they kidding? She glanced around but saw no one, so she set her pencil down and carefully picked up the light bulb. Did she use one hand or two? She had no idea. Tapping the bulb against her other hand, she tried to think. How would one go about lighting a bulb with their hands? Did she have to say anything, or just concentrate on getting light?

She jumped and nearly dropped the bulb when she noticed it giving off a faint glow, but the light quickly faded. Holding the bulb out in front of her, she focused on the bulb and felt a smile come to her face when the glow returned, stronger this time. Grasping the bulb with both hands, she tried harder, the sounds in the gym fading away as she concentrated on getting a brighter light. When the light bulb glowed as brightly as if it had been in a lamp plugged in to an outlet, she felt laughter bubble up and spill out. This was the most amazing thing she had ever seen!

"Oh, nicely done!" a voice said suddenly, followed by cheering and clapping.

Startled, Celia dropped the light bulb and watched helplessly as it fell to the floor and smashed to pieces. "Oh, I'm so sorry!" She looked up and saw Professors Mesbur and Perrin coming across the room.

"Don't worry about it, Celia," Professor Mesbur said, walking over and placing a hand on her shoulder. "We have plenty more."

"That was quite impressive," Professor Perrin said, taking a whisk broom and dustpan out from under the table and handing them to Professor Mesbur.

After sweeping up the pieces, dumping them in a trash can, and putting all three back under the table, Professor Mesbur pulled out a sheet of paper, wrote something on it, folded it in half, and handed it to Celia with her pencil. "You're about five minutes early, but you might as well keep going," he said. "Your next section is with Professor Perrin, and he'll show you the way."

"Right through there," Professor Perrin said, pointing to an opening in the partitions. They headed down a short walkway and into another room, this one brightly lit with a podium and a table and chair. "If you will take the spot behind the podium, I will get settled at my table and we'll begin." He headed for the table and Celia walked toward the podium. "Oh! I need that piece of paper, too," he said, pivoting and changing course midway across the room.

A few moments later they were ready to start. "I'm going to talk to you in several different languages, one at a time," he explained. "If you understand what I say, I'd like you to reply in the same language, if possible. If not, then English is fine. If you don't understand what I say, then just say so, and we'll move on to the next language. Okay?"

Celia nodded, wondering how quickly they were going to run through these since she was certain she was going to stand there in confusion the entire time.

"Here we go," Professor Perrin said, glancing at his notes. "We'll start with this easy one," he said in English. "Now, tell me, what day of the week is it today?"

Celia giggled. "Friday."

"Oh, very good," he said, winking at her.

The next one was definitely *not* English, but Celia was very surprised to find that she understood what he was saying, and she was shocked when she opened her mouth and answered in the same language! Her astonishment grew when it happened again and again; each and every language that Professor Perrin spoke, she could not only understand, but also speak without hesitation.

Dozens of languages and several minutes later, Professor Twombly walked over and said something to Professor Perrin, who glanced quickly at his watch. "It seems we've run out of time, Celia," he said, scribbling quickly on her paper and handing it to Professor Twombly.

Still clutching her pencil, Celia followed Professor Twombly into yet another room. Again she heard loud bangs and shouts echo in the gym, but tried to concentrate on her next exam.

"This test covers a variety of mind tasks, Celia," Professor Twombly said, placing a stapled packet of paper in front of her. "Get through as much as you can, but don't worry if you don't finish. You may begin now."

Celia flipped to the first page and found a collection of codes much more complicated than any of the ones they had worked on in a class that year. Bending over the paper, she got to work. She worked her way through codes and puzzles, and was scribbling away furiously at a final dream interpretation (which she had never tried before), when Professor Twombly told her time was up.

"Have you seen dream interpretations before, Celia?" she asked, writing on Celia's sheet of paper.

"Only what we covered in class."

Professor Twombly smiled at her as she handed over the paper. "Just curious," she said. "You'll need to go through that way next."

Celia went down another walkway and found herself in an area that looked like a rather odd science laboratory or optometrist's office. There were tables set up along the perimeter with machines that resembled microscopes and other more strange-looking contraptions. A large box stood on a low platform in the center of the room.

Celia followed an arrow pointing to the table on her left and found a sheet of paper. It read:

> Look through each machine, and write down anything and everything you see on this sheet of paper. At the end, instructions for the center box are in a slot on the side. Good luck!
>
> Professor Legaspi

Celia stepped over to the first machine and looked through the eyepiece. Seeing nothing but a bright white empty space, she stepped back and frowned. Tapping her pencil on her lower lip, she thought for a moment. This was Professor Legaspi's exam, so it was for sight abilities. There had to be something there.

She looked again and saw what looked like a speck of dust. She stared hard at the speck and soon felt her vision zoom in the way it had the past fall at the Soccovolle tournament. It zoomed once, twice, and she saw a fuzzy outline, a third time and she saw a sketch of an eagle. She zoomed in closer, but didn't see anything else, so she let her eyes return to normal, wrote her answer on her paper, and moved to the next machine.

Glancing at this one, she saw big, bold letters: RAGS. But she faintly saw something else, so she studied it a moment longer. Hidden in the letters she noticed the names of the five coteries.

She moved around the room, encountering things that glowed when she looked at them the right way, things in the dark, things hidden in pictures, and even hidden things written upside down or mirror image. When she reached the end of the tables on the perimeter, she took her instructions for the center box.

> This box is sealed, solid on all sides. Your task is to see what is inside. For some, quite simple; for others, impossible. Do your best to write down what lies within - more detail is more certainty that you are not guessing. Good luck!
>
> Professor Legaspi

Celia nearly laughed. See inside the box? As in x-ray vision? It had to be a joke. But then she thought of all the other seemingly impossible things she had already done at this school, and she decided that it must be something that *someone* could do, so she'd figured she'd give it her best shot.

She took a deep breath and studied the box, trying to decide how to begin. She walked around it, stopping and squinting at each side, but she didn't notice anything changing. It still looked solid and not at all see-through. So she stood in front of one side and stared at it, trying to concentrate on seeing through to the inside.

After a moment, Celia saw a spot in the center of the box start to wiggle, like a bad television signal, and shadows of whatever was inside started to appear in one spot. She concentrated harder on making that spot bigger and soon she was looking through the side of the box as if it was purple-tinted glass. The objects inside seemed like they were lit with the purplish glow of a black light, and Celia could see quite clearly that there was a vase of flowers, a hand mirror, and a pair of old bowling shoes.

She wrote down what she saw, trying to include as much information as possible. Even after glancing at her paper and looking up again, she could still see inside the box. When she finished, she blinked her eyes a few times and her vision returned to normal.

Glancing around, she saw an opening on the opposite side from the entrance, so she headed over and went down another walkway. At the end, she found Professor Legaspi standing in the middle of what looked like athletic equipment.

"Hi, Celia," she said, checking her watch. "You're a few minutes early, but that should be okay. Are you sure you finished everything on my exam?"

Celia held out her answers. "I think so."

Professor Legaspi looked over her exam and said, "Impressive! Very well. Let's get you suited up."

A few minutes later, Celia was wearing a helmet and pads, wondering what was coming next. Professor Legaspi ushered her through a space in the partitions and Celia stepped into a brightly lit arena. Professor Spadaro, wearing his padding and holding his helmet, stood at a water cooler with a cup of water in his hand.

"Ah! My next vict—, er, I mean, challenger," he said when he saw them. "Welcome, Miss Fincastle, to my jousting arena. Your task, should you choose to accept (although you have no choice, because you must) is to make it from one end to the other, past each obstacle, including . . . me."

Celia looked over and saw a foot-wide padded plank running across a pit. Although there were mats all around and foam chunks filling the pit, she was still nervous. She had never been particularly adept at sports and she wasn't very athletic.

"You may make as many attempts as time allows without any penalty," he continued, putting on his helmet. "Are you ready?"

Celia gulped and nodded her head nervously. Professor Spadaro nodded and walked to the other side. Celia grew more anxious as she watched him walk the long distance over to the end of the plank and she realized just how far she had to go across. Professor Legaspi handed Celia a jousting stick, a long pole with padding at each end, and smiled at her. "Cheer up, Celia. No one's made it past him yet, so no pressure."

Celia gave her a weak smile and walked over to the edge of the plank. "Whenever you're ready," Professor Spadaro called, and Celia nodded. She blew out a big breath and stepped onto the plank.

The first section was very soft and squishy, like walking on pillows. Although she wobbled, Celia gritted her teeth, determined she was *not* going to fall. She felt something shift, and then it was like she was walking across the floor. When she reached the second section, she found that it was very wobbly, and the whole section was tilting wildly from side to side. But Celia marched across, never faltering once. The third section looked normal, but Celia discovered that it was extra springy when she was launched a foot in the air on her first step. The first one startled her, but didn't shake her, and by the end of the section she was jumping high in the air, high enough to see Professors Perrin and Twombly in their sectioned areas.

She slowed her bounce and stepped onto the fourth and final section. Professor Spadaro stood at the ready, his jousting stick out in front of him. Celia held hers, too, ready to do battle with her teacher. He smiled at her, an impish grin, and waited for her to make the first move.

Celia narrowed her eyes and marched forward. Padded sticks clashed as they met on the plank. For an instant, Celia thought she saw surprise flash in his eyes before he narrowed them and fought harder. He swung; she ducked. He swept low; she jumped. He jabbed at her; she evaded. She blocked his hits, avoided his moves, until finally, after one of his swings, she whacked him across the stomach, catching him off balance and sending him tumbling off into the foam-filled pit.

He had already climbed out when Celia reached the other side, heaving a huge sigh of relief. They removed their helmets at the same time, and Professor Spadaro smiled at her. "Good work, Miss Fincastle," he said, nodding his head at her. "Professor Legaspi will help you out of your gear."

Celia headed over to the doorway, still breathing hard. Professor Legaspi ushered her back to the room with all the equipment. "You can take off all the padding and set it with your helmet. I'll take your sheet in to Professor Spadaro."

Through the partition, Celia could hear their conversation as she removed all her padding.

"You let her win, didn't you?" Professor Legaspi asked.

"Not at all," Professor Spadaro replied. "I've been going easy on the few who have actually made it across, but not her. I fought hard, and she still knocked me off."

Professor Legaspi laughed. "Sore because you were beat by a girl?"

There was a pause, then, "You don't understand. Unless I'm letting someone win, the only other time I have ever been beaten was by Casimir Coridan."

"Oh." The word was ominous.

Celia moved to the other bench and tied her shoes with shaking hands. A moment later, Professor Legaspi reappeared. "You have one final piece for your exams," she said, "the last section for the ALPHAs."

Chapter Seventeen

"ALPHAs?" Celia questioned.

She nodded. "Academic Level Placement and Habilitas Assessments. They're required for all seventh-years. It's not a graded exam," she explained as they headed through another walkway. "It's just a way to evaluate your abilities so we can monitor your progress at the school and make sure you're in the right classes."

"Oh."

She stopped outside an opening in the partitions. "No one can help you with this section. It is a test of combined abilities, so do what you can. There are no instructions; you must figure it out on your own."

"Okay."

"When you've finished, you'll need to turn all your papers in to Mr. Morven at the table in the hall. Good luck," she said, leaving Celia at the doorway and heading back the other direction.

Celia stepped around the corner and found a single table in the middle of the room with what looked like a pile of rubble sitting on top. Stepping closer, she saw it was a collection of stones, flat on the top and bottom but very irregular around the sides. When she reached the table, she could make out something that looked a little like writing on some of the pieces. She moved the pieces around, and quickly decided that it must be a puzzle of some kind, so she spread the pieces out to see all of them. A few minutes later, she was looking at two phrases, each written in a different language. The first was written with pictures, a little like Egyptian hieroglyphics but different, and the second was written with characters that Celia didn't think she had ever seen before.

Studying the pieced-together puzzle, Celia noticed a message hidden behind the other two, which said to read the second writing upside down. When she walked around the table, the second message suddenly became readable, and it directed her to turn the fourth piece from the right over and read the back. When she picked that one up, she noticed that there were slight bumps on the bottom, and as she ran her fingers over the bumps, like reading Braille, she discovered that it was the key to the picture code. Within moments she had deciphered that code as well, and it directed her to the next room.

The next area felt very cold when she walked through the partition. She didn't see anything, and she wasn't sure what she was supposed to be doing. Wandering around the room, she finally felt that one spot was slightly warmer than the rest of the room, and she knew that her next challenge had to be somewhere nearby. She bent down and studied the floor, and found a thin piece of clear plastic lying there. Picking it up, she felt a slight tingle in her fingers as she held the plastic sheet out in front of her. After a few moments, instructions appeared on the plastic, a flowing, glowing red script, telling her to move to the next room.

Heading to the following room, Celia thought she heard something, a very soft sound. Once inside the room, she found a desk with paper on it. The paper asked her to write down how many different kinds of abilities she had used in the last two rooms, then asked if there were any other comments she wanted to add. Celia was about to head out of the room when she remembered the faint noise she had heard. Listening carefully, she tried to figure out what she heard.

It sounded like a whisper, a single sentence repeating over and over. At first Celia thought it said, "The sand bees are tan," which made no sense to her, but when she listened closer, she realized it actually was "Listen and be certain." She thought there might be something more to the message, but she wasn't sure how much time she had left. Glancing at her watch and seeing that she only had a few seconds before her time was up, she scribbled on her paper and hurried through the remaining doorway. She found herself right in front of the second set of doors for the gym, so she pushed through them and stepped into the hallway. There was a table there, but no Mr. Morven, so she waited a moment until he returned.

"All finished, Celia?" he asked, walking around the corner.

"Yeah, I think so."

"Okay," he said. "Just hand over all your papers and you're free to go." He took the pile from her and instructed, "Make sure you don't say anything about the exams to any of your classmates until after tonight. Once everyone has finished their exams, you can all talk about it as much as you want."

"All right." Feeling like a huge weight had been lifted off her shoulders, Celia headed straight to the refectory for lunch. Most of the other students were still doing last-minute studying for their finals, so the room was unusually quiet for lunchtime. Only the sounds of dishes and silverware clinking echoed in the air.

By Friday evening, the school was filled with laughter and everyone was celebrating the end of schoolwork for the year. The first-years were all getting excited about their upcoming prom, which was happening the following evening. During the prom, the rest of the students were going to the auditorium for an improvised talent show. Anyone who wanted to get on stage and perform could do so. Every table in the refectory buzzed with discussions about one of those two events during dinner.

"Is anyone going to do anything for the talent show?" Libby asked.

"Not me," Celia said.

"We're thinking of doing some ballet," Odette said, leaning over from the table next to them.

"Oh, that would be neat," Maddie said.

"I've been working on some magic tricks," Kitt said.

"Really?" Galena commented. "Sounds great."

"Everyone's waiting to see what the Corpanthera kids come up with for this year," Odile said.

Celia frowned. "Why?"

"'Cause they always do something really amazing every year."

Heath grinned. "Dude, you should hear what my brother told me. He said it's better than anything he's ever seen."

"No kidding?" Rowel asked. "I can't wait."

The talent show was a ton of fun. Heath's brother hadn't been exaggerating about the Corpanthera act. They put on an astonishing acrobatics and physical feats show that had everyone gasping, cheering, and clapping. All the other performers were quite good as well, and Celia really enjoyed watching Odile and Odette dance. It was a great way to wind up the school year.

Chapter Eighteen
Graduation and Going Home

On Sunday morning, Celia woke up and realized that she only had one week left before she headed back to Aunt Agatha's house. She wasn't exactly sure if it felt like home anymore, since she liked being at Renasci so much. She could hardly believe she had reached the end of her first year at school. At times it seemed like the year had flown by; other times it seemed like the days had dragged on forever.

Graduation was on Friday, and everyone would head home on Sunday, June first, which was also Celia's birthday. With plenty of free time before they headed home, the students at RAGS found all kinds of things to occupy their remaining days. Some played games outside, others worked on fun projects indoors. Celia spent most of her week by herself, thinking or reading. There were still so many things that she didn't know, about the demesne, her parents, the Overseer, Casimir Coridan, the position as princep... she felt like everything was somehow connected, but she had no way of knowing and she wasn't at all sure how she would find out.

Tuesday was Coterie Games Day, a little like field day at Celia's old school. The students competed for their coteries in a wild array of activities. There were some of the standards, like the three-legged race and potato sack races, but there were also some more unusual ones, like another one of Professor Spadaro's agility courses and piggy-back Soccovolle, where the person on the ground could only play the soccer part and the person being carried could only play the volleyball part.

Celia competed in the three-legged race with Josh and the wheelbarrow race with Maybell, one of the sixth-years who had stayed over Christmas, and also ran Professor Spadaro's agility course on her own. Since the agility course was an all-school competition, Celia didn't figure she would place very high at all. She didn't think she had much of a chance, seeing as she was competing against some of the students from Corpanthera. To her surprise, she finished third, shocking most of the school and winning big points for Mensaleon. She and Josh had done fairly well in their race, finishing second, but Maybell couldn't stop laughing and they ended up fourth in the wheelbarrow race. It didn't really matter, because there was no official winner, although the team with the most points at the end of the day would get to sit at fancy tables for dinner and be served by the team with the fewest points.

Tattotauri ended up being declared the "winners" by only three points over Mensaleon, and Aquilegia finished last and had to serve them at dinner. Everyone was exhausted by the end of the day, but it had been great fun.

On Wednesday, Celia received a note from Mr. Morven asking her to come down to his office when she had a moment. She wasn't doing anything in particular, so she ambled over to the administrative wing, remembering her last visit to the area. Shaking her head to dislodge the thought, she knocked on Mr. Morven's door and walked in at his invitation.

"Hi, Celia. That was fast."

She shrugged. "I wasn't doing much, so I thought I might as well come down here."

"I just wanted to let you know that I'm going to drive you home from the BUS station. Um, your aunt . . . "

"Let me guess. She's too busy to come pick me up?"

"Well, sort of. It's a combination of that and our desire to keep her as far away from the demesne as possible, just in case."

"Okay."

"Would you like me to travel on the BUS with you, or would you prefer to ride with some of your friends?" he asked.

"I guess it'd be nice to ride with my friends, if you don't mind."

"Sure. No problem." He leaned down and rummaged in a desk drawer. "I'll give you this, then," he said, holding out a long, thin piece of paper with iridescent green ink on it. Celia recognized it as a BUS ticket. "You still have your card?"

"My card?" she asked, confused.

"The one I gave you at the station last fall? With the ram on it?"

"Oh, yes, I do. It's in my duffle bag with the book."

"Oh, good. Don't forget to keep that with you . . . and you might want to think about keeping it in a safe place when you get home."

"All right."

"Okay, then. I'll catch up with you on the platform at the other end. Don't try to head outside without me. If we can't find each other, just pick a bench and sit down and I'll find you eventually."

"Thanks, Mr. Morven."

"Not a problem, Celia. See you later."

On the morning of graduation day, Celia couldn't help but think about Neel and Doxa, who wouldn't be part of the ceremony. Although she was still upset about all they had put her through that year, she felt almost sorry that they had put all the time and effort into seven years at school, only to miss out on graduating at the end. She knew everyone else would think she was crazy if she said anything, since they all now agreed that their behavior had been lower than low, so she kept her thoughts to herself.

She was sitting in the lounge later that day, flipping through the magazine she had bought at the rathskeller at the beginning of the year, when Blaine walked in. "Hi, Celia."

"Hey, Blaine. Are you ready for graduation?"

He smiled at her. "Are you kidding? I can't wait."

"What are you going to do after this?"

Blaine got an odd look on his face. "I've got a few options. I guess I'll just wait and see what works out."

"Oh."

"Listen, Celia... I just wanted to say..." He sighed as he sank down on the chair. "I want to apologize for not sticking up for you this year. I got so busy with all my schoolwork and stuff, and I just didn't make the effort to defend you when everyone else thought you were the one causing all the trouble."

"It's okay."

He shook his head vehemently. "No, it's not. I didn't believe you would do stuff like that, and I should have let you and everyone else know that."

"Really, Blaine. It's all right."

"Well, I disagree, but... if you forgive me for my lack of care..."

"There's nothing to forgive, but if it makes you feel better, of course I forgive you."

He gave a rueful smile. "You sure had a rough year, didn't you."

"It could have gone better," she said, "but it wasn't that bad. Except maybe for Doxa."

He grinned again. “Hey, just think. Next year you won’t have to worry about dealing with her in your room! Maybe you’ll have my sister in with you.”

“Your sister?”

“Yeah, Audra. She’s heading to RAGS next year. If she ends up in Mensaleon, she’ll be in the same room as you.”

“That’d be nice.”

“Yeah, she’s a good kid. I think you’d like her.” Blaine studied her. “I’m going to miss you,” he said quietly. “You’re like my honorary sister.”

“Oh, that’s so sweet,” Celia said. “It’s not going to be the same around here without you. Will you keep in touch?”

“I’m sure I will,” he answered evasively.

“Well, ‘bro’,” she said, “it’s about time for the ceremony, so I guess we’d better get going.”

Graduation was a formal affair, held in the late afternoon with fading sunlight casting a golden glow over everything. They used the Soccovolle stadium, which had been elaborately decorated for the ceremony. The graduates wore the traditional cap and gown, each one wearing a gown in the color of their coterie and a gold tassel on their caps. Their parents all came to watch with pride and happiness as their children received their diplomas. At the end of the ceremony, amid tears and laughter, the graduating class all tossed their caps in the air while the audience applauded, and everyone headed back to the school for a reception.

A huge buffet had been set up in the refectory, and they somehow managed to cram some extra tables in to accommodate the visitors. Balloons bounced along the ceiling and streamers looped all around the room, all in the colors of the coteries. After everyone had eaten as much as they wanted, the new graduates headed to the gymnasium for a graduation party, organized by the second-year students. Everyone else headed off to quarters to go to bed.

Saturday was a hectic day, spent packing, saying good-bye to everyone, and exchanging addresses and phone numbers with new friends. The Mensaleon seventh-years ended up sitting in the chairs in the girls' room on Saturday evening, talking about what everyone was going to do over the summer.

"I get to go all the way to Florida for the summer tournament," Josh said a bit sarcastically.

Celia laughed. "At least you're doing something," she said. "I'm stuck with Aunt Agatha and her bridge club." She got a combination of groans and laughs as a reply.

"I'm going to camp," Maddie said.

"Really?" Libby asked. "That sounds like fun."

"It's my only escape from my brothers and sisters for the whole summer."

"Yeah, all eight weeks of it," Celia teased. "That's such a *long* time."

Maddie gave her a weak shove. "Hey, you deal with them twenty-four, seven, and you see how fast you want to get away from them."

"How about you, Burnsy?" Galena asked.

He cleared his throat as his face grew red. "I-I'm going to . . . um . . . a summer drama program."

"Awesome, dude," Heath said.

"Time for bed, everyone," Professor Twombly said, leaning through the doorway. "Tomorrow will be a busy day, so lights out quickly, please."

The final morning at Renasci was a mixture of happiness and sadness. Celia was glad she had survived her first year, but she was going to miss all the friends she had made once she was back with Aunt Agatha. More than that, she was going to miss the first-years she had gotten to know that year, particularly Blaine. It felt like she was losing a beloved older brother.

Chapter Eighteen

The BUS was already sitting at the station when they went down for breakfast that morning, and Celia nearly groaned at the sight of it, remembering how motion sick she had been on the trip out. Since it was Celia's birthday, some of the students from Celia's coterie tied balloons to her chair in the refectory and wished her a happy birthday. When they finished their meal, they went to complete all their last-minute packing, and then it was time to load on the BUS.

The guys helped them all lug their trunks and bags out to the platform and onto the train. Celia, Maddie, Heath, and Josh decided to share one compartment, so they stowed all their luggage and headed back to get their last few bags. Celia grabbed her duffle bag out of her closet and checked to make sure she had gotten everything else. Stepping out of the closet and closing the door, she saw the empty room and sighed. It looked so lonely and bare.

Maddie came out of her closet. "All set?" she asked.

"Yeah, I guess."

Their professors were all standing in Main Hall to say good-bye. Celia shook hands with Professors Mesbur, Perrin, and Spadaro, but Professor Twombly gave her a hug. "Happy birthday, Celia, and have a great summer," she said, handing her a small wrapped present. "We'll see you in a couple of months."

"Thanks, Professor Twombly."

Professor Legaspi gave her a big hug. "Have a great birthday," she said. "We're working on something that might get you back to the demesne before school starts, so if it works out, someone will be in touch, okay?"

"Okay."

She handed her a small present wrapped in brightly-colored paper and heaped with ribbons. "I hope you enjoy this," she said. "You did a great job this year. I'm so proud of you."

"Thanks." Celia blinked back tears. She'd grown close to Professor Legaspi this year, and as odd as it sounded, she was going to miss her professor.

Higby was standing by the front doors, wishing everyone a great summer vacation. When he saw Celia and Maddie, his face broke out in a wide smile. "Hi, girls. All ready to go?"

"Think so," Maddie said.

"Celia, could you come with me for a moment?" he asked.

Celia shrugged, looking at Maddie. "Go ahead," Maddie said. "I'll just get on the BUS. I'll meet you there."

Higby watched her leave, then turned back to Celia. "I just wanted to let you know how proud I was to be your temporary guardian this year. You did better than anyone could have imagined, even when you had a rough time."

"Thanks."

"I also wanted to wish you a happy birthday and give you this," he said, taking a small present out of his coat pocket. "It's just a little something."

"You didn't have to—"

"I know. I wanted to." He put his hand on her shoulder and gave it a slight squeeze. "Have a great summer, Celia. I'll see you soon." He gave her a wink and then turned to wave to a group of students heading out the door.

Celia wove her way through the crowd of students on the platform, trying to figure out why Higby's wink had sent a jolt through her stomach, as if it was somehow familiar to her. Surely she would have remembered if she'd seen Higby before, and she was certain she had never seen him before last summer.

Her thoughts about Higby fled her mind when she made her way back to the compartment and found it filled with balloons and streamers. She laughed when she saw her friends all wearing pointed cardboard hats with birthday cakes printed on them. As the train pulled out of the station, the entire car sang "Happy Birthday" to her, and Merry presented her with a cupcake complete with a candle.

The BUS ride was quite different from the last one Celia had taken, since she now knew a lot of people and nearly everyone knew her, particularly after the birthday celebration. When they headed back to the dining car, everyone who walked past them wished her a happy birthday, and everyone in the dining car called out the same when she walked in.

They sat in one of the round booths while they ate their meal, and were all surprised when the man at the counter set a small cake in the center of their table. Celia thanked him, then cut and served it to all her friends. It was chocolate with coconut frosting, a big change from the orange-flavored cake Aunt Agatha had ordered last year.

Celia wasn't sure if it was the company or just because she knew what to expect, but she didn't feel as sick this trip as she had last time. They played card games and laughed about some of the things they had experienced over the past ten months, but after a while they all grew tired and took a short nap.

As they got closer to the station, most of Celia's friends handed her birthday cards for her to open when she got home, and Maddie gave her a small present.

"This isn't fair, you guys. I didn't do anything for your birthdays," Celia complained. "How did you know it was my birthday, anyway? I never mentioned it."

Odile snorted in a very ungraceful manner. "Are you serious?"

"What?" Celia asked, feeling like she had missed something.

"Deel, you are so . . ." Odette waved her hands in the air. "Don't pay attention to her, Celia. As for knowing when your birthday is, the entire demesne knows who you are. Didn't you figure we'd know when your birthday is, too?"

Celia felt very uncomfortable. Every once in a while, something like this would happen and remind her that she wasn't just a normal person in the demesne. She sighed. "Fine. But all of you have to tell me when it's your birthday so I can at least give you a card. Deal?"

"Deal!" everyone said at the same time, then burst out laughing.

Celia stepped off the BUS and saw the last person she expected to see there. Doxa was sitting on a bench, watching everyone pour onto the platform and reunite with their families. Celia wondered what she was doing there, but didn't want to have anything to do with her, so she turned to walk the other direction.

"Celia!"

No, surely not. The person who couldn't stand the sight of her all year was calling her name? Celia thought she must be hearing things. She felt a touch on her arm and turned around.

"Hey, Celia." Doxa stood in front of her, only she looked different. She no longer wore heavy eye makeup and her hair was pulled back in a ponytail instead of carefully curled and styled around her face.

"Doxa."

"Celia, I just wanted..."

"Yes?"

"I'm really sorry about everything, Celia. I didn't mean for all of that to happen. I thought I was just playing a prank on you."

"Yeah, well..."

"When Neel asked me if I'd help, I just thought he was going to play a little joke on you and put you in your place."

"I see."

Doxa sighed. "I know you're still upset with me. I can't blame you. If I were you, I'd hate me."

"I just don't understand why you hate me so much."

"I don't hate you... not anymore. I... well, I guess I was jealous, and... I don't know. I'm not making any sense."

Maddie walked over and stood beside Celia. "Doxa? What do you want?"

"I'm just apologizing for what I did to Celia," she said. "I'm sorry for making your year so miserable, too, Maddie."

Maddie's eyes bugged out. "What?"

"Yeah, I know," Doxa said quietly. "I don't really expect you to believe me, and I deserve that. Anyway, I hope someday you can forgive me, Celia." Before Celia or Maddie could find any words to say, she turned and disappeared into the crowd.

"Wow. What was that?" Maddie asked.

"Maybe she really is sorry for what she did."

"Yeah, right. I don't trust her an inch."

"Celia!" Celia turned around and saw Mr. Morven waving at her as he made his way through the crowd. "Are you ready to go?"

"Yeah. My trunk is right there," she said, pointing to it.

"I'll get it loaded in the van while you say good-bye to everyone."

"Hey, Celia, I'll see you next year," Merry said as she passed by with her parents.

"Bye, Merry."

"See you later, Celia," Eliot said as he walked past.

"Have a good summer, Eliot."

"You, too."

"Maddie! Celia!" Galena called from behind them. She waved them over to where the rest of the Mensaleon seventh-years were gathered. "Group hug!"

They all said good-bye and wished Josh good luck at the Summer Tournament, then headed in different directions.

Before Celia knew it, she was in the van with Mr. Morven on her way to Aunt Agatha's house.

"So what did you think of your first year at Renasci, other than the pranks, cheating accusations, and almost getting expelled?" Mr. Morven asked.

Celia laughed. "Other than that, I loved it. I had a great time. I never knew school could be so much fun." She thought for a moment. "Mr. Morven, do you know what happened before my parents disappeared?"

"My goodness, Celia, what brought that up?"

"I've just been thinking about the Coridans and my parents and . . . I don't know anything that happened, so I was just curious."

Mr. Morven thought for a moment. "As I told you before, I was out of the country when it all happened, so I'm not sure I'll be much help to you. You probably should ask Higby about it. He might know more than I do."

"Higby? Why?"

Mr. Morven shrugged. "He was more involved in that kind of thing back then, so I figure he might know something."

"What did he do?"

He frowned as he tried to remember. "I don't think he had any official position, just had an interest in it. Kind of like people getting involved in local politics in the rest of the world. They don't always have a job, per se, but they like being involved."

"Oh."

He glanced over at her. "I'm sorry, Celia. I wish I could help more."

"That's okay."

In what seemed like no time at all, they were pulling into the driveway at Aunt Agatha's. Mr. Morven unloaded Celia's trunk and knocked on the back door, since they had pulled around to the back of the house. A few moments later, Aunt Agatha opened the door.

"Oh, Celia. I didn't know you were coming home today," she said, sounding indifferent about her return.

"I sent you a message a few days ago, Miss Trowbridge," Mr. Morven said.

"Did you? I must have missed it."

He nodded. "May I carry Celia's trunk up to her room?" he asked.

"Certainly."

Celia led him up the back staircase and down the hallway to her bedroom. A layer of dust covered every surface in her room, but otherwise the room looked exactly the way Celia had left it last year. Mr. Morven set her trunk down in the middle of the floor. "Thanks," she said.

He turned to face her. "You're welcome." He studied her for a moment. "Celia..."

"Yes?"

"I know you're curious about a lot of things, and I wish I could give you the answers you're looking for, but...please don't do anything risky while you're here, okay?"

"What do you mean?"

"Just...be careful...and don't stick your nose where it doesn't belong, all right?"

"Okay. But why—"

"Celia!" Aunt Agatha's voice carried up the stairs and they could hear her footsteps on the stairs.

"I don't understand, Mr. Morven. Why are people always warning me but they won't tell me what's going on?"

"Celia," he said, speaking quickly in a hushed tone, "your family was chosen by the Overseer and then disappeared. He specifically selected you as the next princep. No one knows why you didn't disappear with them, but I would think you could see why it wouldn't be wise to take unnecessary risks. Understand?"

"Yeah," she said, resigned to the fact that she wasn't going to get any more answers.

"We're doing as much as we can, Celia," he said softly, a note of tenderness in his voice.

"I know."

"Celia!" Aunt Agatha appeared in the doorway. "Will your... *guest* be staying for dinner?"

"No, Miss Trowbridge, I have to be on my way, but thank you for the invitation."

Celia tried to hide a smile when she saw the look on Aunt Agatha's face.

"Very well, then," Aunt Agatha said, looking between them with curiosity. "Celia, I'll be in the parlor. I'd like to see you once you've finished."

"Yes, Aunt Agatha."

"Hm." She looked at each of them once more and then spun on her heel and left. Soon they could hear her footsteps on the stairs as she went back down.

"Did Professor Legaspi tell you we're trying to figure out a way for you to escape this prison, ah, I mean, house?"

Celia giggled. "Yeah."

He smiled at her. "You're a good kid, Celia. Happy birthday, and I hope you have a good summer."

"Thanks for everything, Mr. Morven."

A few hours later, after being ordered to dust her room (and the entire parlor while she was at it) and wash and dry the dinner dishes, Celia closed her bedroom door and pulled out all her birthday cards and presents. She opened the cards carefully, giggling at the funny pictures and sayings and picturing each person as she read the cards. When she had opened all the cards, she turned to the presents. A little while later, she had a small pile of new treasures around her.

Chapter Eighteen

Maddie had given her a small scrapbook, filled with pictures and sketches of things to help remind her of their time at Renasci. Celia looked longingly at the picture of the front doors of the school, wishing she was back there already. She laughed when she read the note Maddie had written next to the picture of the coterie statues in the commons: "I never want to see purple paint again!"

Higby had given her a small notebook with a purple pen. On the first page, he had written, "Purple for your coterie, but also because you behaved the way only a person of nobility could this year. Keep in touch and I'll see you soon."

Professor Twombly's present was a small purple lion zipper pull, which Celia put on the zipper on her duffle bag. Professor Legaspi's present came in a small jewelry box, and when Celia opened it, she pulled out a locket on a silver chain. Carefully opening the locket, Celia saw two pictures already placed inside the locket. She noticed a note in the bottom of the jewelry box. It read:

Celia,

I don't know if you have any pictures of your parents, but I thought you might like to have a locket so you can always carry them close to your heart. These pictures are old, from a year before you were born, but they are the most recent ones I have. I'll see you soon. Happy Birthday.

Professor Legaspi

Brushing away tears, Celia fastened the necklace around her neck, then held the locket tightly in her hand. She still didn't know what had happened to them, but holding their pictures somehow made her feel closer to them.

Standing her cards up on her desk so she could see them all, she felt a wave of loneliness. She missed everyone already. It would only be two months until she headed back to school for the next year, but right now two months seemed like an eternity.

She got ready for bed and flipped off her light, then stared at the constellations on her ceiling. Remembering the last time she had stared at those stickers, she realized that she was not the same person she had been then. No matter what happened after this, she had come a long way in the past year, and she had a feeling that her adventure was only beginning. With thoughts of her year at Renasci filling her mind and a smile on her face, she drifted off into a peaceful sleep.

About the Author

Melissa Gunther lives in Florida where she continues her work on the Celia's Journey series. She loves to hear from readers and is always happy to answer questions, except maybe the ones about how far in the series she's written. Visit her online at www.melissagunther.com.

Books available from Melissa Gunther:

Key to the Past

Celia's Journey - Book 2
Available in Hardcover, Paperback, and e-Book

The Book in the Attic

Celia's Journey - Book 1
Available in Hardcover, Paperback, and e-Book

Turn the page to read an excerpt from

Key to the Past

Celia's Journey - Book 2
Available now!

Chapter One
Mail

Morning sun poured through the paned-glass window and spilled over the inert form buried under the covers on the bed. Birds chirped from the tree outside, but the heap on the bed simply rolled over to face the other direction, not realizing it was now facing the brightly shining sun. Eyes scrunched and there was a grunt, followed by a big yawn, and then the form on the bed sat up and stretched.

Celia Fincastle rubbed her eyes, looked out the window at the blue sky, and yawned again. She'd stayed up late the night before, opening all of the birthday cards and presents from her friends at her school, the Renasci Academy for Gifted Students. It had been the best birthday she could remember, even though it included heading back to Aunt Agatha's house after her first year at Renasci and despite the fact that Aunt Agatha hadn't even acknowledged her birthday.

Celia shifted to the side of the bed and slid her feet into her slippers. She stood and stretched, then went to her closet to get her robe. Seeing the collection of birthday cards lined up on her desk, she smiled, remembering all the friends she had made last year. She glanced at the clock and saw that it was still early, but she knew Aunt Agatha would be awake already. On her way to the door, she caught a glimpse of her reflection in the mirror and paused. She'd forgotten she'd worn the necklace to bed.

Professor Legaspi, one of her teachers and faculty mentors, had given her the necklace for her birthday. The round silver locket held pictures of her parents, whom Celia hadn't seen in ten years. She knew nothing about what happened to them, only that they disappeared just before she turned two years old. Soon after, Celia had come to live with Agatha Trowbridge, her distant but only remaining relative.

She opened the locket and studied the smiling face of her mother and the roguishly grinning face of her father. Looking back and forth between the pictures and her own reflection, she tried to figure out if she looked like either one of them. After a few minutes, she sighed, closed the locket, and headed downstairs for breakfast.

"Oh, good, you're awake," Aunt Agatha said as Celia walked into the kitchen. "We have a busy day today, so you'll have to eat quickly. No dawdling."

"What are we doing?" Celia asked, pouring herself a bowl of what looked like cardboard squares and rabbit food yet claimed to be cereal.

"I have some very important meetings to attend, and... Is that a new necklace?"

Celia touched the silver locket. "Yes, it was a birthday present from... a friend."

"How nice. What a delightful birthday... oh, no!"

"What?"

Aunt Agatha pressed a hand to her forehead. "Your birthday! How thoughtless of me! When was it again?"

"Yesterday." Did Aunt Agatha honestly think that she would believe that her aunt had forgotten when her birthday was? Until last year, Celia's birthday had been a celebration for

Aunt Agatha—one year closer to sending her off to boarding school. Celia bit her lip to keep from saying something that would get her in serious trouble.

"My goodness, I feel just awful that I forgot about your birthday! How terribly inconsiderate of me!"

"It's okay, Aunt Agatha."

"Oh, I must do something about this. I'll have to call all my friends and invite them over for tea. Yes, that would be splendid! We can have finger sandwiches and a prune tart. How delicious!"

Celia tried not to gag at the thought of a prune tart. Surely she wouldn't have to endure *that*. "Really, Aunt Agatha. You don't have to," she said, a note of panic creeping into her voice.

"Oh, and you can wear that delightful purple hat of yours. Everyone just loved that hat last year." She rose to her feet and swept from the room saying, "I must get working on this right away. There's no time to lose!"

Celia sighed as she dropped her cheek onto her hand. She hated that purple hat. Besides the fact that it looked like a chicken, it brought back memories of last year at school when someone had painted the mascot statues in the commons purple and dressed them in purple lion costumes. Celia had been framed for the prank and got stuck cleaning all the statues.

And *prune tart*!? It sounded awful. The chocolate and coconut cake she'd had with her friends on the trip home yesterday had been much better than that. She sighed again as she realized that she had the whole summer in front of her before she could go back to Renasci again.

"Hurry up, Celia!" Aunt Agatha called. "We have to leave in half an hour. Don't be late!"

Celia rolled her eyes and sighed for a third time. It was going to be a very long summer, indeed.

Chapter One

By mid-June, Celia had resigned herself to another six weeks of misery with Aunt Agatha. Every day was basically the same as the last, so the past two weeks felt like two months. Celia would get up and eat breakfast, when her aunt would announce that they were going to another one of her teas, luncheons, bridge club meetings, or some other collection of social gatherings. Since Aunt Agatha wouldn't let her wear anything "scruffy," Celia was forced to spend the vast majority of her time in uncomfortable and hideous dresses, usually accompanied by an equally uncomfortable and hideous hat of some sort.

Celia had been forced to endure the promised prune tart, which had been as horrible as it sounded, made worse by the collection of gossipy old ladies who had come over for tea. She found her mind wandering for much of the afternoon, thinking back to the birthday celebration she'd had with her friends from school. It wasn't much of a competition, that afternoon with her friends and the delicious cake versus this stuffy gathering of Aunt Agatha's friends and the disgusting prune tart, so Celia tried not to compare the two, but that didn't stop her from wishing she were anywhere other than where she was.

The only thing that had been worse than Celia's birthday tea was the Grandmother's Afternoon Tea, where all the ladies in Aunt Agatha's circle of friends brought their granddaughters for the event. It was designed to give everyone a chance to meet the granddaughters they all talked about so much so people could put a face with a name, but Celia had a sneaking suspicion that it was just an opportunity for everyone to show off their granddaughters and brag about how great they were, and she'd done her best to get out of the event.

Mail

"But Aunt Agatha," Celia had said, using what she hoped was her most persuasive voice, "I'm not *really* your granddaughter, so I don't think I should be going with you. Won't everyone else decide that they should be able to bring someone other than their granddaughter?"

"Oh, pish posh, Celia. I'm not about to let everyone else show off their granddaughters while I sit in the corner and watch. You're going, and that's final."

"Couldn't I—"

"Absolutely not. I said you're going, and I don't want to hear another word."

Try as she might, Celia could not convince Aunt Agatha to let her skip the tea, so she was forced to endure three hours of listening to snobby girls who were being groomed to become identical copies of their snobby grandmothers, who each thought her granddaughter was the greatest thing since sliced bread.

"Oh, my Abigail is just the smartest little thing! You should see how her teachers rave over her."

"Well, my Veronica has the best voice you ever heard. I always say that she's going to sing at Carnegie Hall someday."

"Have you seen little Penelope? She's so adorable! I've told her parents they should send her pictures out to an agent and get her into modeling."

"Well, *my* mom says that the people who go to *my* school are the best students because we go to the best school."

"Yeah? Well, *my* daddy says that I'm his little princess, and everyone else isn't good enough for me."

"I've never *heard* of your school. RAGS? How appropriate. Is that what you wear for your school uniforms?"

She'd figured that no one there would have ever heard of her school, and that was just fine with her. Renasci wasn't the average school, and the students who attended the school were not your average students, either. The school was for people with very unusual talents and abilities, or gifts, which let them do things that most people could only dream of attempting. Even though the people at Renasci didn't try to keep their school a secret, most people refused to believe that such abilities existed, so they had never heard of the school.

Collapsing on her bed after that torturous afternoon, Celia was certain that was the last straw. If she had to go to another one of Aunt Agatha's meetings, her brain was going to explode. She rubbed her eyes and studied the constellation stickers on her ceiling. How she missed her bed at school, with the windows that let her see the stars, which were brighter and more numerous than here at Aunt Agatha's house.

Sighing, she glanced around the ceiling, then bolted upright, her heart pounding with excitement. For the stars on her ceiling were glowing blue, and that could only mean one thing: someone from the demesne was trying to contact her.

She looked over at her desk, then scrambled to her feet and hurried over to see what had arrived. She found two envelopes sitting there, and grabbed the ivory-colored one that was sitting on the top. "Celia Fincastle" the envelope said, and she quickly opened it and pulled out the letter.

Dear Celia,

I trust you are doing well at home with your aunt and enjoying your summer break. It occurred to me that you haven't learned how to send mail in the demesne, so you have no way of contacting any of us. To remedy that, I have enclosed an address where you can send correspondence. Should you need to reach anyone, simply send out a letter to that address and someone will make sure it reaches the correct individual. However, please be sure that your name and address are not visible on the outside of the envelope when you mail it.

I am assuming your aunt will not wish to act as your guardian for this year either, so I will be contacting her about my position as temporary guardian again, if that is acceptable to you. Should she agree, I will perform the same duties as last year, signing your ERs and handling any necessary disciplinary action (although I don't anticipate that being a problem for you this year).

Sincerely,

Higby

Havensmoor via A-BUS 3rd Station

Despite the fact that the letter said nothing about getting her away from Aunt Agatha, it was nice to hear from someone in the demesne, and Celia was quite excited about being able to send mail out to other people.

She turned her attention to the second envelope, this one plain white. "Celia" was printed in silver ink on the front in even letters. The back flap on the envelope was stamped with the image of a silver eagle. She carefully opened the envelope and pulled out a sheet of light gray paper.

Dear Celia,

I hope you are having a good summer holiday. We heard from Maddie that she's heading to camp in July, and both we and she wondered if you'd like to go with her. She should be sending you a note soon with the rest of the information about the camp, in case your aunt is curious. The camp runs the two weeks before school starts, so you'd head straight to school from camp. I know it's not much of a help to get you out of the house right before you'd be leaving anyway, but I guess two fewer weeks is better than nothing.

Your packet of information for this school year should be heading your way soon, but don't worry about getting all of your books and things. We'll make sure you have everything

you need when you get here. See
you then!

Warmest wishes,

Professor Legaspi

Summer camp? Celia had never been to camp before. Was the camp just for kids with unusual abilities, or was it for everyone? Did it matter? She could get away from Aunt Agatha a whole two weeks early! To make it even better, she'd get to see Maddie, too! Madelia Hannagan was her best friend, an energetic blond-haired girl who often talked before she thought. They'd met on the way to school last year, and had been friends ever since.

She carefully folded the letters and returned them to their envelopes, then put them in her closet with the pile of birthday cards she'd set on a shelf. She couldn't ever remember getting mail before, other than last summer when she first found out about Renasci, so it felt kind of special to get *two* letters, even if they didn't come in the regular mail.

For the next week and a half, Celia waited every day for the mail to arrive, hoping she'd hear something from Maddie. She sat outside on the front steps, watching carefully for the mailman, then stood, shifting from foot to foot with anticipation, while he retrieved their mail from his bag. She flipped through the mail, her hope fading with each item not bearing her name, until she reached the bottom of the stack and still had nothing from Maddie. Then she'd drop the mail on the sofa table and hurry upstairs, thinking maybe something had appeared on her desk, only to be disappointed when she saw her empty desktop.

Finally, on a Friday near the end of June, Celia saw a bright pink envelope in their pile of mail and knew it had to be from Maddie. Sure enough, it was addressed to "Miss Celia Fincastle" in Maddie's curly handwriting. Celia rushed inside, leaving the rest of the mail in the parlor, and headed up the stairs two at a time. Once she was safely inside her room with the door closed, she opened the envelope and pulled out an equally bright green piece of paper.

Dear Celia,

I hope you are not too bored at your aunt's house this summer. My annoying siblings have been up to their usual trouble, making my life miserable the way they always do. My little brother decided that it would be a good idea to smear toothpaste all over the mirror in my room and my sister thought it would be fun to use my clothes to play dress-up. I never thought I'd say this, but I can't wait to go back to school!

Professor Legaspi heard about the camp I'm going to next month, and she thought you might like to go, so I'm officially inviting you to come to camp with me. I sent the brochure, too, so your aunt will know that the camp really exists and she's not sending you off to who-knows-where (not that it sounds like she'd care). I really hope you can come. It would be so much fun to have you there.

I'd better go - my brother is trying to tie all my shoelaces together.

See you soon (I hope!),

Maddie

Celia laughed out loud at the antics of Maddie's brothers and sister. She could see Maddie getting really irritated with her younger siblings, particularly when they tried something like tying her shoes together. But although she found the descriptions funny, what really put a smile on her face was the actual invitation to go to camp with Maddie. It meant she only had to endure three more weeks with Aunt Agatha.

Made in the USA
Middletown, DE
13 July 2016